D0193098

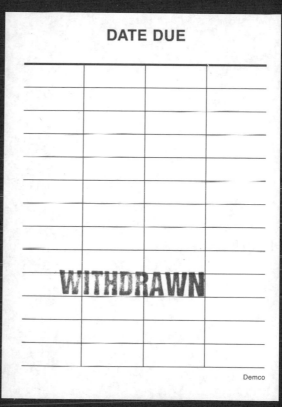

The

Library

of

Fates

The
Library
of
Fates

ADITI KHORANA

RAZORBILL

An Imprint of Penguin Random House

RAZORBILL

An Imprint of Penguin Random House
Penguin.com

Copyright © 2017 Aditi Khorana

Penguin Random House supports copyright. Copyright fuels
creativity, encourages diverse voices, promotes free speech, and
creates a vibrant culture. Thank you for buying an authorized
edition of this book and for complying with copyright laws by not
reproducing, scanning, or distributing any part of it in any form
without permission. You are supporting writers and allowing
Penguin Random House to continue to publish books for every
reader.

ISBN: 978-1-59514-858-2

Printed in the United States of America

1 3 5 7 9 10 8 6 4 2

Design: Eric Ford

For those who seek a better world,
and for those who fight for one every
day, I dedicate this book to you.

We shall not cease from exploration
And the end of all our exploring
Will be to arrive where we started
And know the place for the first time

—T. S. Eliot, from *Little Gidding*

AUTHOR'S NOTE

OFTEN THE MORAL of a story is culled out at the end, but in the case of *Library of Fates*, I felt the need to state it up front: when we act with only our selfish interests in mind, disregarding the rights and experiences of others, everybody loses. But when we act in the service of the greater good, even if it costs us something—even if it costs us a lot—we are deeply and profoundly transformed by love, empathy, and wisdom. And so we transform the world.

I know that many on our little planet are feeling a great deal of despair and terror today; I know this because I feel it too, this unsettled dread that descended upon me after the jolt of the 2016 U.S. presidential election. In the weeks that followed, I couldn't write. I was in a state of deep mourning, worried for the safety and well-being of friends and family, the state of the environment, of civil rights, of civil discourse. I had recently completed a manuscript about a louche, patriarchal dictator's slimy advancements on an idyllic kingdom. Now life appeared to be imitating art.

But I also knew that it was not the first time the forces of hatred and ignorance had somehow usurped power from those who seek goodness and equality. It was not the first time we had experienced grave disappointment in the systems and institutions we trust, or in humanity itself. Sadly, we know that hatred has always existed, even before this recent election.

But it stings every time, doesn't it? It shocks us to the core, leaving us feeling exposed and raw. I am a woman, an immigrant, brown, a writer. I grew up in a world that made no effort to hide its disdain for me. I have spent a lifetime shielding myself and those I love from the contempt cast against anyone in this society who is considered Other.

That's why I wrote this book, and the one before it, and why I'll continue to write the ones that come after. Because I know that many times in our history, people like you and me have had to confront a culture of malevolence and antipathy and uproot it like a weed. And then we have to replace it with a new culture. A far better one. One in which we all matter, regardless of our race, gender, religion, or who we love. One in which our stories matter.

And we will. Because we're not broken. And we won't be silenced. It is up to us to build webs of goodness wherever we go, up to us to uproot injustices and expose them to the light. So be brave, keep fighting, and I will fight alongside you.

Aditi Khorana

Parable *of* the Land *of* Trees

*L*ONG AGO, *there was a land entirely occupied by some of the most beautiful and oldest trees in the world. These trees had inhabited the Earth longer than humans, longer than the vetalas —the immortals who roamed the planet alongside humans till they all but disappeared.*

They were wise trees and had existed on the Earth for such a great span of time, they had learned how to speak. They offered their visitors fruit and shade. They told captivating stories and made people laugh. They were servants to the land and to those around them.

Those who had the good fortune to stumble upon the Land of Trees said that the experience stayed with them forever. They returned to their homes and spoke of this ethereal world, and so, word began to spread about the Land of Trees. Waves of new explorers trickled in, and soon visitors came in droves, marching into the land from all corners of the Earth.

But these new visitors wanted more from the trees. They sought to own the trees and the land that they lived on. They spoke of opening up taverns and lodges and inns so people could stay when they came to visit. They wanted to build roads, bridges, an infrastructure that would allow individuals to come by the thousands so that they could experience the Land of Trees. But there was one problem with this . . .

They needed the wood from the trees to build all of these things. And so they began to chop down the trees in order to build inns and taverns and roads and bridges. One by one, the trees came down, axes cutting into their trunks. Saws slicing away at their roots and branches.

And soon, the Land of Trees was filled with inns and taverns and roads and bridges. Some trees survived, but they were so devastated by the loss of their family and friends that they stopped speaking, stopped laughing, stopped sharing their voices. Their despondency, their mistrust became silence, and the forest was no longer filled with laughter, with wisdom, with stories.

For some time, people continued to visit, but instead of the Land of Trees, what they saw now was a land that had devolved into just another place on a map.

After some time, people stopped coming, and now the Land of Trees is just like any other place. A place whose magic has been erased.

But perhaps one day, you'll find yourself walking through a forest, and maybe if you listen closely enough, and maybe if you ask from the very bottom of your heart, one of the trees might hear the longing in your soul—the longing for connection, the longing for something deeper that resides so far below the surface of the world in which we choose to live out our day-to-day. And you'll hear it, the voice of one of those trees, calling back to you, telling you that the world is alive with mysteries, and that in order to understand them, one must first learn to be still, to listen, and the world will unveil itself to you, as though it was waiting to do so all along.

Prologue

I STILL REMEMBER the first time my father told me the Parable of the Land of Trees. It was night, and outside my window, a soft quilt of mysterious darkness had settled over Chanakya Lake. But I felt safe under the gauze of the white silken mosquito net that hung over me, and my father's presence reassured me. He sat at the edge of my bed and pointed out past the lake, past the mountains, to a horizon shrouded in mist. What he was really pointing to was a time that existed before us, to a world neither of us could even be sure had ever really prevailed.

"Have I ever told you the Parable of the Land of Trees?" he asked me, his dark eyes fixed on that elusive brim between earth and sky, before they turned to look back at me, a wistful smile twitching on the edges of his lips.

I shook my head. Outside my window, lanterns lit up the

sterns of houseboats on the lake, their twins reflecting in the water, suggesting another world underneath that channel, a mirror to the one we inhabited now. I wondered about the people who slept on those boats, who lived in that sphere I had still never seen. I thought about all the places I had never visited, that I had heard about only in the stories people told me.

And then in the gauzy lamplight, over the quiet, contented chirping of insects calling out to one another in the night, my father told me the tale. I didn't understand then how stories have a way of staying with us long after people are gone. That night, I simply held on to his words: somber and thoughtful. I listened to his voice: calm, soft, measured, wise. It was how I would always remember it, taking for granted that it would always be there. I didn't know then what I know now: that everything—my father, this moment, every experience that molds and shapes us—is ephemeral, evaporating into the air before we have a chance to grasp on to it, before we can truly even understand what it means.

One

PAPA WAS STANDING on the balcony outside his library when I arrived to meet him. From the doorway where I stood, I could see the sun setting over the lands he had inherited from his father, that for so long I had thought I would inherit from him one day, turning the hills and plains the color of burnished gold. Far out in the distance, snow covering the mountaintops glistened like a gilded scrim sparkling in the early evening light.

Blue and silver minarets rose above the walled city of Shalingar's capital—Ananta. A layer of marine fog settled over Chanakya Lake, revealing miniature houseboats wearing elaborate gardens on their roofs like soft, mossy hats. They sailed placidly across the flat, misty surface of the basin.

But I was anything but placid. As I crossed the vast sanctuary cut of auric filigree and tomes, its gold and crystal domed ceiling dousing every shelf and book in honey-colored light, I measured my breaths, as though controlling each inhalation were the key to mastering my fate itself.

I approached the balcony, and from there, I could hear the sound of the festivities below in the streets. Cannons exploded, making the stone walls of the palace tremble. And just below those walls, dancers swathed in white silk, green and red ribbons around their waists, twirled in the streets like spinning tops. The brazen blast of horns and the *clop clop clop* of horse hooves resounded through the palace quarters. Children flung rose petals into the sky. They fell back down into the mud streets, transforming the lanes between homes into blushing rivers. Elephants adorned in patchwork costumes embellished with mirrors, tassels, and festive silk ribbons made their way up these very rivers, carrying Macedon's most important dignitaries on their backs. Brightly colored lanterns illuminated their path, like diyas lighting Emperor Sikander's way to our home.

My father stood, watching the festivities. When I approached, he turned abruptly, as though I had interrupted him from a dream, or perhaps a nightmare. "Sabahaat Shaam," I said, giving him a warm hug.

He started for a second. I realized that he had never before seen me this elaborately dressed and coiffed. My cheeks were covered in rouge tincture, my lips streaked with crimson; my lashes were curled and painted black like thick spider's legs. I was wrapped in a magenta and gold sari, my hair piled high over my head.

Earlier that day, Mala, my lady-in-waiting, and a retinue of her helpers had buzzed around me, a hive of activity that revolved around beautifying me from head to toe. It was a dance that took place whenever an important dignitary came to visit the kingdom, but today the hive spun and sped as though an inaudible tempo had accelerated everyone's movements without warning.

"Hold still, dear girl. When a great king arrives, one must look presentable," Mala had said as she combed out my snarled hair, untangling the knots with her capable fingers.

A great king.

A great king who held the fate of our kingdom, as well as my own fate, in his hands.

Papa regained his composure and smiled at me. "Sabahaat Shaam," he said before he looked back at those packed streets before us. "I forget sometimes how lovely the kingdom is at this time of day. Not the dancers or the carnival down below . . . but the light," he said, glimpsing the sky, shaking his head in disbelief. "It's as though the sun and the moon want to offer our little kingdom their best."

"Luminaries," I said to him. "That's what Shree taught me in our astronomy tutorial—the sun and the moon are luminaries. And the way Shalingar bends toward the ocean . . . ," I said, mimicking the curvature of the Earth. "It's the light reflecting on the water."

Papa looked at me and laughed. "Or perhaps it's just magic," he said, and his eyes sparkled as he challenged me.

I shook my head. "No such thing."

"Maybe you're right," he quietly responded, and for a moment, I was regretful of my words because a mask of seriousness transformed my father's face again. "One day, after you've seen the world, you'll understand just how special Shalingar is."

"I know how special it is, Papa." I sighed. "If I could stay here forever . . ." I couldn't finish the sentence.

"You always did speak of traveling the world, didn't you?" he wistfully asked. "Now you'll have the opportunity to do so." But I could hear the lack of conviction in his voice. We both knew that this, what was about to transpire over the next few days, was not what either of us had in mind when I spoke of traveling the world.

"Sikander was a friend of yours once, wasn't he?" I changed the subject.

If he had once been a friend of Papa's, how bad could he really be? I wondered. I had, for the past several weeks, asked everyone I knew a variation of this question.

"They're all just . . . stories, aren't they?" I had queried Arjun, my best friend, the night before as we slowly walked the grounds together.

"Of course they're just stories," Arjun had mumbled.

"Like that thing about how he had all the advisors on his father's council stoned to death?"

"I'm sure that's not true." Arjun shook his head vehemently before he pressed his lips in a thin line. But his silence for the remainder of the walk didn't inspire confidence.

◻

Now my father turned to me, and the light of the sunset caught his eyes, transforming them to gold. We looked alike, my father and I; people often told us this. I had his hands, with their long, tapered fingers, his smile, broad and easy, and his dark, wavy hair.

"Friends . . . something like that. But it's all in the past. I haven't seen Sikander since you were a baby. Now we're starting anew." The uneasiness in his voice was difficult to ignore. I assumed he didn't want to discuss it. It had never been his way to be open about the past.

But I knew *some* things about Sikander and about Macedon beyond what my tutor, Shree, had taught me about the Silk Road and Sikander's conquests. I knew that my father had first met Sikander when they were both young scholars at the Military Academy of Macedon. And that they *had* been friends, once upon a time, at least according to Bandaka, Papa's advisor and Arjun's father.

That was before Sikander took the throne by assassinating his own father and declaring himself the new emperor. After that, he battled his way through Anatolia, Syria, Phoenicia, Judea, Bactria. After his overthrow of Persia he became Sikander the Great, who led the greatest and fiercest standing army of all time. In just fifteen years, he had nearly quadrupled his territories, largely through battle. *Who was he really, though? Who was he back when my father knew him?*

I attempted a different tack. "Did you like Macedon?" I asked Papa.

"It's . . . very advanced in some ways. Buildings so tall they block out the light. Giant arenas that took hundreds of years to build. They're used for fighting: slaves fighting one another to the death. People cheering like madmen over it. Everyone has a slave, practically." He shook his head. "They don't believe in equality between the sexes. To question the leadership is considered a sin. And they like war. Very much."

I was quiet as I considered that it didn't matter anyway what Macedon was like. I would see it from my window in Sikander's harem, living among his other wives. I wouldn't visit the great cities of the world, or rule over my kingdom the way my father had. I would be nothing more than a prisoner in Sikander's bejeweled zenana of toys.

I knew the thought of this sickened my father, just as it horrified me. I wanted to believe that my fate wasn't yet sealed, but we both knew that my father's options were limited. He could agree to Sikander's proposal of marriage to me, and Shalingar would remain stable and have a powerful ally. Or he could refuse, and Sikander would undoubtedly take umbrage, as he was often known to do.

In fact, we were expected to be thrilled, honored that Sikander was seeking to build diplomatic relations with our little kingdom. That was Sikander's new strategy, now that he had battled half the world. Or rather, that was the only choice left for the tiny kingdoms he hadn't yet conquered. Agree to all of Sikander's terms with regard to the negotiation of trade relations, developing trade routes from the east

to the west, and the fate of your daughters and sons, and
Sikander would be your most powerful friend.

Displease him, disagree with him, question his motives,
and another outcome awaited you.

What concerned my father, beyond my own future, was
the future of our kingdom. While Shalingar would have an
ally in Sikander once I took his hand in marriage, would it
also mean that Macedon's ways would bleed into our own?

In just a few weeks, Arjun was expected to make the
journey to attend the Military Academy of Macedon—the
best military academy in the world. For the longest time, I
had desperately wanted to join him, and I still remembered
the day that I learned that the Academy didn't accept girls. I
was devastated to learn that the fate of a woman in Macedon
was so circumscribed. There were no women on Macedon's
Leadership Council, and all the diplomats and scholars sent
from Macedon to Shalingar were men. Women weren't
allowed to own businesses in Macedon. Or work, for that
matter. They weren't allowed to attend school, or walk down
the street unescorted.

"How come you never went back to Macedon?" I asked
my father now. It was an obvious question. My father traveled all over the world on diplomatic trips, but he had never
returned to the place of my birth.

Papa continued to look out past the horizon. The parade
in honor of Sikander's visit was thinning now, the tide reced-
ing, and most of Sikander's advisors were already within the
palace walls, waiting for us to come greet them.

I looked at my father expectantly, waiting for his answer, well aware that there was something else embedded in my inquiry about his time in Macedon. It was a question within a question, like those dolls I played with as a child—the ones that nested inside larger versions of themselves. I was really asking him to tell me something, *anything* about my mother, whom he had met in Macedon during his time away.

I wondered now if Sikander had known my mother too.

"There was no reason to," he said as he looked back toward the walled city. I followed his gaze, noticing the way whitewashed homes blushed in the early evening light, an empire of pink. That was what my father was talking about when he mentioned the light.

I thought about things like that sometimes—how many elements it took to create the simplest of things—a pink sky, an unusually perfect day, a happy family, a deep friendship, a moment of pure delight.

I wondered too what it took to undo these things. It seemed to me that undoing something was far easier than creating it.

"I wish your mother were here now, to explain things to you." Papa abruptly interrupted my thoughts.

I glanced at him in shock. He had never mentioned my mother before, and as much as I had hoped that he might, that day it still stunned me to hear those words coming from his mouth.

She was the mystery I most wanted to unlock. It called

to me in my dreams, a vision of her, green eyes just like mine, and her voice telling me how much she loved me, how much she missed me. How desperate she was to meet me, wherever she was . . . if she was even still alive.

"What . . . kinds of things?" I asked carefully.

"Amrita, what's about to happen . . ." My father shook his head. "I wish I could go back in time and undo things." He paused before he added, "And I wish your mother were here to tell you about marriage . . . I have so many regrets, and now it's coming back to haunt me, the past, and I—"

"Your Majesties?" Arjun's low voice called from the doorway. My father and I both turned, and I found myself doing a double take when I saw him.

He was handsomely dressed in a crisp blue and gold khalat rather than his everyday kurta pajamas or slacks. His hair, usually a mess because he was always running his fingers through it, was combed down. He looked taller somehow, more like a man than the boy who chased me around the mango grove outside his parents' quarters.

"It's time," he announced to us, a tight smile on his lips.

His eyes caught mine for a moment before he quickly looked away.

"Go on, Amrita. Arjun will escort you," my father said, before he gave me a kiss on the forehead.

I squeezed my father's arm to reassure him. His words about my mother lingered in my mind, what he had said about his regrets. I opened my mouth to ask him more, but the moment was already gone.

"Go on," he said again, more gently this time. "They're waiting for you downstairs. I'll be there soon."

I nodded slowly before I crossed the library toward Arjun, noting his broad shoulders, the stubble on his jaw, the loose smile on the edge of his lips, his dark eyes examining the shelf to my right. I followed his gaze: Something sparkled amid the tomes. I discreetly ran my fingers across the dark wood till I discovered something cool and delicate wedged between two books. I realized what it was even before I saw it.

A ring.

I gasped, turning to look back at my father, making sure he didn't notice me snatching the bauble into my palm. I quietly inspected the treasure that had been hidden expressly for me. In the place of a gemstone, the gold delicately curved into the petals of a jasmine bud. I slipped the ring on my finger. It fit perfectly.

"Thank you," I whispered, looking back into Arjun's face, returning his smile.

"For good luck," he responded, his eyes twinkling.

Hidden gifts: It was our language; it always had been.

It started when we were children. Arjun was allowed to leave the palace whenever he wanted, something I envied. I was allowed to leave, but going out into the world beyond the palace walls was such a fraught production that on most occasions, I avoided the entire nuisance of it. For one thing, at my father's insistence, I had to cover my face with a veil.

"We have to protect your identity," my father insisted.

"We don't want you to lose your anonymity and not experience life in a normal way. Or worse, become a target," he always added, his voice stern.

And then there was the matter of my having to be escorted by a member of the palace retinue, which made leaving the grounds decidedly less fun than I hoped. But Arjun had traveled the world with his parents and, more recently, on his own.

When we were children, every time he went away, I cornered him upon his return, demanding to know what he had seen. Every time, he was vague.

"I went to a temple."

"Which temple?"

"It's high up on a mountain, with a slanted roof and lanterns hanging from the rafters."

"Who goes to this temple?"

He would shrug. "People."

"What kinds of people? Where do they live? Whom do they pray to in the temple?" Impatience creeping into my tone.

Arjun would sigh. Or sit down, or bite his lip, running his nervous fingers through his hair, apprehensive that his answers would never placate me in a way that was satisfying to either of us. "It's really not all that interesting, Amrita. And I'm no good at describing things anyway. You're the one who tells stories."

"You're the one who gets to travel."

"So?"

"So at least bring me back something."

And so he did. From the ocean, a shell. From the desert, a dried fossil of a sea horse. From the temple, a thread of jasmine. From a shop, a silk scarf. I had a collection of things that Arjun had brought for me from the outside world, that he would hide in all corners of the palace for me to find. Sometimes he left me clues about where his presents were hidden. A note tucked into my schoolbooks, arrows made of stones that I would find in the mango grove outside his living quarters, and occasionally, a sly gesture or glance.

I had, over time, made peace with the fact that he spoke better in gifts than he did in words.

Now I turned the ring in my hand as Arjun and I crossed the wide, pillared corridors of the residential west wing, past the potted palms and portraits of my ancestors, our feet clacking on the marble checkerboard floor.

"I had it made," he whispered. "An artisan in Shalingar. I know jasmine is your favorite flower. You can't carry the fragrance with you all the way to . . ." He went silent for a moment, as though he didn't want to say it, as though he couldn't bring himself to acknowledge it. "And I wanted you to remember . . ."

That was all he said, his eyes fixed on the guards, dressed in emerald and gold khalats, who saluted us as we made our way down the corridor. He refused to look at me, but I couldn't help but watch that profile I was so familiar with that it may as well have been my own. His regal nose, his square jaw, his full lips tightening into a line as his face fell into a mask of composure.

"It's good luck," I repeated his words.

"Too bad you've never believed in luck," he said to me, and I caught a brief smile fleeting across his face.

"Maybe I should start now. I need it," I told him.

"You'll be fine. You're good with people. He'll . . . love you."

"Perhaps it's better if he doesn't," I whispered under my breath as we turned toward the grand stairway. I tried to smile, attempting to shore up my confidence.

"Unfortunately, I don't think that's an option," Arjun responded. "It's impossible not to adore you." He was still looking straight ahead, and his words released a torrent of butterflies in my stomach.

I wanted time to stop. I wanted to turn, to run, but where? I could already hear the brass band playing Shalingar's national anthem in the gallery below.

In the quiet hollow of my chest, I was lamenting the fact that I was powerless in the face of my own fate, and something within me was screaming, flailing against all the walls of my own existence, fighting for another outcome, for another choice.

But on the outside, I remained calm. I did what I knew to do whenever I greeted dignitaries: I slipped a cool mask of composure over my face. I held my head high, flashing the diamond-studded shoes Mala had selected for me, my fingers light on the redwood banister as we descended the grand stairway into the Durbar Hall, a vast gallery with a glass dome and frescoes of Shalingar's history painted into the ceiling.

"Are you sure you want to wear it?" Arjun asked, his eyes glancing at my finger.

I nodded. Wearing Arjun's ring felt like an act of defiance but also reflected something true within me.

I knew why my heart was racing. And it didn't have to do with my fear of Sikander.

I wanted to choose my own future.

I didn't want to be Sikander's bride.

What I wanted was too impossible to say aloud, too dangerous, too fraught.

And yet I knew that I desired it with my entire heart: To stay in Shalingar. To be my own person. To serve my people. And to be with those I loved—Papa, Mala, Bandaka, and Shree. But also Arjun, I realized in that moment. Especially Arjun.

Two

M Y HEART WAS POUNDING like a drumbeat as I descended into a sea of red coats. They stood in formation as the band played Shalingar's national anthem.

"Where is he?" I whispered to Arjun, squinting my eyes as I smiled at the crowd of men standing before me.

They didn't smile back. Their faces were somber, immovable. Their large, rectangular bodies formed a wall of sameness. Even their haircuts were identical.

"I can't recognize him," Arjun said. "All I've ever seen is his likeness on a coin."

Shree, Arjun's mother, had shown us the coins, along with maps of the region, giving us lectures on the Silk Road, teaching us Macedonian greetings, which we employed the moment the band stopped playing.

"Kalispera." I nodded as I bowed before a tall,

broad-shouldered man with silver hair. He nodded back at me, his eyes narrowing as they took me in. I quickly looked away.

"Kalosìrthes." Arjun shook hands with another man whose palms were at least three times the size of mine.

When the musicians started playing Macedon's national anthem, I knew this was a signal. Our own guards saluted in formation as a man walked across the threshold of the hall, his feet plodding heavily across the parquet. He too wore a maroon jacket, but his was trimmed with gold, medals across his chest.

I had held those coins in my hand, inspecting them so carefully, trying to identify who he was from those gilded discs. But it was tantamount to reading my fortune in tea leaves.

He looked past me and Arjun, his head held high, his hand over his chest as he listened to the brass chorale that seemingly went on forever. *Was their national anthem a war chant?* I wondered as I watched him.

In person, he looked nothing like the face on those coins. In fact, I would have been hard-pressed to find anything exceptional about the physicality of the man standing before Arjun and me. He wasn't tall or broad like his men. He was slight and carried his body as though entirely aware (and dismayed) that he had somehow been assigned the wrong one.

I carefully studied his face. It was creased with deep lines, his hair almost completely gray. He looked much, much older than my father even though I knew they were about the same age. His face looked weathered, severe, humorless. There was no evidence of all those victories. Or maybe it *was* evidence of what a lifetime of military victories can do to a person.

I was still watching him when the music stopped. For a moment there was silence.

It was Sikander who broke it.

"Chandradev." He greeted my father by his first name. His voice was a jeer, or maybe it was just the Macedonian dialect.

I turned to see my father, descending the grand stairway. His uniform contrasted sharply with Sikander's. My father was dressed in a simple raw-silk tunic, the only ornament on him the wedding ring he always wore.

He smiled. "Sikander," he said, walking past me and Arjun so he was standing face-to-face with the man who, it was rumored, had stoned his father's entire council to death.

Tension gripped my shoulders as I watched Sikander's visage unexpectedly open into a smile. I noticed that his front teeth were broken and that they had been capped in gold. I caught my father's expression as he took note of Sikander's teeth. For a moment, he looked taken aback by the sight, but he recovered quickly as Sikander reached to embrace him.

When they stepped back from each other, Sikander softly said, "It's been a very long time."

He was standing a mere half pace from my father. I tried not to think of how many people he must have killed in his life, how many people had died in battles he had waged.

"It's been far too long. It's an honor to welcome you to my home, Sikander," my father said. He hesitated before he said, "Meet my daughter, Princess Amrita."

"Your daughter—" Sikander's eyes caught mine. He looked startled for a moment before he spoke. "Ah yes, the last time I saw her, she was but a baby."

"Welcome, Your Majesty." I bowed before him, and he laughed. It was a short, staccato sound, not a real laugh.

"No need for that," he said, touching my bare shoulder. His hands were ice cold, making me flinch. He quickly stepped back, his head tilted to the side.

"She looks just like her mother," he said. My father opened his mouth.

"You knew my mother?" I interjected, before my father had a chance to speak.

"I did, little one. A very long time ago. She was quite a force to be reckoned with," he said, his eyes manically bright.

I turned away from him and caught my father's eye, waiting for him to say something, anything. But my father was impossible to read, his eyes flitting quickly away from mine. Perhaps my interruption had forced him to reconsider his words, or maybe he hadn't anticipated the mention of my mother.

But shouldn't he have? I wondered to myself.

I wanted him to take charge of the situation. I wanted him to deliver a response that would quell my curiosity, shift the axis of power that Sikander had somehow managed to capture the moment he mentioned my mother.

But he didn't. Or he couldn't.

Instead, it was Sikander who turned to my father, narrowing his eyes. "Surely your father has told you about her?"

Three

M Y EYES SCANNED the Great Hall. Orange trees grew from large blue-lacquered pots around the edges of the space. On their branches hung brightly colored gold lanterns, imparting a warm, golden glow in the large, stately room.

The dining table was decorated with copper platters covered with figs and pomegranates, rose and marigold petals scattered across their surfaces.

There was always beauty here. *Shabahaat.* It was one of my favorite Shalingarsh words. It meant beauty, grace. Our language had nearly fifty words for the different varieties of beauty, but *Shabahaat* also included a certain subtext; it alluded to how beauty made one feel: full, whole, transformed. And I desperately needed to feel whole rather than the fractured emotions I was currently experiencing.

A thick, discomfiting tension hung over us, as though we were enclosed in a hut made of kindling on the hottest of days.

"Don't you want to be a part of civilization, Chandradev? It's certainly charming, this . . . kingdom of yours. Very quaint. But I know how we can bring the grand avenues and lofty stadiums of my kingdom to yours. Consider it a gift. A gift that comes at a price, of course."

"Typically, things that come at a price are by definition *not* a gift," my father intoned, his finger resting on the sharp, golden edge of his thali, the platter filled with mounds of sumptuous food.

I glanced at the immense spread of food before us: spicy prawn curry dotted with cashews and pomegranate, black lentils in cream with wild greens, roasted brinjal with ginger and tomato, raita frothy with fresh green flecks of coriander and cucumber, tomato-raisin chutney, tiny orbs of lemon pickled in sugar syrup, glass after glass of ruby-colored wine.

But Papa had barely eaten a thing. So had I. I couldn't stop thinking about what Sikander had said about my mother, and I didn't doubt that it had thrown my father off too. He wasn't his usual self. He was distant, irritable in a way I had never seen him before.

I could barely concentrate on the conversation transpiring before me. Why hadn't my father mentioned anything about my mother in all these years? Why had he always cut me off or changed the subject when I attempted to inquire about her? What was he keeping from me? And to what end?

I looked across the table at Arjun, who smiled at me

before he glanced at my ring. Just looking at him flooded my heart with affection. I caught myself staring as the lanterns lit up the golden planes of his face, the angle of his cheekbones, and forced myself to look away.

"I'm going to get right to the point, Chandradev," Sikander said. "It's taken me fifteen years to establish trade between the east and the west."

"And it's been very good . . . for Macedon."

"Not just Macedon, Chandradev. The Silk Road has been good for everyone."

The Silk Road: When I first heard of it as a child, I imagined a path made of reams and reams of gold silk. I imagined traders, monks, entire clans of Bedouins traveling along it, barefoot so as not to mar the pristine fabric under their feet. It took me years to understand that the Silk Road of my imaginings was nothing like the real thing, even if I had never seen the real thing with my own eyes.

"And I know just the thing that you can bring to the table, so to speak."

"Enlighten me, Sikander," my father said, narrowing his eyes.

"Chamak."

Across the dining hall, there was silence. Bandaka put down his spoon. Shree raised her eyes. Arjun and I glanced at each other. For a moment, all that could be heard was the startled chirp of insects.

My father leaned back in his chair, his face drawn, his jaw tensed. "That's a complicated request, Sikander."

"It's not a request, Chandradev," Sikander responded crisply. Again, silence. This time Sikander shattered it with a sharp laugh that startled me. "That's why I'm here. To say hello to an old friend, to discuss our trade relationship. And, of course, to meet your beautiful daughter," he said, turning to smile at me with his golden teeth.

I shrank in my chair, forcing a small smile in his direction, but his gaze was so intense that I had to break it. I imagined what it would be like to be married to him. The image of him kissing me with that mouth filled with gold teeth startled me and made me want to retch.

"You don't know this about my kingdom, Sikander, but I don't have any control over chamak. It's not a regulated substance. It's a drug—"

"A drug that isn't available anywhere else in the world!"

"A drug that's mined and guarded by an ancient tribe that lives in an undisclosed location and communicates with the rest of society only on their own terms, through their own intermediaries—"

"But they communicate with you, Chandradev," Sikander said quietly.

"Through messengers whom they select and deploy, but never directly."

"Then bring the Sybillines here. Make introductions. I'll talk to them."

Bandaka shook his head, interjecting, "They would never agree. They don't leave the caves. And, with all due respect, Your Majesty, one can't just think about a boost to our own economy and irresponsibly send caravans full of chamak to other lands. We have to consider the consequences."

"What consequences? You already trade small amounts of it with neighboring kingdoms," Sikander said.

Shree stepped in, authority in her voice. "With neighboring kingdoms, yes. And small amounts—that's the key. But we have to limit its trade. Chamak can be good or bad, but ultimately, the Sybillines are the custodians of it—they've studied its uses for thousands of years, and we have to acknowledge its power. If it were to get in the wrong hands—" She hesitated and looked away.

"One could easily go to the mountains, mine the stuff with or without the Sybillines," Sikander said with exasperation in his voice.

"It's not that simple," Bandaka responded. "Chamak responds to the Sybillines—it's a living substance. It loses its power if it's mined by someone else."

Sikander placed his palm on the table before him. "Then we force the Sybillines to mine it for us."

My father interjected. "They would likely rather give their lives than live as slaves. They live within a compound of caves that's impossible to find. People have tried to find them and died trying. And they are a fiercely ethical people. Sikander, you don't understand—the Sybillines communicate only with those they *want* to communicate with—"

But Sikander dismissed my father. "Anything is possible if there's a will. There must be a few we can persuade."

"No one has even *seen* a Sybilline in centuries, Sikander!"

Sikander sighed, exasperation registering on his face. He looked at my father like he was reasoning with a belligerent child, one who didn't know what was good for him. "You knew me all those years ago. Did you ever think I'd become emperor of the greatest kingdom there ever was? Did you ever think I'd become Sikander the Great?"

My father was silent.

"I learned quite a bit from you back then, Chandradev. Maybe now it's your turn to learn something from me. You're a maharaja of a kingdom. And you're being pushed around by a gang of chamak farmers and Earth-lovers who live in caves?"

"Chamak is a temperamental substance, Sikander." My father raised his voice. "It has the wiles of an infant. It can be tended to only by the Sybillines, or it's just a powder."

"Silver dust," Shree added.

"You'll be a part of our trade route, part of the modern world! Imports pouring into your kingdom, visitors coming in from across the world. Why fight this, Chandradev?"

"No one in Shalingar suffers from poverty. Everyone is taken care of here." And then my father added the part that we all instantly knew he shouldn't have. "Not like in your kingdom," he said.

I glanced at Arjun, who looked back at me, startled. I knew right then that my father needed saving in that moment, and instinct kicked in, the urge to protect him. But I can't say my own curiosity didn't play a part in what happened next.

"Your Majesty, I'd love to learn more about your time at the Military Academy," I said. I was looking down, but the moment the words were out of my mouth, I knew I needed to go on. I looked up, my eyes meeting my father's. "What were you like? What was my father like? And my mother . . ."

Sikander didn't look at me. His eyes were on my father, who sat at the head of the table, glaring back at him.

"Your mother was a magnet, a star, the sun to all our moons," Sikander said, skipping to the information he seemed to understand I most wanted to know. "Beautiful, courageous, brilliant, compelling. Good at so many things that sometimes I wondered if she could possibly even be human." Sikander's face softened for a moment before he continued, his next words directed solely at my father. "Brother. We have history. Do you remember that time we snuck off campus together and went into town, drank bottles and bottles of wine into the night, just the three of us?"

But my father said nothing. He simply pursed his lips together.

"She told us that story, that parable . . ."

My head whipped back in Sikander's direction. *The Parable of the Land of Trees.*

"She was quite a storyteller." I could tell he was drunk from the way he slurred his words. I didn't care.

"What was she like?" I whispered, my eyes fixed on him. Everyone at the table hushed, hanging on Sikander's every word.

He leaned back in his seat and looked at me, his eyes

tracing my shoulders, my bare arms. I looked away, uncomfortable, slightly afraid.

"Quite like you, actually. Brilliant, witty, very protective
of those she loved. She had a fighting spirit, coming from
that family she was born into . . ."

"Her family?"

"Your father really hasn't told you any of it, has he?" He
grinned, glancing back toward my father, whose silence was
beginning to infuriate me. I avoided looking at him across
the table, even as I felt a pang of disloyalty.

"I don't know anything about her," I said. And as I said
it, I knew that I had chosen a side, but hadn't my father kept
everything about my mother from me my whole life? Wasn't
he simply standing by as Sikander marched into Shalingar to
make me his bride, technically against my will? I was owed
something. An explanation. That was all I was asking for. It
wasn't very much, I realized, and this realization made me
even angrier.

"Your mother came from the aristocracy of Macedon.
They were very liberal in their politics. Troublemakers,
intellectuals, revolutionaries. The kind that don't fight. The
kind that talk." He shook his head and laughed. "They were
very outspoken about their vehement dislike of my father's
rule. None of them survived, of course."

My heart stopped. "What do you mean?"

"There was a raid on their home, sometime before your
father left Macedon with you." He turned to me, pressing
his hands together in a strangely watered-down mea culpa.

"My father didn't like his critics very much. It had to be done. Her parents — your grandparents — were taken in for questioning. Her brother too. They died in prison, as far as I know. But your mother, she escaped."

"Escaped?"

"They weren't able to locate her. She's still on the loose, as far as I know. In hiding, I suppose. So your father never told you that you have criminal blood in your veins, eh?" He laughed, looking back at my father. "I'm sure she wonders about you too."

"You mean she's—" *Alive. My mother is alive.*

But Sikander was lost in his own thoughts. "Every man at that school was in love with her, but she was quite taken with your father," he said, pointing his spoon at my father. "It was back in the days that the Academy accepted women. Not anymore. I find them to be an unnecessary distraction."

At that very moment, my father's gaze caught mine from across the table. He looked from me to Sikander, and I could tell from the frozen expression on his face that he had completely lost control of the situation.

"We were such . . . idealists back then, weren't we?" Sikander went on, lifting his knife and turning it in his fingers before he drove it into the spiced quail sitting on his plate. "But much has changed since then. We've changed. We live in modern times . . . I wish I had your idealism, Chandradev, but I live in the real world. Not in a land of magical talking trees."

We were all silent, stunned. I glanced at Arjun, who

furrowed his brow at me. Sikander looked around the room at his advisors, then at my father's.

He choked out his words in anger, emphasizing each one. "Fairy tales mean nothing to me. Stories have never saved anyone. Time moves forward, and you have to decide: Do you want it to move on without you? Think of the future of your kingdom. *Think of Amrita's future,*" he said, and he pointed his hand at me, a gesture that made me shrink in my chair. "Right now, you have a choice. What happened to this Land of Trees of yours—that's just the nature of the world. One can't resist the world forever. And if you resist now, you won't have the choice later."

Four

SEVERAL SETS OF EYES turned to look at me as I burst through the door of the Map Chamber, holding back my tears. I hadn't expected to see all of Papa's advisors there with him: Shree, Bandaka, Ali. I glanced around the room. His entire council of advisors was meeting past midnight, the large wooden table before them covered with maps and scrolls of parchment filled with frenetic text. Papa's security detail was there too, all of them still dressed in their khalats. They must have reconvened right after dinner.

An emergency meeting, I realized. I quickly wiped away my tears, embarassed. It was instinct by now. I remembered the words Mala had recited to me since I was little: *Royalty does not make a scene. Royalty behaves with dignity, poise, decorum, grace, compassion. Royalty remembers responsibility, maintains their composure, knows they are constantly being watched. Royalty must be brave, strategic, loyal.*

In bursting in on my father, or in betraying him by asking Sikander about my mother, I had displayed none of these characteristics. Yet I was simultaneously furious and confused. My father was the only one who could clarify everything for me, and he knew it.

Dinner had ended on a tense note, with Sikander curtly excusing himself to retire to the guest quarters and my father disappearing soon after. I sensed I would find him in here, where he was most at ease and entirely in control, but I wasn't expecting him to be in the midst of an emergency congress.

"You're all dismissed." He turned to his advisors. "Turn in for the night. We'll convene early tomorrow morning and start where we left off."

Shree's voice carried a hint of worry. "But, Your Majesty, we still haven't come up with a solution—"

"And we will. Tomorrow."

I watched guiltily as Papa's advisors and security trailed out the door. And then there were just two of us, standing on either side of the Map Chamber. My father at the head of the heavy wooden table carved from a banyan tree that Arjun and I used to play under when we were children, and me by the door, waiting for him to explain.

We looked at each other across the dimly lit room, maps of Shalingar, of Lake Chanakya, of Persia, Macedon, the entire east, surrounding us. I had studied those maps so carefully, memorizing capitals, learning about topography, the economy, trade. I had painstakingly studied the customs and beliefs of all the lands south of the Jhelum River and many of the lands north of it too. I knew the history of every kingdom that surrounded us, including our own, but I didn't know my own past. I didn't know who I was. And I couldn't help but conclude that it was my father's fault.

But my father was quiet. He simply pressed his palms into the table before him and watched me silently, and I could tell he was trying to decide what to say.

"Sit down," he said softly, and I came around the table as he pulled a chair out for me.

He poured a tumbler of water from an earthen carafe and placed it before me, squeezing my shoulder with his other hand. Then he sat down and looked out the window, taking a deep breath. My eyes followed his to the highest mountain in the distance. *Mount Moutzu.* I remember Mala telling me its name, *The Mountain of Miracles.* It was on the way to the Janaka Caves, where the Sybillines supposedly lived.

Mala had told me a fable about the mountain when I was a child. It was the site where the Diviners, the first humans, met with and built an alliance with the vetalas, the cunning and beautiful ghouls that haunted people's souls. No one had seen a vetala in hundreds of years, but it was believed that they once wandered the Earth as though it was theirs.

The Diviners, the vetalas, talking trees. Sikander was right—they were just stories, and stories couldn't save people. Maybe those stories did more harm than good by giving us false hope. All they did was reinforce our faith that the world was once made up almost entirely of magic or miracles. But where was that magic now, when we needed it?

"That's why you told me that story again and again and again," I said to my father, seeing for the first time that he must have thought of her each time.

"It was . . . her favorite parable."

There was an awkward tension between my father and me, and I realized how difficult it was for him, discussing my mother.

"You should have told me, at the very least, that she's still alive!"

"There's no way for us to confirm that. You saw the way Sikander is. It could all be manipulation in order to—"

"It doesn't matter!" I yelled. "You knew that she might be alive, and you never even bothered to mention it?"

"It was far more complicated than you know. And if I didn't tell you, it was to protect you—"

"That's rubbish!" I yelled again, stunned at the ferocity of my tone.

He nodded, as though he understood that my reaction was warranted. "I've tried, over the years . . . to tell you about her, and to find her. I know how difficult this is for you to understand, but Sikander is attempting to drive a wedge between us, and she—"

"You allowed that to happen, Papa."

"I should have told you," he quietly said. "Tell me what you want to know. Ask me whatever you'd like to ask," he said. He waited me out patiently.

It was all I had ever wanted to hear. I held my breath, but my head was spinning. Now that the opportunity had presented itself, there was only one thing I wanted, no, *needed* to know.

"How do I find her?"

"That, I can't tell you," he said.

"But she's in Macedon?"

"I don't know."

"Why isn't she . . . *here*? With us?" I asked, tears filling my eyes.

"We needed to keep you safe. We had a plan, but the day we were supposed to leave Macedon and come here, she disappeared."

"I don't understand. She was supposed to come here?"

My father nodded, slowly. "We had gone into hiding. There was a time when I even considered staying in Macedon, or going someplace else. Hiding our identities. I thought about giving Bandaka the throne. He was . . . *is* my best friend, just the way Arjun is yours. But in the end, we decided to come back to Shalingar. Only, she didn't come with us."

"Why not?"

My father sighed. "It was a complicated time. Sikander had just taken over the throne. Macedon was in a volatile state. And she came from a family that actively questioned the leadership. It was an unstable period for all of us."

Nothing he was saying made any sense to me. "But you were friends," I whispered.

My father shook his head. "A long time ago, we were

friends. And then we . . . weren't. My understanding . . . my hope was that Sikander had changed. I haven't seen him or spoken to him in years. But it's becoming increasingly clear to me that he hasn't changed. And that you . . . cannot marry him."

"What does that mean? I thought you had an agreement. We can't simply break it, can we?"

My father opened his mouth to speak again, but it was no good, what he was telling me. It was too late, and there was so much I didn't know, and even though his words about breaking the promise of marriage to Sikander sent a shot of relief through my nerves, I was too terrified to get my hopes up only to have them shattered.

"It doesn't matter," I realized aloud, getting up and pushing my chair in. "In a few weeks, I'll be in Macedon." My stomach turned at the thought of leaving home, of marrying Sikander, even of the regret I knew my father would feel, perhaps for the rest of his life.

And yet I was still furious with him; I couldn't help it. Only one thing kept me going. "I'll find her myself," I said before I turned on my heel and walked out of the Map Chamber, leaving my father behind.

I saw it as I approached my chambers. At first, I wasn't sure what it was. Wedged into the doorframe of my bedroom, a slip of parchment. A note. I unfolded it, recognizing the handwriting immediately.

The Mango Grove. Come find me.

Despite everything that had happened, I couldn't help but smile. I looked up and down the corridor with its high ceilings and open skylights. Not a soul in sight. Mala's door, right next to mine, was closed.

Quickly, I shuffled to the back stairwell at the edge of the east wing. I threaded the maze of the servants' quarters, slipping out the kitchen door, as Arjun and I had done a million times before.

Only this time, it felt illicit. Recently, I had noticed that my heart pounded like a drumbeat as I approached these meetings with him, so loud that I was afraid it would wake up everyone sleeping in the palace.

I considered for a moment that no one in the palace was sleeping tonight. Papa's advisors were strategizing, their heads negotiating a million political calculations a minute, even as they rested on silk pillows. It was unlikely that Papa was sleeping either, considering the conversation we just had.

But I left this fleeting thought behind as I exited the stone walls of the palace residence and emerged on the grounds, met by a balmy breeze that smelled like a mixture of jasmine, mango, and cut grass.

The grounds were quiet, empty. And the sky was a navy quilt embroidered with diamonds. I tiptoed quietly on the trail to the mango grove, noticing the arrows made of jasmine petals that Arjun had most certainly left behind for me. The moonlight illumined silver spiderwebs between the leaves of trees. Mangoes hung like ornaments from delicate branches that looked like fingers in the dark.

I continued to follow the arrows. By morning, the groundskeepers and the breeze would have swept them away, but right now, they were the kind of gift that was precious precisely because it was ephemeral. Arjun had always specialized in such bequests—the kinds that required thought and effort but ultimately existed only for a moment before they were gone, leaving behind a memory slipped into one's heart like a parchment note left in a doorframe.

I followed the arrows into the cut grass that tickled my bare feet. It was about fifty more paces till the edge of the grove, and once there, I could see a light glowing in the center of the thicket.

All of a sudden, I felt nervous. My stomach fluttered as I caught a glimpse of him seated on a mirrored cushion amid a nest of patchwork blankets and throw pillows, waiting for me. He was surrounded by lights—at least fifty diyas and a handful of lanterns. I wondered when and how he had found the time to set all this up.

I sat down beside him, feeling too shy to speak. Luckily, he was quiet too. It was as though we both understood that something had shifted between us. Perhaps it was the knowledge of my departure bringing things to a head, and yet, despite the jumble of thoughts and emotions churning within me, I still wasn't sure how to act or what to say.

I opened my mouth, and as I did, I knew that I was somehow squandering this moment, killing the magic in the air.

"I can't believe my mother's still alive," I said. "I can't believe Papa never bothered to tell me. I feel like my mind has been caught in some sort of storm, like I'm in the eye of it, and if I don't find her, or at least find out what happened to her, I know the storm will ravage me."

"You'll find out. I'll help you," he said, laying a hand on my arm. His fingers felt electric as they slipped between mine, taking my breath away. I tried to appear nonchalant to hide my fear, my excitement, the whirl of a million feelings roiling within me.

"I want this to be over," I said to him.

"If only so we don't have to dress like characters from a Persian fairy tale," he whispered, making me laugh out loud.

"Shhhh . . ." Arjun squeezed next to me, his arm against mine. "We don't want to wake anyone."

"My father says Sikander's trying to create a wedge between me and him."

Arjun nodded, his eyes on me the entire time. He tucked a stray strand of hair behind my ear, his thumb trailing my neck, leaving behind a line of goose bumps. "I think he's right." He paused for a moment before he added, "You know I'd do anything for you, right?" he said.

"Anything?" I teased. I wanted to ease this tension between us. It felt so dangerous that it couldn't possibly be good for either of us, like attempting to light a fire stick near a field of hay. But then again, it was Arjun, whom I had known my entire life. My best friend.

"Anything," Arjun insisted.

There had never been any space between us, any hierarchy. That's how my father and Bandaka were too. Bandaka had grown up within the compound of the palace, and his father had been my grandfather's advisor. My father and Bandaka had played together as children.

It was just the same, I told myself. We were just like them.

Until Arjun's fingers slipped into my hair. Gently, he tilted my face back until my eyes met his. The only thing I could hear was my own heartbeat, startlingly loud in my ears.

There was no decision, no reflection, only impulse. An impulse so clear that it was as though it had been there all along, all these years, waiting for us to uncover it.

And we did.

I lifted my face to meet his, noticing everything about him as if for the first time, the curve of his lips, the plane of his jaw, his warm, dark eyes. His hands clasped my thigh, pulling me closer and closer until our bodies were entwined.

And when we kissed, I was stunned by how soft and yielding his lips were, eventually giving way to a ferocious urgency, a desperate need to hold me and never let me go.

Five

"EVERY KINGDOM has its traditions," Sikander announced.
It was morning, and we were convened in the gallery
once again—Papa, Sikander, their advisors, and of course
Arjun and me. I wondered if anyone could tell from the dark
circles under my eyes that I had been up all night with Arjun
in the mango grove, talking, laughing, kissing, until the first
rays of dawn chased us back into the palace to get dressed
for another day.

A day that I could face only because I knew I would see
Arjun again. And yet I also lamented this fact. How many
days did we have together, now that we had discovered this
magnetic alchemy between us?

He had held me tightly against him outside my chamber,
his face meeting mine.

"It's not over," he whispered to me. "This is just the
beginning."

"But how?"

"We'll figure it out. You and I . . . we can do anything together," he said, kissing me one last time before returning to his quarters.

But what we could do was still up in the air, unclear, at least to me.

I turned back to Sikander, who was loudly pontificating to us.

"In Bactria, negotiations begin after everyone observes a circus show. In Anatolia, there is the sacrifice of an animal. Considering the union that will bring our two kingdoms together," he said, nodding at me with a patronizing smile that showed off the mouthful of gold, "I'd like to bring a Macedonian tradition to Shalingar."

"So it starts," mumbled Arjun under his breath.

It took everything in me not to look at him when he said this. I leveled my gaze at my father, whose face was stern and unmoving. "Please go on," he said.

Sikander's mouth twisted into a mischievous grin. "As you know, Chandradev, I love to surprise."

I wondered what he meant by this, but my father's face gave nothing away.

"I come bearing gifts," Sikander continued as he nodded to some members of his retinue who disappeared for an instant, only to return with hundreds of large golden chests. One by one, they were placed before my father and me.

"There was no need, Sikander."

"Come now, old friend. You wouldn't refuse a gift for your daughter, would you?"

And then, at a mere inclination of Sikander's head, his footmen opened the chests to reveal troves of jewels—cut emeralds, sea-blue sapphires, rubies the color of blood. Gold coins, shimmering in the light of a thousand diyas, illuminated the Durbar Hall. Reams and reams of buttery silks spilled forth across the marble floor.

More footmen arrived, carrying pots that contained unusual varieties of flowers—horn-shaped and bell-shaped poufs of purple and magenta, others that looked like flames. "The first gift." Sikander nodded. "The gift of beauty. For your daughter," he said, smiling at me. "The greatest treasures the world has to offer."

He smiled again, and I tried not to stare at his teeth.

"Sikander, you've outdone yourself—" my father began, but Sikander interrupted him.

"It's the first time I'm meeting this little one in sixteen years," he said, smiling at me.

I bristled at being called that. My mind flashed to the night before, Arjun kissing me, undoing my blouse, his hands on my stomach, his fingers dipping into the waistband of my petticoat.

Stop, I told myself. I could tell that my face was reddening, and I wondered again if everyone in the room could tell what had happened between Arjun and me.

But Sikander merely turned back to his footmen. "The second—a gift of power. A cavalry of trained horses—for your army. Just outside the palace," he said, waving his arm toward the grounds.

My father's chin lifted, his eyes narrowed. "I thank you

for your Nawaazish, Sikander." But Papa's cold tone told me
that he was dubious of this gesture of generosity.

Sikander smiled a circus-master's smile, but something
about the way his mouth twitched, or the way his eyes
scanned the room nervously, made me slightly anxious. "And
the last gift, of course, is the most important one."

Once again he gestured to the door, but his eyes were
still on me, inspecting me carefully. I looked away self-
consciously as four footmen, led by a man with sharp features that appeared as though they had been chiseled in
stone, brought in a large golden box.

"Nico, my head of security, has been guarding it with his
life the entire journey to Shalingar." Sikander pointed to the
man with the sharp features. Nico bowed before us, and his
eyes lingered on me for a moment before he turned back to
the box.

"Well, open it." Sikander smiled, glancing from my father
to me. He rocked on his heels, his arms clasped behind his
back. He looked like a magician, delighted at his own tricks.
Something about the amusement on his face made a chill go
up my spine.

I looked at my father, and he nodded. I stepped forward,
reached for the latch on top, and flung it open.

Inside the box, something moved. I jumped back, startled.
Sikander smiled.

I stepped closer. Inside, the creature writhed. Skin, hair,
fingernails. A mouth. It was a *person*. When she looked up,
her eyes squinting into the light, I realized that she was a
girl. A girl my age.

My heart began to race.

Her skin was pale, practically translucent. Her hair was woven into copper-colored braids. But it was her eyes that struck me. They were lavender, and they flashed fear.

I backed away till my shoulder bumped Arjun's. He grabbed my elbow, but his grip did nothing to reassure me.

"An oracle," Shree whispered. "I've never seen one before." Her eyes widened in shock.

"Sikander." My father's voice was tense. "You are truly" — he stopped, took a deep breath — "too kind," he quickly said. "But you must know we don't keep slaves in Shalingar." I could see from his eyes how disturbed he was at the sight of a girl my age chained and trapped in a box.

"Not a slave." Sikander shook his finger vehemently at my father. "A gift of vision. An oracle. Some say they're anomalies, freaks of nature. But I say they're quite magnificent." He grinned at my father. "Come now, Chandradev, I remember your fondness for *prophecy*." He stressed the last word, and my father's eyes flashed anger at the sound of it.

"She can't stay here," my father tersely responded.

"Of course she can," Sikander went on, ignoring him. "She must be kept in darkness. She needs silence. Solitude. Her gifts are only effective under such conditions. And with the chamak that your kingdom trades in, her powers are magnified."

"She cannot stay here!" My father raised his voice.

"Are you refusing my gift?"

"She's not a *gift*. She's a girl. A human being. What

exactly is the meaning of this, Sikander? Are you threatening me? Are you threatening my daughter, my kingdom—"

Sikander smiled, his voice even. "I'm merely offering you a gift. The best my kingdom has to offer."

"If the best your kingdom has to offer is its cruelty to human beings, a lack of democratic values, slavery—"

"It's not his gift to refuse," I cut in, my voice surprisingly calm. Everyone in the room turned to look at me. My eyes met my father's, but I was speaking to Sikander. "Your Majesty, I thank you for your . . . generous gift. What is her name?"

Sikander was silent for a moment. He turned to his man.

"Her name is Thala," Nico responded.

"I will take Thala to her chamber. You said she needs to be kept . . . in darkness?" My voice was flat, unaffected.

"Answer her, Nico," Sikander commanded.

"She's most useful when she's kept in darkness," Nico sternly replied. I tried not to cringe.

"Well, that's settled." Shree smiled a tense smile. "Now, shall we convene to the State Room for discussions, Your Majesties?"

My father was glaring at me, but I knew I had done the right thing. Someone needed to take control of the situation, and my father was too emotional. I had never seen him like this before.

I gripped my bracelet tightly, thinking through my next steps. All I knew was that there was no way I could leave the palace with this cruel man.

I bowed before Sikander, thanking him again. I waited till Papa and Sikander and their advisors had left the room.

"I'll have the guards escort the two of you," Shree mumbled to me before she took off to join them.

"Do you want me to come with you?" Arjun whispered in my ear.

I shook my head. "I'll find you later," I said to him. Once he was gone, I released a terrified breath.

I couldn't keep my eyes off the girl. Her thin shoulders trembled, but no one had reached out to help her. Somewhere in the palace, someone slammed a door with a loud bang, and she flinched at the sound. I noticed that her small hands were bound in rope and that she had cuts on her wrists, bruises and burns on both her arms and legs. On her left shoulder was an image—a tattoo of a swirling, living thing with tentacles. It took me a moment to realize that it was a tree. Her eyes scanned the space around her until they met mine. And even without her saying the words, I knew what they conveyed.

Please, they said. *Please help me.*

Six

I TRIED TO SEE OUR WORLD through her eyes, and I felt as though I were observing the palace grounds for the first time. What struck me was how vibrant and expansive they were, even on a gray day like this. Rolling emerald greens, peacocks with their shimmering train of turquoise feathers tipped with a million yellow eyes dancing in the light drizzle. Large palms swaying in the wind. Plumes of hibiscus, groves of ripe yellow guavas. I plucked one off a tree and offered it to Thala.

She looked at me as though she didn't know what to do with it.

"You can unshackle her," I said to our guards, and they removed the iron shackles from her feet, the rope that bound her hands together. I tried to look away from the cuts on her arms and legs, but it was impossible.

She was stumbling more than walking, so much so that the guards had to prop her up.

"Are you all right?"

I tried to hand her the guava again, and she stared at it for a long time, finally taking it and turning it in her hand.

When she looked up, I noticed her eyes were rimmed red and looked faraway. *Chamak.* I recognized it. I had witnessed these symptoms only in the ascetics who came the palace grounds once a year, asking for alms, blessing the palace, and occasionally delivering messages from the Sybillines, but Thala's eyes resembled those of the saddhus—hollow and red, her pupils dilated.

I choked back the jet of emotion spouting within me. *She's just a girl, my age, in a condition that terrifies me, that no girl should ever be in.* How could every type of control—over her destiny, her mind, her body—have been taken from her? I wanted to reassure her in some way, let her know that we had no intention of harming her, but I didn't know what to say.

"We're taking you to the Temple of Rain," I said to her in Macedon. She squinted her eyes into the sun, a groan emerging from her throat. It was a despairing sound of resignation, as though she didn't care where we were taking her.

I wasn't even sure if she understood me, but I kept talking.

"You'll be safe there," I told her. "It's . . . not a temple, exactly. Well, we're not quite sure what it is. I suppose you'll just have to see it to understand."

She said nothing. It was only when we reached the

mouth of the temple that she uttered the first words I ever heard from her.

"Theé mou!" she gasped in awe.

"Don't be scared," I whispered as we began to head down into the Temple of Rain, a stepwell made of stones. We descended a grand stairway, sinking through a series of carved corridors and pavilions until we could no longer see the light of day. The guards had brought lanterns with them, and the oily orange glow of fire lit up the subterranean friezes and colonnades that filled the cavern.

We quickly descended another flight of stairs, turning into a doorway. I watched her pressing her palms to the wall, feeling her way down the dark corridor.

"It's all right. It's dark, but you're safe," I said to her.

Nobody knew who had built the Temple of Rain, how long it had existed before us, or even why it had been built.

Once I had asked Shree about it, and she simply shrugged her shoulders. "The Ancients," she had responded. "They must have known what they were doing. But I certainly don't."

In the current dry season, the Temple of Rain was a stony subterranean maze, filled with elaborately carved pillars, doors that led down twisting hallways, some that wound themselves in dizzying circles around the structure, others that dead-ended into walls.

There was folklore that the Temple was haunted by vetalas, immortal spirits who could enter and inhabit anyone's body. It was believed that vetalas roamed the Earth freely for many years, inhabiting the bodies of humans after they died. Vetalas had all sorts of powers. Some of them could fly. Others had the ability to heal any wound. They were known for their trickery and brilliance, and also their loyalty and their beauty. But humans were mistrustful of vetalas and had wiped them out. Even so, some people, like Mala, believed that vetalas still existed, that they hid among us, pretending to be human.

"They're the most loyal creatures; they'd do anything for those they care for," Mala once told me.

"Except they don't really exist," I said to her, and she raised an eyebrow.

"They exist for anyone who believes in them. And you'd best not be creeping around dark places at night if you never want to encounter one."

But we didn't listen to her, Arjun and I. When we were younger, in the dry months we played hide-and-seek in the Temple of Rain. There were endless places to hide. Even now, I didn't know where all the pathways and corridors led.

But when it rained, the entire stepwell—doors, stone rooms, pillars, and all—disappeared into a cistern, filling to capacity and submerging the Temple.

Thala was running her hands over the ornate columns and eroded reliefs, and even in the dark, I sensed curiosity in her eyes.

"We don't know who built this, or why. Many of the carvings on the walls . . . they've been eroded in the rains or defaced."

We arrived at a cell, and I asked the guards to leave us. They handed me the key, bowed, and took leave, placing a lantern at my feet so that I could safely return back to the palace. I hated that I had brought her here, to a dark, enclosed space, but it was the only place I would be able to speak to her alone that wouldn't raise suspicion. When I turned to look at her, she didn't seem surprised that I had stayed behind. I wondered if she knew what I wanted to ask her.

In the cell was a basin of water, a tumbler, a blanket, and another lantern.

I dipped the tumbler into the water and handed it to her. She slurped at it, thirstily, downing the entire thing, coughing violently before handing it back to me. I refilled it and placed it back in her hands.

Then, I tore a strip of fabric from the pallu of my sari and dabbed it into the water, reaching for her arm, making her flinch.

"It's all right," I told her as I began to clean her wounds. Her body tensed in fear. I knew I had to distract her, calm her. It was dark, but I could make out a relief of a giant face on the wall. I pointed to it.

"My friend and I . . . we're always speculating about this place . . . Maybe it was a place of worship? Or a refuge? It could have been a prison. Or a subterranean city."

"Why would anyone bother to beautify a prison?" she whispered in Shalingarsh.

It took me a second to make sense of what she had said. In the distance, I could hear the sound of insects chirping, and then their echoes. I took a deep breath, swallowing my shock. I placed my hand on the curved wall of stone beside me.

"You speak . . . my language?" I asked.

"I speak many languages," she whispered. "Once upon a time, I was a person. Just like you."

"You *are* a person," I quickly responded. I looked up from her cuts and saw her face, illuminated in the lamplight. She was partially obscured by the shadows of iron bars in the door to the cell, but despite those shadows, I could make out her features, delicate and fine-boned.

"It's been a long time since I was treated like one," she said, watching as I cleaned the cuts on her ankles.

I thought about the chains and the ropes again. The scabbed cuts and burns on her arms. I thought about her trapped in that box. How long had she been in there? Just the thought of it made it hard for me to breathe.

"Why are you here?" I asked her.

"Because they brought me."

"No." I shook my head. I wasn't even sure I believed in oracles, but I did know that offering Thala as a gift was a strategic move on Sikander's part, maybe even a trick. He knew my father and I—our entire kingdom—abhorred slavery. He understood how much it would disturb us to see a small girl in a box, chained and beaten. But he still brought her to us. Why? Was my father right about it being a threat? Or was there something else? Something we didn't yet know?

"You must know why you're here," I said to her.

But she ignored my question. "You have to help me," she

whispered. Her voice shook, but I could hear the determination in it. Slowly, carefully, she reached for me with her free hand, touching my shoulder. "They keep me chained day and night. I must return home."

I nodded. "I'll do anything I can to help you," I promised her, and I knew I would. That I had to.

"I have a home, a family . . ."

Carefully, gingerly, I touched her hand to comfort her. She gripped my fingers tightly.

"I will help you, I promise," I assured her. "But you must tell me—"

She cut me off. "You will release me," she said. "I'm sorry for what it will cost you." Her voice didn't waver this time, and her eyes were resolutely fixed on me.

I was taken aback for a moment. "What do you mean?"

She pointed to the key in my hand. "There's a key. But you don't yet know where to go. I will show you the way."

"I don't understand," I said, shaking my head. Her eyes were still hazy, and I wondered if she was even cogent. But I asked her again: "Why are you here? Why did he bring you?"

"It won't matter. There are more important things. You're about to go on a journey."

My heart sank. "To Macedon, you mean."

She looked away. "He loves you, you know."

"Who? Sikander?"

"The boy you kissed in the mango grove. He'll save your life."

The hairs on the back of my neck stood up when she said that.

She closed her eyes tightly before she opened them again. "And what you're desperate to know," she said.

I waited.

"About your mother. Why they never spoke of her." Her voice was low and conspiratorial. "I know the answer to this."

The mention of my mother was so unexpected that I paused to take a deep breath. Had Sikander instructed her to say these words to me? Had he sent spies after me to catch me with Arjun? I wasn't sure whether to believe her, to trust her. As it was, she was high on chamak.

I wore a mask of detached curiosity on my face. "You do?"

For a moment, Thala didn't answer. She closed her eyes, and when she opened them again to look back at me, I noticed that they had changed color. They were green now. I was startled at the sight of them.

Her voice was a frightened whisper. "He came bearing gifts," she said. "Heed the warning in the gift."

She paused and closed her eyes again, and this time when she opened them, they were the color of gold. The color of my father's eyes that day when he looked out over the hills of Shalingar. The color of chamak in the light of the rising sun. Just the sight of them made me inch backward. I sensed a power in her that had been subdued by all the beatings, all the humiliations, all the assaults to her humanity, but it was there: She was one of the most powerful individuals I had ever encountered.

"You will recognize the signs of the attack," she told me. "But it's already too late. Your fate has been written. All you can do is go back and say goodbye."

"Attack? Goodbye? What are you—"

"The animals will run loose. A fight will break out in the west. He says he wants friendship. He says he wants an alliance. Don't believe what he says."

My heart began to race. "Sikander? You mean he—"

"Once upon a time, I was just like you. A girl, free. You feel sorry for me now, but once upon a time, I had a family, a mother, a home. And then it all changed. You'll understand what that feels like soon enough," she said, and I felt the color drain from my face. "I'm sorry for it. I truly am."

Seven

"Is Arjun here?" I asked, trying to keep my voice measured and calm. Within minutes, he emerged from his quarters, dismissing his footman.

We walked the lofty corridors of the palace together in silence, our feet clicking on the marble. We observed parrots and bluebirds building nests on the rafters of the Durbar Hall, watched the way peacocks proudly wandered in and out of the interior courtyards. We pointed at the slippery movements of bright blue fish swimming across the pools in every verandah that Tippu the gardener lovingly watched after, traversing the terraced floating gardens that lined the balconies on the second floor of the palace. We ventured past the neem and walnut and lime trees that had grown into the palace compound, as though they were a part of the structure.

We pretended we had somewhere important to be, smiled and nodded to the footmen and cooks and gardeners and other members of the palace staff as we made our way past them, but the moment the door to my bedroom closed, he pressed me into a wall, his mouth on mine, the stubble of his chin nuzzling my neck, his palms on my waist, his fingers slipping up into my blouse. We kissed until I was dizzy and lightheaded. For however long it was, I couldn't speak, couldn't think; there was nothing else I wanted but the heat of his body against mine, the feeling of closing any space between us.

It was dark outside when I finally slipped away from his arms to draw my curtains.

"Aren't your parents expecting you back in your quarters?"

He shook his head. "They're still in a meeting with Sikander's advisors. I don't think they're going to let out till late tonight. Is Mala going to come check on you?"

"She'll come by in the morning."

"So . . . can I stay?" he sheepishly asked, and I took his hand, pulling him into the bed with me.

We lay there together silently, and I felt a contentment wash over me. His arm was wrapped around my waist, my head buried in his chest, his other hand grasping a fistful of the cloud of my hair surrounding us. My body was aflame with a euphoria I had never before felt. And then I remembered Sikander, and my stomach lurched.

Perhaps Arjun sensed it. Or maybe he felt exactly what I did. Still, I wasn't expecting him to say what he said next.

"Run away with me."

I choked out a laugh. "Are you serious?"

"I wish I weren't."

My heart began to race again, but not out of passion. I glanced around the familiar walls of my abode, the ceiling painted a bright cerulean, the white lacquered cupboards, the mosquito net over my bed. All of a sudden, it seemed like an entirely different world. I shook my head, overtaken by a fear that silenced me. A seesaw of terror, panic on both sides of an impossible equation: Losing Arjun and being Sikander's bride was bad enough, but what if we were caught running away? What would Sikander do to us then?

And yet, I wanted desperately to flee.

"I've traveled the world," Arjun told me. "I can show it to you. I've always wanted to; now here's our chance."

I opened my mouth to speak, but he placed two fingers on my lips.

"Nobody in Shalingar knows what you look like. We could hide. It would just be you and me, together."

"Sikander and his men know what I look like."

"We'll lie low. We'll get help from people in Ananta. We'll—"

"How would we even get out of the palace without anyone noticing?"

"There's a way out through the Temple of Rain. I heard my mother talking about it once. It's an emergency escape route."

"But why didn't I—"

"You're not supposed to know. For your own protection."

"And my father?"

Arjun looked back at me, but from the expression on his face, I could tell that he hadn't yet worked out the answer to that particular question.

"Your father doesn't want you marrying Sikander. He was right. The oracle was a threat."

There was a protective note to his voice, but I found myself thinking about the oracle again. I promised I would return, but her words left me shaken; after I departed her cell, I fearfully locked the door, my hands shaking, and ran from the Temple of Rain as fast as I could.

"She told me that we shouldn't believe Sikander."

"Who?"

"Thala, the oracle."

"What else did she say?"

"Something about an attack. Animals running loose, a fight in the west. That we can't trust Sikander . . . It didn't all make sense. I think she was hallucinating. And I don't even believe in that sort of thing, but—she knew other things too."

I didn't mention what she said about Arjun loving me, about how he would save my life, but all of a sudden, I wondered if it was possible that he might. That maybe we *could* actually run away together.

"What could it possibly mean, Arjun?"

"It doesn't matter, Amrita." He was holding my face in his hands now, urgency in his voice, desperation in his eyes. "I can't let you end up like her."

"I can't just run away and leave my father. Imagine what Sikander would do in retaliation!"

"Your father would want you to go. He knows you'd be safer with me than with anyone in the world."

"You're acting crazy because I snuck you into my chambers, and because everything is changing, and because we'll be apart for the first time in — "

"You're right. I *am* acting crazy. But it's not for any of those reasons. It's because I love you, Amrita."

He had said the words that silenced me.

So the oracle had been right on one count, at least.

"If you love me too," he continued, "run away with me. Don't think about the things that scare you. Don't think about all the things that could go wrong. You and I, we're a team. We always have been. If anyone can pull this off, it's us. And I can't possibly spend the rest of my life — "

But he didn't need to say anything else — couldn't, actually, because right then, I reached for him and kissed him, his mouth against mine, his strong hands clasping my waist. He pulled at the pallu of my sari, untwisting it around me, kissing my neck, my shoulder blades, his tongue tracing the exposed skin of my décolletage. I unbuttoned his khalat, pressing my face into his chest, till we were just skin on skin, just mouths and hands, till I couldn't tell where I ended and he began, our arms and legs entangled, our eyes fixed on each other.

"All right," I said, pulling away from him. "If we were to run away, how would we even — "

But Arjun already had a plan. "The morning after Sikander's last dinner here, we can leave before dawn, slip out of the palace. Meet me at the mango grove, and we'll go out the Temple of Rain. I'll take care of everything. Just be ready," he said, an intensity in his voice I had never before heard.

It was real, I realized.

He was right.

We *could* run away.

Maybe my fate wasn't sealed yet.

Eight

"RISE AND SHINE!" Mala's voice cut through the humid air in my bedroom like a scimitar, making me jump.

I had been plagued by nightmares all night: Mala coming in, drawing the curtains as she did every morning to start getting me ready for the day, only to discover Arjun in my bed, scandal registering on her face. Arjun and me running in circles through the Temple of Rain, lost and confused. Sikander tossing me into a box and locking me in there, while I screamed and banged against it with all my might.

"That's quite a reaction," Mala said. "I hope you haven't been up to mischief." She placed a tray with chai and warm biscuits on my bedside table. I looked around the room. Arjun was gone.

A single magenta hibiscus bloomed from a glass vial. I touched its petals, trying to distract myself from thoughts of him.

"Why would I be up to mischief?" I mumbled, my face reddening as I discreetly glanced around my chambers. Just then, my fingers discovered a loose scrap of parchment under my pillow. I pulled it into my fist, watching Mala as she buzzed around the room like a hummingbird.

"It's a busy day today. Breakfast with His Majesty's guests, a tiger hunt, a banquet at the end of the night. Several dress changes, sorry to say." I watched as Mala began to lay out my clothes for the day, scouring my wardrobe, pulling forth tunics and lenghas and saris and scarves.

Normally, I would have expressed annoyance, but today, I simply watched Mala as she zigzagged around my chambers, grabbing a bangle from a jewelry box, a pair of shoes from my wardrobe.

I thought of how Mala had cared for me since I was a child, waking me up every morning before breakfast. Feeding me slices of guava when I was hungry. Telling me stories. Combing my hair. Laying out my clothes. Making sure that I was on time to things. Scolding me when Arjun and I ran out in the rain without our shoes. Hugging me whenever I made her proud. These were only a few of the things Mala did for me.

"Come now, why are you still sitting? Let's run you a bath."

But all of a sudden, my eyes were filled with tears, and I was overwhelmed by the realization that I was leaving home and that Mala wasn't coming with me.

Neither were Bandaka and Shree, Arjun's parents. Nor

were the hundred or so people who inhabited and operated what was practically a village within the palace compound: guards and cooks, gardeners and medicine men, ladies-in-waiting and council members. Even a zookeeper for the palace zoo that had been built at my great-grandmother's insistence. These people were my family, and Shalingar Palace was my home. And then there was my father. Whether I was leaving with Sikander or Arjun, I would probably never see any of them ever again.

Another thought crossed my mind: What would happen to all of these people, my family, if Arjun and I ran away? Would our transgression put their lives at risk as well?

"What now, girl? I don't have time for your tears today," Mala said sternly. But she glanced at me a second time, and I could see her soften. She sighed and sat down at the edge of my bed.

"It's scary and unnerving, I know. Leaving home, leaving Shalingar. Their customs are different, their way of life. Still, you'll come visit. And Master Arjun will be in Macedon for his military training. And I suspect your father'll take some trips to Macedon too, now that you're to be there."

I nodded, but now a torrent of tears was running down my face. I hated that I was keeping things from Mala. I never kept anything from her.

"Girl, this is going to be hard for you to understand since you grew up in a palace, everyone giving you exactly what you wanted the moment the thought of it fell into your head. You've had a charmed and blessed life. Nothing but fortune.

I used to worry that that kind of pampering would make you soft. But you're not soft. You're braver, fiercer, smarter than you think. Use those parts of yourself and you'll never blame anyone else for the conditions of your life. It'll be your own, no matter what happens, no matter who you're married to or where you are. No matter what anyone says."

I nodded, wiping away my tears. I felt the urge to tell Mala what Arjun and I had discussed last night. I wanted to tell her that I was in love, but I knew I couldn't, so I simply hugged her as tight as I could.

Mala squeezed me back before she got up again. "No time to dawdle now. What's this?" she said, lifting up Arjun's sock from the floor.

I opened my mouth to say something, my heart racing, but just then Mala drew the curtains open. Bright sunlight poured into my bedroom. She pressed a palm to the window and put down the sock, bringing her hand up to her mouth. "What the—"

I scrambled behind her. The sight outside my window made me dizzy with panic. A loose zebra, running across the grounds.

"How did it . . . ?" Mala began. "Someone must have let it out of the zoo."

I felt a cold stab of fear in my heart as I thought about Thala's prophecy.

Mala shook her head, but her eyes remained fixed on the grounds below. "Nothing but commotion today. Look." She pointed at the guards scurrying after the zebra. "What

a nuisance. And when we're already stretched thin deal-
ing with guests. Something about the alignment of the stars
today . . ."

"What do you mean?"

"We just learned about some strange activity on the western border, possibly a tribal war. We've sent a convoy, some
intermediaries. I tell you, when trouble comes, it doesn't
leave till it's done its full work. And the council's been up
all night in the Map Chamber. They're still at it; God knows
what they're discussing in there . . ."

But I was already tossing on my robe and fleeing out the
door, running as fast as I could down the corridor before she
could finish.

Nine

"I'M SORRY to be disrupting your meeting, but there's something you need to know!" My face gleamed with a sheen of sweat, and my voice came out a mangled scream. I cringed at the desperate sound that echoed across the chamber.

My father was standing at the head of the table, surrounded by his advisors. Before him was a roll of parchment filled with frenetic, curlicued text. Once again, several pairs of eyes snapped up in my direction. Mala was right—they had been up all night, strategizing. I glanced at the parchment with interest.

A treaty.

"What is it, Amrita?"

I assessed the faces looking back at me, regretful that I had barged in on their council meeting for the second time in a matter of days, but I knew I had to put aside everything—my sense of propriety, any feelings of betrayal or anger that I had toward my father. I had to tell him what I knew.

"The oracle. She said something about animals running loose, some sort of fight on the western border. She told me we can't trust Sikander. She said something about an attack. I know it all sounds vague, but—"

"There was a breach at the royal zoo this morning," Shree offered.

"And Mala mentioned something about activity on the western border," I said.

"A tribal war, most likely. We're looking into it," said Bandaka.

"Papa, you know I don't believe in such things, but—"

"We're handling it, Amrita." He looked around the room at his advisors before he turned back to me. "We're putting the finishing touches on a treaty. One that keeps you safe. You're not marrying Sikander," he told me. "You're not going to Macedon with him. Your betrothal is no longer on the table; it's not open for negotiation."

"But what about Shalingar? What about—"

"We're agreeing to all of Sikander's terms, but he doesn't get you. And we keep Shalingar secure."

"But . . . how is that possible?"

"It's possible because I can't allow this . . . marriage. The treaty focuses on trade relations, tariffs, allowing Sikander access to our ports. But the alliance won't be built on a marriage."

I looked back at my father, tears in my eyes. I wondered

how much he was giving up to keep me away from Sikander. That was all he had ever wanted, to keep me safe.

"Thank you, Papa," I said to him.

"Thank your brilliant family," he said, gesturing around the room. "These are the best legal minds in Shalingar. And they all love you very much."

I smiled at Shree and Bandaka and Ali, my hand instinctively reaching toward my heart. "Thank you," I whispered before I went to my father, embracing him.

"And I'm not ready to see you go yet," he whispered in my ear. "Now, don't worry about a thing. We've got it all handled. We're presenting this information to Sikander today . . ."

I didn't hear the rest of what he said. Because behind my father, out the window, I could see an elephant running across the grounds.

And I wondered if, despite my father's best intentions, it was simply too late for us all.

I carefully uncurled the note in my hand as I walked out of the Map Chamber, and in Arjun's fastidious handwriting were the words:

> *My love,*
>   *It took everything in me not to stay in bed with you, not to wake up with you this morning. But then I thought, I get to wake up with you every morning for the rest of my life. I can't wait for the adventures*

that await us. I have always loved you. I will always
love you.

Your Arjun

A smile inadvertently spread across my face.

I had an intuition about where I would find Arjun. I walked down the interminable main corridor filled with elaborate displays of shields and swords till I arrived at the east courtyard. It had always been one of our favorite places to meet: a verandah of white marble and light, filled with ferns and palm fronds. Lush vines crawled up marble columns into the hazy sunlight that poured through the open roof. A small pool filled with fluorescent blue fish, darting this way and that, shimmered in the center of the space. A marble fountain gurgled, as though in a constant state of delight. Sparrows and parrots flew down from the edge of the roof into elaborate nests. Off in a corner was a hammock, surrounded by fragrant jasmine plants.

"Arjun?" I whispered, and he emerged from behind a palm tree, his hair a mess, dark circles under his eyes. But he looked happy to see me.

"So you've been up all night too?"

His face opened into a smile and he pulled me into his arms, running his fingers through my hair, kissing me softly at first, and then more ardently.

"How can I sleep when I can't stop thinking about you?" he asked.

I breathed in his familiar scent, my hands on the sides of

his neck. "I can't stop thinking about you either," I told him as I buried my face in his chest. "My father is—"

"Working on a treaty to present to Sikander. I heard."

I nodded into his collarbone. "I saw a zebra. And then an elephant. And the fight on the western border—"

"I know."

"What do you think?"

"I think your father is doing the best he can, but Sikander has been known to turn his back on treaties. What's stopping him from simply saying no? I've been thinking about our plan, researching routes from here to the east. I know so many people along the way who would help us." He hesitated before he added, "Sikander's last dinner is tonight."

Even though I knew this, I couldn't quite wrap my mind around how fast it was all happening. "So that means we leave . . . tomorrow at dawn?"

Arjun reached for me, stroking my arm.

"Are we being selfish, Arjun?"

"I don't know," he said, leading me to the hammock, gently lifting me into it. I watched him for a moment before he grinned, slipping in with me. We began to laugh.

"If this were a magic carpet, we could just fly away in it," I said.

"Too bad we don't live in a Persian fairy tale."

"We only dress like we do. For Sikander."

Arjun laughed, and I kissed him again. I wanted to close my eyes and stay here, in this hammock, curled up in his arms forever. It felt like the most natural thing in the world. After all, this was how we had been since we were children. Only now, the desire between us had spoken, made itself clear.

"I love you, Arjun."

"Thank God for that. I was afraid you were just using me for my body."

I giggled, wrapping my arms and legs around him, and for a moment we were literally like two seeds in a tamarind pod. "Could you blame me if I was?"

"I guess that would be all right." He shrugged, a smile across his face.

We were quiet for a moment before I asked, "If we leave, can we go find my mother?"

"You think he's telling the truth about her being alive?"

"Maybe I'm just hopeful. We'll be all alone. I can't imagine never seeing Papa ever again." Tears pierced my eyes. "Who else do I have?"

"You have me," he insisted. "You'll always have me." His voice was fierce, his hand held my face, and I could see from his eyes that he meant it. "I can't imagine never seeing *you* ever again."

"Remember that story Mala used to tell us about the vetala and the Diviner?" I asked him. "I was thinking about it the other day, but I couldn't remember it."

It was the first love story Mala had ever told me, and now that I was in love, I couldn't stop returning to it in my mind.

"I remember. The Diviners hated the vetalas; the vetalas hated the Diviners," he said as he stroked my hair. "But they had some sort of agreement. They left one another alone.

Until one day, a Diviner stumbled into vetala territory. She feared they would eat her soul, take her body, but instead, one of them fell in love with her."

"How did it end?"

"The vetala was immortal and the Diviner wasn't. So it ended with her dying and her vetala lover waiting centuries for her to be reborn, scouring every corner of the Earth in order to find her."

"No wonder I forgot it. It's too sad."

"It's all just folklore anyway, isn't it? That's what you always said."

Before I could respond, I heard a quiet crack, followed by a rustling sound. I froze. Maybe it was just the wind. Or a twig snapping. But we were in an enclosed space; there was hardly any wind here.

"Did you hear that?" I whispered, trying to hide the frantic hitch in my tone.

"Hear what?"

And then I heard it again, except this time there was a scurrying sound that followed it. I pulled away from Arjun, trying to extricate myself from the hammock.

Something dashed around the edge of the courtyard, but it was impossible to see what—or who—it was from where we were, with all the palm fronds around us.

Maybe it was just a mouse, but my heart was beginning to race. "What was that, Arjun?" I whispered, beads of sweat forming on my upper lip.

I could see that he was nervous but he didn't want to scare me. "Probably just a small animal."

"What if someone saw us?"

He shook his head. "Nobody ever comes here."

"Tippu the gardener does. We do."

"Yeah, and that's it. Tippu isn't going to tell on us."

"What if he *heard* us?"

"Then he heard us," Arjun whispered. "We'll be fine. I'm not going to let anything happen. Just . . . we should return to our quarters. Say your goodbyes to everyone . . . I mean, not literally, but in your own way."

I took a deep breath. "You'll be at the banquet tonight?"

He smiled a false smile. "Looking forward to it," he said. "Do me a favor," he added as I got up and brushed myself off. "Charm him tonight. I don't want him to suspect anything."

In less than twenty-four short hours, my life would change. I would leave my home, my family. And what awaited me out in that vast world I had barely seen a fraction of? It was the great Unknown, and it both frightened and thrilled me.

Ten

"*THESE*," MALA SAID, her eyes wide, her hands holding up a sculptural pair of platform shoes studded in diamonds.

I hesitated, looking at the precarious and sparkling footwear: a combination that didn't inspire confidence. I hesitated. "Can't I wear sandals?"

"Girl, why don't you just greet him in your pajamas, with grit in your eye and with your hair a snarled mess?"

I blushed. I could tell that Mala was just hurt because she had hand-selected the shoes for me, but she was right. I remembered what Arjun had said about charming Sikander.

"All right." I looked at Mala with affection.

When Mala turned her back, I grabbed the key to Thala's cell. I had taken it with me and hidden it in the top drawer of my dresser. I wanted to go check on her tonight, after the banquet. I was determined to help her, and I also secretly wondered—given what Arjun and I had discussed—if she had anything more to tell me.

"Mala, how come you never said anything about my mother?" I asked.

Perhaps it wasn't the best way to say goodbye, but I was closer to Mala than practically anyone in the world, save Arjun and my father. Why hadn't she ever told me anything?

Mala didn't look surprised. She put down the wooden comb in her hand and looked at my reflection in the mirror.

"You never asked."

"I thought it was a sensitive topic."

"Since when have you hidden behind sensitive topics? Your mind is like the tentacles of Makara the Spider."

I laughed, remembering the fable Mala used to tell me when I was a child. Makara was the creator, destroyer, and sustainer of the world. He created the world through his dreams and sustained it through his thoughts, destroying it every ten thousand years before he started again.

"I used to love that story," I said to her.

"I know. And I loved telling it to you," she said as she wiped away a tear.

"I'm going to miss you, Mala," I said, looking at her. Mala and I were rarely sentimental with each other, but how could I not be tearful and nostalgic on this night? "You've been the closest thing I've ever had to a mother."

"And you've been a daughter to me," she said. "Maybe that's why I never brought it up. Perhaps I was jealous of the possibility that you could love someone more. Blood is blood, after all."

I shook my head. "That's not true. What you and I have is thicker than blood. I couldn't possibly love anyone more."

Mala raised an eyebrow and put a hand on her hip as she regarded me in the mirror. "But?"

"But I don't know who I am."

"Girl, who you are isn't about who gave birth to you or who raised you. One finds out who he or she is over the course of a life."

"How do I do that?"

"Through your actions, through your choices."

"I'm afraid my choices are limited, Mala. It seems that I don't have any good ones."

"But your life isn't limited. Your spirit isn't limited. Develop some swagger, girl. You'll need it. You don't know it yet, but the rest of us do. Your life is going to unfold in unpredictable ways. You're far more powerful than you know."

"But what if you had to do something that could potentially be difficult for the people around you to understand . . . or recover from . . . ?"

"Take the risk, girl."

"What do you mean?" I was taken aback, my body instinctively tensing at her words.

"If you were a girl who always took risks, I'd tell you to slow down, be conservative, think twice before you leap. But from the time you were born, you were careful, thoughtful. You took others' feelings into consideration. That's why you never asked anyone about your mother. Or if you tried and saw that it made people uncomfortable, you stopped. You were so concerned about causing others pain that you squelched your own needs. Don't ever do that again. Take the risk, and don't look back."

"But, Mala—"

"That's all I can say, and that's all the advice I'm going to give you. Your instincts are good. You have a good heart. Don't hesitate. Don't waste time. Don't apologize. You'll always think about others; it's your nature. That runs in your blood, after all. Look at what your father's done for this kingdom, and his parents before that. But you can't help others if you don't help yourself first. Do you understand what I'm saying?"

I nodded, dumbfounded. Did Mala know what I was up to? She wouldn't let on, and I told myself I was being paranoid. And yet . . .

"Now go on. Your retinue will escort you to dinner. I'll be here when it's over so you can tell me about it and we can get you into your pajamas. All right?"

I got up slowly, watched Mala as she closed tins of rouge and lip tincture, put brushes made of fox fur away. Then I grabbed her and hugged her tight. "Thank you, Mala," I whispered.

"Thank *you* for being my girl all these years," she told me.

"It appears your staff has its hands full with the zoo breach." Sikander leaned back, taking a sip of his wine. He wrapped

his arm around the back of my chair as though he were a
resident and not a guest of our palace.

"It's not a usual occurrence, but we've got it handled."
My father smiled a tense smile.

Shree had told me that today's negotiations had gone
"well enough," but they weren't finished yet, and I could see
that my father was still not entirely himself.

"What do you mean by *well enough*?" I asked her.

"The terms of your betrothal haven't been settled yet.
So don't say anything," she told me as we were descending
the stairway for dinner. "Pretend you're marrying him as
planned."

My heart sank. Even though Arjun and I had made our
own plan, I had carried within me a tiny wisp of hope that
my father's negotiations would work. That I wouldn't have
to run away after all. But now I knew I would have to take
the matter into my own hands. Come dawn, Arjun and I
would be gone.

"But we're not done yet," she quickly added. "That's the
thing about negotiations. They take some time." Shree's voice
conveyed a false optimism intended, I knew, for my benefit.

The atmosphere in the Courtyard Hall was heavy with an
unrelenting strain that had descended upon us with Sikander's
arrival and churned thicker and thicker with each passing
hour, turning mere anxiety into a solid mass of panic, like
milk into butter.

Groundspeople and guards had been out in the hot sun
and humid air, corralling animals, all day. The zoo breach

was immense. Hundreds of animals had been let out of their cages and wandered the grounds, scared and confused. It was an unusual occurrence indeed.

But the confusion in my own mind felt far worse than the commotion at the palace; it threated to overwhelm me completely. I thought about what Mala had said to me about taking a risk, about putting myself first. Still, she couldn't possibly have endorsed my running away from the palace with Arjun had she known about it.

I looked across the dimly lit hall at Arjun, who smiled at me, his eyes shining at the sight of me.

"The two of you." Sikander turned to me, pointing his knife at Arjun. "I never see one of you without the other. I knew another couple like that once." He glanced at my father.

"We're not—we've just . . . we've known each other our entire lives." But I could tell that he sensed something more; it was impossible not to. Whatever had transpired between Arjun and me over the past few days was so powerful, I feared that everyone around us could smell it from a mile away.

"Now, that's a special kind of relationship, isn't it? A lot of history there. A lot of . . . affection."

I blushed.

"Careful." Sikander raised a finger at Arjun. "You'd be surprised at how much trouble that kind of affection can bring."

For a moment, I considered whether Sikander was threatening Arjun, but I quickly put the thought out of my mind.

I turned to him, trying to change the subject. "I'm very

curious to learn more about Macedon. I've been studying the language since I was a child."

"Have you, now?"

"My father tells me it's a captivating place. He told me about the tall buildings, the arenas, the . . ."

That was it. Everything else my father had told me made me think it was a soulless place of hierarchy and fear.

"I'm quite captivated by *you*, actually. You'll make an excellent queen," he said, as he ran his finger along the length of my forearm. I wanted to cringe at his touch, to cry out, to scream, but instead, I simply smiled and bowed my head.

"It would be my pleasure to serve you, Your Majesty." The very words made me want to vomit.

"And yet, your father believes otherwise."

"Pardon?"

"It would appear that he doesn't believe I would take good care of you," he said, loudly, so everyone at the table heard.

For a moment, there was a shattering silence. Until I remembered Arjun's words and added quickly, "You know, one might consider that I am actually Macedonian by birth. I was born there, after all." The room hushed, waiting for Sikander to react.

Luckily, he laughed. "I hope we can return you to your place of birth," he said, a smug smile across his lips, the gold teeth flashing in the candlelight.

I knew it in my bones in that moment: There was no way I would go anywhere with Sikander.

And yet, as I glanced around the Courtyard Hall, decorated gorgeously for tonight's banquet, I also understood how difficult it would be for me to leave Shalingar Palace. The beauty of the room contrasted sharply with the tense atmosphere. High above us were slat rafters from which star-shaped lanterns, each holding a candle, swayed in the wind. The candles illuminated the olive trees Tippu had brought back from his trips to Judea, ivy from the east that crawled up palm trees and marble columns, and local blooms of hibiscus. Beyond the slat rafters, one could see nothing but a square of navy blue sky and the bright light of millions of stars.

The dining table was decorated with large wooden platters that held cut mango, guava, and bright magenta orchids.

My father was sitting across from me, watching me carefully over his golden thali. He looked concerned that I was sitting next to Sikander, but I knew I could handle it. I just needed to get through this dinner, through the night.

Finally, dessert was served. "You know, Chandradev, it's been a pleasure learning about your kingdom." Sikander threw a smile in my father's direction before he picked up a golden spoon and plunged it into his bowl of rice pudding. "You've been an excellent host, and I know there's quite a bit you've had to contend with in the time I've been here." He shook his head vehemently. He was talking fast, his fingers drumming down on the table before him. "A breach at the zoo. Those skirmishes on the western border."

In that moment, it was as though all the air left the room.

My father froze. "How did you—"

"I know everything, Chandradev. I have eyes everywhere. On the western border, in Shalingar, in every territory that spans the region." He took a sip of his chai, put down his cup, and smiled. "You've sent quite a few of your troops out there to quell the situation," Sikander added.

"And?" My father furrowed his brow. I could tell that he was trying to maintain his composure but that he was just as shaken as I was.

"Chandradev." Sikander spread out his palms as though offering my father a gift. "The activity on the border—it's not a tribal skirmish. It's my army. And my colonels are there, waiting for a signal from me."

My entire body went cold. I glanced from my father to Arjun. My heart raced in fear.

"I considered offering you the job of satrap, Chandradev. I thought maybe you'd care more about your own interests. But I've realized that I simply can't leave these sorts of decisions up to you."

My hands were trembling violently.

"Amrita, leave now," my father said to me. "Arjun, go with her." His instincts were, even in this moment, to protect me.

I couldn't move, but Arjun got up, came around the table, and reached for my arm. I ignored him.

I could stab him right now, if I wanted, I thought. *I could grab Arjun's sword from his belt and stab Sikander in the throat.* But my hands refused to cooperate.

Sikander stood up too and faced my father. "So I have

some new terms that I'd like you to hear." He turned to me, a lascivious smile across his face. "I've taken quite a liking to your daughter. She's very spirited," he said.

Arjun's hand tightened around my elbow. *Or I could grab the knife on the table before him and stab him repeatedly.*

"We had an agreement, and now you want to break it." Sikander shrugged.

I shivered at the mention of this, and this time Arjun successfully pulled me away from the table, but I couldn't move farther than that.

"If you think I'm going to sell my daughter to you—"

"No one's talking about selling, Chandradev. You should know by now that I take what I want." He snapped his fingers, and soldiers appeared from the front entrance to the hall, all dressed in their maroon uniforms, each of them brandishing a sword. All of a sudden, I couldn't breathe.

I began to piece it all together. Sikander wanted to keep our soldiers busy in the west. *The east* was what he was interested in. That was where the Sybillines were. And they were exposed, completely unprotected.

Arjun drew the sword he always wore on his belt, but the soldiers stood on the other side of the Courtyard Hall and appeared to take no notice of us—it was my father they wanted. Within seconds, we were outnumbered. *Where were our guards?* And then I remembered: *the zoo.* A sinking feeling in my stomach.

He had thought through every detail of this attack. He had never had any interest in negotiating anything with my father. And my father was so concerned about me, he didn't even realize that we had been compromised.

"We could be done with you in a day. Less. A few hours."

More soldiers poured in from the east wing, one after another. He was right. We were more than outnumbered. My legs trembled with fear as I noticed two of them, only about ten paces away, brandishing their swords at Arjun and me. One of them smirked in my direction. It took me a second to realize that it was Nico, the man who had been responsible for transporting Thala to Shalingar.

"Don't be scared, Princess. We'll take good care of you," he said. "Sikander wants you in one piece." He laughed then. I looked at Arjun, his jaw tensed. He kept his eyes on Nico, his sword drawn before him.

"You have to run, Amrita," Arjun whispered. "I can fight them off. I'll catch up." He surreptitiously glanced in the direction of the corridor that led to the west wing. It was empty. We *could* run. Sikander's soldiers hadn't flooded our side of the palace yet. And I had always been a fast runner.

But what about my father? I couldn't just leave him. I looked at him now, regal and brave, standing in a sea of red coats and swords. A tiny sob escaped my lips as I thought about what Sikander was capable of.

"Go now," Arjun said. "Through your quarters," he whispered in my ear. "Through the mango grove. Go to the Temple of Rain. Wait for me there."

"I'm not leaving my father, Arjun!" I whispered back.

"You have options, Chandradev." Sikander turned back

to my father. "I want you to know that. I'm a reasonable man. I won't tell my colonels to attack Shalingar unless you give me reason to. You know what I seek: the open trade of chamak—on my terms; control over your territory, including that of the Sybillines; and, of course, your daughter. I'll take good care of her, I assure you. She'll be happy in Macedon. As she said herself, one could claim that she is a Macedon by birth . . . and born to a Macedonian mother . . . perhaps an opportunity to reunite them." He laughed.

I thought about what Sikander was demanding and wanted to scream. For my father, though, I would marry Sikander. I would go with him to Macedon.

"Run, Amrita, now," Arjun whispered in my ear.

I shook my head. What I wanted to do was run to Papa. I wanted to fight off all those soldiers. I wanted to kill Sikander. I had never felt such hatred for another human being.

I thought of Thala's words. *He says he wants friendship. He says he wants alliance. Don't believe what he says.*

"Do what you will to me," my father responded. "But leave my child be."

I looked at my father's eyes, and in an instant, I could read them, as I always had. *Amrita, go now*, they were saying.

"I'm through with you telling me what I can and can't have, Chandradev. And besides, I never asked."

And with that, Sikander nodded to one of the guards.

It was a second. A blink. The flap of a bird's wing, the moment it takes to say *hello*, or *goodbye*. So quick that it made me think of all the insignificant seconds that we throw away.

And all the seconds that we don't too. The seconds that we hold on to, that we return to. I thought about standing with my father on his balcony that morning before Sikander arrived, talking with him. I thought about how much I loved him. I considered the fact that all it takes is a second for life to completely change.

And then I saw the sword flash before my father, watched him drop to the ground. There was something so absurd about it that at first, I couldn't make sense of what had happened. But when I saw the blood pooling at the front of his shirt, the way his lips trembled, and the startled look in his eyes as he brought his hands to his chest, his palms stained crimson as he pulled them away, I knew that this wasn't the kind of injury he would recover from.

I wouldn't recover from it either.

"Papa! No!" I screamed when it all came together. I tried to run toward him, but Arjun grabbed me.

My father's eyes met mine for the last time that day, for the last time ever. His words came out choked. "Amrita, RUN!"

Arjun pushed me in the direction of the west wing, and I ran, my feet slapping the marble floors, everything around me a blur. Behind me, I heard the clanging of swords, and as I turned the corner, I saw Arjun slice through the uniform of one of the guards before he knocked a sword out of Nico's hand, and then Arjun turned, running behind me, a band of soldiers on his tail.

"The west wing, NOW!" he yelled. I ran toward my chamber, choking back sobs, tears streaming across my face.

Something within me wanted to defy the reality of what had just occurred right before my eyes; I didn't want to believe it.

We could get help; we could call in the palace healer. A medicine man, the best medicine man in the world.

But I knew that no healer would be called. And even if he was called, it would be too late. I had seen my father's face as he fell, the color draining from it, his hands trembling. I had seen the blood, vast pools of it. I had seen him choking on his last breaths, a sight I would never be able to erase from my mind.

The walls bleared in my peripheral vision. I cut across another corridor, running as fast as I could. I turned to make sure Arjun was behind me; he was, only paces away. The gap between us and the soldiers was widening. They didn't know the west wing, at least not as well as we did. Arjun threw a large palm plant down across the passageway.

"Keep going!" he gasped. I turned into the main hall. There were five different doorways. We had a shot at losing Sikander's soldiers. I dodged back through the main court-yard. Tippu the gardener was watering a large banana tree.

"Tippu! Hide!" I yelled to him.

Arjun caught up. "Get off the grounds, Tippu. Leave the palace. Tell everyone. The palace is under siege," Arjun said.

It wasn't till I heard those words that I truly knew it was real.

Tippu nodded and then ran from the courtyard as Arjun grabbed my hand. We had a little bit of a lead on them, just barely. I turned to look at Tippu trying to make it out of the palace as fast as he could. I hoped he would be able to warn people in time.

I was panting hard by the time we reached my quarters. Arjun slammed the large wooden doors shut behind us. He locked them, then shoved a bureau in front of them. The only other entrance to my chamber faced the back of the palace. Beyond that was the mango grove and then the Temple of Rain.

Mala had been sitting on the settee, reading a book, but the moment she saw me, she stood up. She stopped short, her face registering alarm at the state Arjun and I were in.

"Sikander—he . . . the maharaja—" Arjun started. "Soldiers after us. We—"

Mala nodded. "You need to leave the palace now."

She grabbed some things from the top of my bureau—a scarf, a skin of water, bandages, a bag of coins. I watched as she stuffed everything into a satchel. I realized that she had left them out for me. For us.

She knew. She was the one who had heard us in the courtyard. She knew about our plan. Only, it was going into effect hours earlier than expected, because we had no choice but to run.

Mala placed the satchel in Arjun's hands before she turned to me. "Here, girl, take this," she said, handing me a golden dagger. I glanced at it. There were three rubies on the handle.

"What is it?"

"It's the key you need to get out of here. Keep it on you

at all times." She quickly looked from my face to Arjun's. "Follow the stone markings. They'll lead you outside the palace."

"What stone markings?" I shook my head, terrified sobs escaping my lips.

"Arjun knows. They've always been there, in case of an emergency, so the royal family can make a speedy exit, but sometimes one has to adjust one's eyes," she said, before grabbing my shoulders and looking me right in the eye. "Listen to me, girl. We're going to get you out of here! You need to be brave," she said just as there was a loud bang against the door. I jumped.

"They're breaking in," Arjun said as we heard an even louder thud.

"There's no time, go now!" Mala said, leading us to the back door of my chamber.

From the doorway, I could see the mango grove. I couldn't stop to think of all the summers that Arjun and I had lazily wandered among those trees, picking mangoes and eating them with our bare hands.

Now this grove was the only chance we had at escape from our own home.

"Be safe," Mala said to me as she cupped my face in her hand.

"What about you, Mala?" I asked.

"I'll be just fine."

"The dagger—the key—I don't understand—"

But before I could finish asking my question, we heard

the terrifying sound of wood splintering, the door cracking open.

"Amrita, it's your duty to warn them," Mala said.

"Warn whom?" I asked, but there was no time.

"The cartographer will tell you everything. RUN!"

When I saw the tears in her eyes, I knew: We would never see her again. But before I could even fully make sense of it, before I could register that this was our last goodbye, Arjun grabbed my hand and pulled me to the grounds.

I turned to look back, and I immediately wished I hadn't. I saw Mala—squirming against the tight grip of a soldier, a knife against her throat. It was Nico.

My heart felt as though it stopped beating right in that moment.

"Let me go, you rascal! Who do you think you are?" she screamed.

"Arjun, we have to help her!" But he kept pulling me along.

"Don't worry. Won't hurt one bit," I heard Nico say.

"No!" I shook my head in fear, but before I could even think, I saw a flash of silver, a thin line of red spreading into the shape of a smile across Mala's neck. Terror in her eyes. She dropped to the ground just as I heard a scream, my own.

"Run, Amrita!" Arjun cried.

And I did. Branches and leaves scraping my face as we ran, harder and faster. My lungs burned, my feet ached, but I couldn't bring myself to look back. Couldn't bring myself to look at my beloved Mala, now gone too.

It was only once we arrived at the mouth of the Temple that I turned back to my home, the only home I had ever known. I knew for certain now: I would never see it again.

"Don't look back!" Arjun's voice snapped me back into focus. "Just go!"

I could hear the sounds of hundreds of feet marching through the grove, twigs and branches breaking. *They were right behind us.*

We descended those stairs that we had run down so many times as children, laughing and playing hide-and-seek, until finally, we were in the dark. I felt around the walls with my fingers until I unearthed a lantern and lit it with shaky fingers.

"The markings . . ." I shook my head. "I don't know what she's talking about."

"Up there." Arjun pointed to the ceiling, and there they were, right above us. Arrows. I had never seen them before.

"Don't worry, Amrita. We'll get out of here. We'll be safe," he said, but his voice was tense.

Safe. Just the word made me want to cry. Perhaps I would be, but what good was safe when my father was gone? And Mala! I couldn't believe it. Even if Arjun and I survived this attack, nothing would ever be the same again. I quickly wiped away my tears.

"And the dagger—Arjun, what did she mean by that?"

"I don't know about that," he said. "She probably gave it to you for self-defense."

"She said to warn someone, that it was my duty—"

"We'll figure it all out once we get out of here," he said to me, his fingers slipping to the inside of my arm. "I know people beyond the palace walls. They'll be able to help us."

He was talking to soothe me. Arjun always knew how to calm me down when I was nervous or scared, but he must have been thinking about his own parents too, whether they were still alive, whether they had somehow managed to escape, whether they would be taken prisoner by Sikander. But if Sikander hadn't spared my father, what hope was there for Shree and Bandaka?

Arjun craned his neck, frantically investigating the cavernous space. "This way," he said, pulling us around a bend. He angled the lantern in his hand as he pointed to the ceiling.

"All those years that we played hide-and-seek here," I said, "and we never bothered to look up."

My eyes bounced from him to the carvings, disfigured bodies, eroded torsos, faces whose noses had been cut off. This whole place told a story, carried within it so many secrets, but we would never know exactly what those secrets were.

And what were the secrets around my life? Around my mother? Around the conditions of my parents' meeting, their separation? What would make Sikander hate my father so much that he would simply . . . I couldn't even think of what had happened.

Another thought occurred to me: If there was a secret escape plan in case of an emergency that I had never known about, what other truths had been kept from me?

What had I failed to observe?

There was so much I was ignorant of that it terrified me.

Like these hieroglyphs, these arrows above us—if I hadn't been told to look for them I might have simply mistaken them for scratches in the rock, but there was a pattern to them, a chain of hints that led out of the Temple of Rain and into the kingdom of Shalingar.

What was the pattern to my life that I couldn't yet see?

"Where will they take us?" I asked.

"We're going to find out," Arjun said. I looked up at his face, lit only by the glow of the lantern, his dark eyes watching me carefully. "Come on, let's go. We don't have a lot of time."

But I found myself stalling. "I'm afraid, Arjun."

"I know. But right now, we just need to stay alive."

We followed the arrows, twisting and turning down the stone tunnels, until we came to a part of the Temple that I recognized.

I tripped over a jagged rock, and Arjun caught me.

"It's these shoes," I said, realizing that I had been running in the platform diamond-studded footwear that Mala had selected for me. I quickly removed them, thinking about how she had painstakingly chosen them for me. I couldn't bring myself to leave them behind. I grabbed the satchel out of Arjun's hand, stuffing them inside.

It was silly, but they were all I had left of Mala. I swallowed the lump in my throat. *I will never see Mala again. Never wake up to the sound of her voice again. Never hear the stories she told me about vetalas and Diviners. Never feel her hands combing my hair.*

Just as I was thinking this, we both heard the tromp of

feet in the distance. "They know we're in here," Arjun whispered. "Faster, follow the trail!"

I looked around at the familiar reliefs on the walls. The air in this part of the Temple was filled with dust, my lungs struggling to inhale.

"Did everyone else in the palace know? About a getaway plan? An exit in case of an emergency?"

He nodded. "You'll have to cover your face when you leave the palace. I'll explain everything," he said.

Spiraling farther down into the bowels of the temple, we reached a familiar doorway, wooden, with iron bars. A delicate hand reached out through the bars, and I almost screamed in terror, but Arjun grabbed me, his palm across my mouth.

"Help me!" she cried.

"Quiet!" Arjun whispered. "You'll give us away!" His face was white with fear.

"Please release me, or I'll be stuck here for the rest of my days. I'll die in here!"

"Keep going, Amrita!" Arjun told me, his voice stern.

I hesitated. "We can't just leave her, Arjun."

He reached for my face, turned it toward him so I was looking right into his eyes. "My job is to protect you, to make sure you get out of here alive," he said. "Amrita, listen to me. We can't take her. She'll slow us down. Look at her—she's high on chamak! She's barely alert."

I had seen what Sikander's men were capable of, and the thought of leaving a young innocent in their hands terrified me.

But Thala interjected before I could object. "I know what happened to your father," she spoke quickly, in whispers. "I know Sikander killed him. I'm sorry."

At Thala's words, I inadvertently let out a sob, and Arjun pulled me close. "Amrita, we have to keep moving," he said gently.

But Thala must have anticipated Arjun's reluctance, because what she said next changed all of our fates in ways we could have never predicted. "I know how you can bring him back from the dead," she whispered. "There's a way. It can all be undone. Please, free me, and I'll show you the way."

Eleven

I STOPPED SHORT. "What did you say?"

"She's pulling your leg, Amrita. I'm sorry, but he's . . . gone," Arjun said to me, touching my face with his hand, his finger tracing my cheek. "It can't be undone." There was a tenderness in his voice, but his words jarred me.

By now I could hear boots pounding on stone, not so far in the distance. I turned to look back. Any minute now, they would find us.

"It *can* be undone," Thala insisted. "In Macedon, there's a story about reversing fates, changing the past. If you give me a chance, I can help you."

"She *can't* help you." Arjun's voice was frantic now. "She's trying to trick you, or she's lying. Please, Amrita, we're losing time." I looked at his face. I had never seen such fear in his eyes.

"Oracles don't lie," Thala insisted. "We're incapable of lies. And I've been right before. Ask her," she said to Arjun.

It was true. Thala had been right about everything. The animals running loose, fighting in the west. An impending attack. *He says he wants friendship. He says he wants an alliance. Don't believe what he says.* It had all come true.

Maybe she *could* undo what had just occurred. Maybe she could help me bring my father back from the dead.

The sounds of feet marching through the tunnels were getting louder and louder. We had seconds to escape. I reached for the large iron key tucked into the waistband of my sari and slipped it into the lock. It jammed, and I struggled to turn it. Arjun took a deep breath, his hands in his hair.

"Amrita," he said. "Hurry, they're almost here!"

Finally, something gave way and the key turned, creaking loudly.

Thala breathed a sigh of relief.

"Let's go," Arjun said, and as he did, I saw a single red coat turning a corner, his sword drawn.

Arjun saw him too, instinctively pulling at his sword just as Thala emerged from the cell. She was out, but the soldier stuck two fingers between his lips, and a shrill whistle pierced the air around us.

I froze, panicked.

And then we heard them, hundreds of feet, marching toward us.

"Go!" Arjun yelled at us, but I had no intention of leaving without him.

Arjun leapt toward the soldier, swinging his sword with all his might.

"Take her away from here!" he yelled to Thala.

Thala grabbed my hand and pulled me away as Arjun fought the soldier to protect us, to protect *me*. Against the clanging of metal, I heard the scuffle of bodies, the heaving of breaths. And then they came, one after another. Arjun fought them, one by one.

"No!" I screamed. "I can't leave him," I sobbed as Thala dragged me away, deeper into the darkness of the Temple.

"You have no choice," she said, hushing me. Her voice was comforting, but her words sliced through me like a knife, gutting me. I couldn't breathe, couldn't think.

Thala gripped the lantern and, with her spare hand, tugged my arm, and even though I resisted, something snapped within me, some survival instinct that propelled my feet to keep moving.

I ran, tears streaming down my face, the soles of my feet torn and bloody by now, and yet, I continued to race through those stone passageways, Thala holding my hand.

He would have never abandoned me. We had a plan. We were supposed to escape together. We were supposed to go into hiding together.

And I had simply left him behind, my best friend of sixteen years, the love of my life. I had left him to fight for my life with his own. I had saved myself while he battled countless soldiers. What kind of person did that make me? Mala had told me to be brave, to take risks. But the truth was that in the face of a crisis, I was a coward.

I thought about the other thing Thala had said: *Arjun . . . he loves you. He'll save your life one day soon.*

I ran harder. Mala, my father, Shree, Bandaka, Arjun. They were all gone, or left behind. What was I even doing, trying to survive? What was I surviving for?

I couldn't stop the tide of thoughts that threatened to overwhelm me. I had seen too much today, too much violence, too much death. And I couldn't help but feel as though I might have been able to prevent it. My father telling me to run, Shree and Bandaka with swords against their throats, Mala dying at the hands of one of Sikander's men, and Arjun stemming the tide of those soldiers so that I could escape.

We ran and ran and ran for what felt like days, stopping only to make sure we were still on the right path. The arrows continued to lead us somewhere, but where?

"Come on!" Thala said, still holding tight to my hand.

By now, we were in a part of the Temple of Rain that I had never seen before. The corridors narrowed, and instead of the high ceilings that I was used to, the walls were beginning to close in on us. All of a sudden, I felt as though I couldn't get enough air into my lungs. I choked on my breath, and my hands and feet were clammy and wet.

"I don't like small spaces," I whispered. I stopped, pressing my hand into the wall. "I can't. I don't think I can do it. I can't go farther."

Thala turned, looked at me, her eyes a bright blue. "We're almost there," she said. Her voice was calm.

"How do you know?" I felt like I was going to pass out.

"I *know*," she said. "You have to trust me. I'll get you out of here, I promise. It's just a little bit longer. The only way out of here is through this passageway."

I hesitantly nodded, knowing I had no option but to follow her. The walls continued to curve in on themselves, and I wondered if anyone had ever attempted to make an escape through this vast network of tunnels before.

We arrived at a juncture where the tunnel narrowed. Thala put down the lantern.

"I can't carry this anymore," she said. "Go ahead of me," she instructed me. And I knew what she was saying. We would have to crawl the rest of the way.

I shook my head, my entire body trembling in fear at the small, dark hole before me. "I can't."

This was it. I knew I simply couldn't go on. My brain was a blank; the only word I could contemplate was *no*. I had lost the will to survive. I had lost the will to live. My legs began to tremble. I felt cold sweat on my brow.

"You can. I'll be right behind you, I promise," she said, her voice forceful.

"No," I whispered. "You can leave me here. You can go on. But I can't go."

Thala reached for my hand. "Trust me. I'll be there with you the entire way."

I shook my head.

"Look at me," she said. "Do you know what I've gone through in my life? Do you know the kinds of things I've experienced? If I can survive all that, you can crawl through this tunnel. Even if they're gone, you're still alive. And your only job now is to try to survive."

I don't know what it was—the bare conviction in her voice, or the fact that I couldn't think straight, or simply that she was right. I was still alive. And I couldn't imagine what Thala had lived through, but she was my source of strength in that moment.

I took a deep breath and got down on my hands and knees, a small whimper escaping my lips.

"Only a few more paces," she whispered. I tried to look straight ahead, tried to keep breathing, but by now, my whole body was shaking and tears were flowing freely down my face. Still, I kept crawling, my tears mixing with dirt. The taste of mud and terror in my mouth, flashes of such acute fright that I didn't know if I could survive it. My hands so cut up from the jagged rocks beneath me that I could barely feel them anymore. My whole body damp with sweat, my thoughts nothing more than a blur of panic.

"You can do this. You have the heart of a warrior. A rebel," Thala said.

"I don't know what you're talking about," I cried, but I thought about Sikander's words at dinner. He had told me that my mother came from a family of revolutionaries.

Then again, according to him, they were *the kind that don't fight. The kind that talk.*

Not to mention that none of them had survived Sikander's father's attack on their home.

But maybe she had.

"My mother . . . is she still alive?"

"Yes."

"You promise you can help me bring my father back?" There was a desperate need for assurance in my voice.

"I promise."

I imagined a reunion between my parents, the three of us together, happy. A sob escaped my lips.

"Okay," I said, and I stumbled through the dark tunnel.

I closed my eyes, feeling my way through the dusty shaft with my hands. I landed on something furry and fought the urge to scream as it disentangled itself from my fingers, squeaking as it ran the other direction.

My whole body was trembling with fear when I felt something hard and square before me.

"There's . . . something here."

"What is it?" Thala cried.

I felt the flat surface of it—a box. No. A lantern! I felt around with my hands until I found a sulfur stick. I struck it against the wall and lit the lantern. But the light only illuminated a sight that sickened me with fear.

We were facing a dead end, a wall of stones. And there was no room to turn.

"No, no, *no!*" I shook my head, sobbing.

I was dizzy with fright now. We would be stuck here, starve to death in a space that was just barely large enough to hold me, balled up and covered with dirt.

"There!" Thala cried, pointing to the ceiling. "Look up! We're here."

I craned my neck and squinted to see what she was pointing at. It took me a moment to make out what it was: a golden triangle hung from the ceiling. A handle of some sort.

I reached for it, and as I did, a chunk of dried dirt fell to the ground before me, revealing a small corner of gold attached to the handle. I looked closely, running my hand over the surface of it.

"It's a design of some sort," Thala said, moving her palms over the surface to remove caked mud from hundreds of years of flooding.

I watched as an engraved tableau revealed itself to us with every stroke of Thala's hand.

Next to the handle were three rubies, arranged in a triangle, mimicking the pattern of the rubies on the dagger Mala had given me. But there was more: elaborate carvings that appeared to tell a story. A fortress-like structure. It looked like the Temple of Rain with its grand stairway and elaborate pavilions. A forest full of trees. Some of the trees had faces chiseled into their trunks. Their branches looked like limbs. They were . . . alive.

"It's just like the parable," I whispered. "The Parable of the Land of Trees, it's depicted here . . . ," I said in amazement.

I was sitting up on my calves now, removing the dirt with both hands, trying to make sense of the discovery at the end of what was the most difficult journey of my life.

"There's more . . . ," I said as I noticed engravings of people flying through the air. A hilltop, with the sun rising just beyond it.

As I removed more dirt, I realized that the golden surface wasn't just a work of art.

"It's a door!" Thala said. But I was too mesmerized by the story before me to respond to her.

I traced my hands over the carvings: two people standing before a series of caves. Behind them, a large procession.

"Who did this?" I whispered to Thala. "Someone carved this door, they built this temple. What was it?"

But Thala wasn't listening to me. She reached up and pushed the door open.

My eyes stung as they adjusted to the light. It was day. The sun was shining. After being in that dark, cramped space for so long, the very idea of light stunned me, made my eyes tear as though they were witnessing sunlight for the first time.

Thala reached for the lip of the doorway, hoisting her body up, crawling into a world that I realized terrified me perhaps even more than burrowing my way through a dark tunnel. And yet, I also knew I had to come out. All of it, all the sacrifices made on my behalf, crawling through that terrifying passage, it was for this: to come out the other end.

Thala reached her long, slender arms back down for me, and I noticed the tattoo on her shoulder again. It was an image of a tree, its branches and roots coiling around her collarbone. "Don't worry, it'll be all right," she said, as though she were speaking to a skittish animal.

I reached for her hands, and she lifted me up into a small and empty alleyway. My breathing was heavy, ragged, my lungs screaming for air. But we had made it. We were free.

Twelve

I PRESSED MY FACE to the cold cobblestone beneath me, crying so hard that my entire body shook.

My thoughts were fragmented. Broken sentences sparked like fireflies from the recesses of my mind, barely registering before they flickered out again. All I could feel was pain.

Thala placed a gentle hand on my shaking back, but I barely took any notice of her.

I wished I had died right there in the palace with my father and Mala and probably Arjun too. I *should* have died, I told myself. I had survived all the people I loved. Worse than that, they had all perished trying to protect me, trying to help me.

I didn't deserve to live.

Finally, I heard Thala's voice. She spoke in careful Shalingarsh. "You can cry for another five minutes. And you can grieve. But then we have to go. We have to keep moving. We're not safe."

But where would I go without Arjun? *I've traveled the world. I can show it to you*, he had said to me. *I know people who can help us*, he'd told me.

Who did I know in this unfamiliar world? Where would I go now?

I watched as Thala closed the hatch door to the tunnel, and the moment she did, all evidence of it disappeared. The earth swallowed it up as though it had never existed. The only thing that remained was a row of cobblestones in the small covered alleyway where we had found ourselves.

There was a finality to it that made me want to claw at the ground with my fingernails, go back in time, go back to my father and Mala and Arjun, to the familiarity of my old life. I felt an ache so intense that it felt as though I had been gutted. I had been cut clean of my entire past, like a fish flailing on land, desperate for the safety of cold blue water.

But that same terminality appeared to put Thala in a completely different mindset.

"I'm free," she murmured, laughing, though it sounded like a cough.

I resented the giddy relief in her tone, and then I remembered the box, the chains, the rope. I couldn't fault her for feeling euphoric.

Her voice was softer when she spoke again. "Please. If anyone knows what it feels like to lose . . . everything, it's me," she said, touching my arm. I finally looked up at her face. She was covered in mud, just like me, but under all the dirt, I could see her russet hair, her delicate features. A sharp nose, fine cheekbones.

"I know how difficult it is," she said, crouching down next to me. For a moment, there was compassion in her eyes. "But it gets easier."

"Does it?"

Her voice was gruff when she responded, as though it was difficult for her to soften, even for a minute. "The truth is, it doesn't get easier for a long time. No one tells you that. It aches less and less every day, but it never completely goes away. But we have to keep moving. They're not likely to stop looking for you . . . Your Majesty," she added, furrowing her brow with a formality that appeared ridiculous given the circumstances.

"You needn't call me that," I whispered, still unable to take my eyes off the spot in the ground that I had just emerged from. "You saved my life. And besides, no one would ever believe me if I told them who I am. My father made sure to keep my identity hidden my whole life."

"That might be a good thing," she said, and I remembered what Arjun had said about keeping my face covered. I fished a scarf from the satchel Mala had packed and wrapped it over my face.

"Let's go," Thala abruptly said as she marched forward.

I had seen the walled city every day from my window, but on my visits, I had walked only the main avenues and thoroughfares, and that in a rush, with a retinue huddled around me like a cocoon.

I had never known the sounds of Ananta.

Now I heard the metallic tinkling of wind chimes, hurried footsteps, unabashed laughter, the long, shrill wails of vendors advertising the best fruit or toy or fabric. I tilted my head to hear the whistle of wind rustling through the leaves of miniature banana and palm trees that lined the lane I was standing in.

Above us was a roof made of elaborately patterned indigo and white tiles. I looked at the whitewashed walls around us, draped in curtains of pink and purple vines. Weeds grew between the cracks in the stones under my feet. In the middle of the alleyway, a broken glass bottle, its green-blue shards shattered everywhere. Just behind me, someone had scrawled LIVE IN THE ZEPHYR OF SPIRIT in purple ink.

I looked out from the enclosed alley, and in the distance, I could see a tiled blue and white fountain, gurgling.

"Shoo! You're blocking my path!"

Thala and I quickly scampered to the edge of the alley. A woman dressed in an orange and gold sari assessed us. There was pity in her eyes. She must have thought we were vagrants.

She pursed her lips together and reached into a gold satchel in her hand, plucking out a small silver coin with her fingers. She held the coin out to me.

"Come now, take it," she said, impatience in her voice.

Slowly I reached for the coin, turning it carefully to inspect it. My father's face graced one side of it.

"Now go on," she said.

And something about that prompt, about her stern and instructive tone, made me stand up taller.

"Go, go, go! You must have someplace to be now, don't you?"

Before I could respond, I found myself behind Thala, marching into the mandarin orange–colored light of a new dawn in Ananta.

I was startled by the sight before me: a cheerful redbrick town square, bustling with activity; groups of people chatting or playing games as they sipped their morning chai and shikanji under large green umbrellas.

Along one side of the plaza was an open-air market, with vendors selling globes of claret pomegranate, so ripe that their skins burst open with seeds. Tiny perfect green mangoes, the size of my fist. Sticks of dried chili and bunches and bunches of small yellow grapes, tumbling off the wooden carts that housed them. Fish with silver scales tiled one cart, and there were other carts and vendors still, hawking colorfully painted wooden dolls and animals made of bits of string and clay, earthen vessels for cooking, and brightly colored patchwork quilts dotted with mirrors that sparkled in the cantaloupe-colored light.

A woman peddling threads of jasmine walked by, barely taking notice of us. Their fragrance filled my nose, making me think of Arjun, of the ring he had given me. I still had it on my finger, and I looked at it longingly.

Arjun. Would I ever see him again?

"Keep walking," Thala urged me, interrupting my thoughts. And so I did.

My eyes couldn't take it all in fast enough. The buildings in the town square were a stark white, but they all had red tile roofs that they wore on their heads like low hats. A clock tower chimed and two small doors opened, releasing a dozen or so wooden birds, painted red and blue and yellow.

And in the distance were the lofty blue and silver minarets of Ananta's temples, mosques, and churches.

A trio of musicians finished tuning their instruments and began to play a folk song, the cheery staccato notes contrasting with how I felt. A group of young girls in low-waisted yellow saris began to dance, twirling string of bells on their wrists as they moved, laughter escaping their lips as though they were deliriously happy for this new day. Even the sky—too clear and too beautiful to be reasonable—appeared to be taunting me.

"We should clean up," Thala said, her voice slicing through my thoughts like the blade of a fan through heavy air. "And then I'll tell you everything you need to know."

"Tell me now," I insisted. I couldn't wait.

She closed her eyes. When she opened them her irises were black.

"Your friend, Arjun. He's safe."

I exhaled a sigh of relief. "He is?"

"Yes. He's been taken captive. Sikander plans to use him for his knowledge of the kingdom, and his knowledge of you."

"And Bandaka and Shree?"

"They've been taken captive as well."

I felt a fresh set of tears piercing my eyes.

Thala closed her eyes again, and when she opened them, they were lavender.

"Your eyes—"

She nodded. "It's a characteristic of oracles. That's how they hunt us down, how they enslave us. Our eyes change color whenever we have a vision. It's usually subtler. The chamak enhances it. They've been lacing my food with it, force-feeding it to me for months now. An experiment," she said. Her voice carried no emotion, and she looked away when she said this.

I remembered Shree telling me once that chamak was dangerous for an unformed mind, and I wondered about the toll it took on Thala.

"That's why Sikander says he wants chamak. So he can see the future. And so he can control its trade and become the most powerful man in the world."

"Isn't he already?"

"There's no limit to his greed, to his desire for power."

But something else was eating away at me. "What did you mean when you said they hunt you down?"

Thala hesitated, looking away from me. Finally she met my eyes, her face immobile. "In Macedon, they treat us like second-rate citizens, and yet, they rely on us for our visions, our talent. They hunt us like animals, enslave us, trade us on the open market. Entire empires are built on our predictions. They run experiments on us, give us all kinds of concoctions to enhance our powers. And then, when they're done with us, they dispose of us," she said.

"That's horrific." I shuddered.

She went on. "Sikander couldn't have built his empire without the aid of oracles. Or his army of slaves. One man's will carried out by a regiment of the unwilling. And yet we all helped him. We had no choice. Death or a life in slavery."

"His entire army is a mercenary army?"

Thala nodded. "The desperate, the poor, orphans, young men who have lost their families, their homes. Sikander's empire absorbs them; they become a part of his machine. Most of us are so young when he takes us from our homes, we have no say."

"How old were you when you were brought to Sikander?"

"I was nine," she whispered, looking away. But I heard the hint of devastation in her voice.

To distract myself from the shock of her words, I dug my fingers into the satchel Mala had given me, pulling out a scarf and the skin of water and handing them to Thala. She drank thirstily and then offered the water back to me before she wrapped the scarf around her russet-colored hair, which would have made her stand out conspicuously as a foreigner in Shalingar. Once it was securely wrapped around her face, only her eyes exposed to the world, she looked at me. I wondered who, if anyone, she had shared her story, her words, with. I considered what her life must have been like before she became Sikander's slave.

We continued to walk through the crowds, and I watched despondently as people around us went on with their day as though nothing had changed. Some of them exchanged and bartered goods, haggling with vendors. Elderly men and women hobbled with canes. Children played with marbles or drew patterns on cobblestone with brightly colored chalk. Monks clad in orange robes silently strolled the packed lanes just outside the square. Teenagers on their way to school, judging by the books in their arms, held hands and giggled, or quietly whispered secrets to one another.

Even though the palace was under siege, no one in the kingdom of Shalingar seemed to know this. But soon they would.

We should have known was all I could think. When Sikander attacked Bactria, there was a rumor that he did it so quietly and swiftly that the people of the kingdom didn't even know it till days later, once the military had been turned, the granaries had been looted, and the royal palace overtaken.

"Are you going to return to Macedon now?" I felt a pang of panic in the pit of my stomach. *Would she leave me too?*

Thala shook her head. "I won't leave you, don't worry. I'm indebted to you."

"For what?"

"I'm free for the first time in years."

I nodded, but I wasn't sure what to say. Perhaps I had helped her, but I hadn't been able to save those I loved the most.

She must have read my thoughts, because she took a deep

breath and said, "It's not over yet. You're the heiress to the throne. As long as you're still alive, there's . . ." But she didn't finish, as though the word *hope* didn't exist in her vocabulary.

"I don't even know how to navigate my own kingdom by myself."

"I'll help you. And there must be other people in Shalingar we can approach for aid."

"I don't know a single person in Shalingar." I shook my head. "And look at me." I gestured to my filthy clothes, my matted hair. "Who would ever believe that I'm Princess Amrita?" I whispered.

"Think," Thala said. "There has to be someone you know, someone we can speak to."

"Mala said something about a cartogapher. She said it was my responsibility to warn someone."

"That's a good place to start."

But my mind was already trying to untangle what had just occurred. "How could we have trusted Sikander?" I whispered. "We were fools. We greeted him with a parade, acrobatics shows, music, and dancing. And he planned on attacking all along."

"You *didn't* trust him. Why would you? Sikander is full of tricks," Thala said offhandedly, stopping before a vendor selling sandals made of braided leather and pieces of linen. She selected some linen and two pairs of sandals and then bargained with the vendor in simple Shalingarsh. Once she was done, she nodded to me, and I handed him the coin the woman in the orange sari had given me, along with some of the silver in my satchel. He barely took note of us as he placed the shoes, the linen, and some coins in my hand.

Thala collected the fabric from me and then led me to the fountain at the center of the square.

I quickly removed the scarf and glanced at my reflection in the pool of water before me. I could barely recognize my tear-streaked and muddy face. My clothes were filthy from crawling through the Temple, drenched in sweat. My throat was parched.

But Thala was right, I was alive, and some instinct had propelled me to stay that way, despite myself.

Thala lowered a wooden pail into the water, and when she brought it up, I was startled at how clean and refreshing it looked. We drank it thirstily, cupping our hands and trying to take in as much as we could, before she refilled the skin and dampened the cloth she had purchased from the vendor. Then she sat on the ground before me, wiping my feet clean. I looked down at them and gasped. I hadn't even noticed till now how badly cut up they were or how much they ached. I watched as Thala carefully cleaned my wounds, remembering how I had done the same for her when she first arrived at the palace. It made me feel humbled, cared for.

"Thank you," I whispered.

She didn't respond. "You risk infection," she said. "We'll have to get you some herbs for those cuts." Her tunic was torn, and I noticed again the curlicued tattoo on her shoulder, whorls of black ink. I pushed back her sleeve.

"What is it?"

She looked around before she pulled her shirt over her shoulder to show me. "The Tree of Life. It's an old symbol, from the time of the Diviners. I'm a descendant of the Diviners."

I nodded. "So are the Sybillines."

She looked up at me, a drunken smile across her face that made me nervous. She was a survivor, and I admired this in her, but there was also something unpredictable about her reactions. She was gruff one moment, then lucid, then it seemed as though the chamak had overtaken her mind, making her eyes cloudy, a loose smile across her lips. "My people wear the mark of the Tree of Life when we choose to commit ourselves fully to the Gift. I chose that life when I was nine."

"Why a tree?"

"Because the Diviners derived their power from the Earth, and trees were considered the wisest living things on the planet once upon a time. The Parable of the Land of Trees is a famous tale where I come from. But it's told all over the world."

"Does it still exist—the Land of Trees?"

"That I don't know. But it did once. In the time of the vetalas and the Diviners. They had their conflicts, but they ultimately felt the same way about the forests, the oceans, the land. That's why they were able to coexist on the Earth for so long."

"You know about the vetalas?"

"Everyone knows about the vetalas," Thala said. "In Macedon, they're called the Tithons. In the east, they're the Xians. They used to dominate the Earth, but they've been edged out, hunted down by men like Sikander."

"Do you know what happened to the vetalas and the Diviners?"

Thala shrugged as though she could barely care. "What always happens. A fight that made them forget all the things they had in common, and all their gifts. That's why they went extinct."

It made me think of Thala's gift. "How long have you had visions?"

"My whole life."

"So you knew all of this would happen."

"It is written. I told Sikander it would happen." She shook her head. "That if he decided to attack, you would escape. He knew that if he forced you to marry him, it would give him legitimacy, but that wasn't meant to happen. He didn't like my answers, but I cannot lie—those with the Gift, we're not capable of lies. From time to time, I would try to evade his questions, trick him. But sometimes I would get caught and be punished," she quietly said, and I looked at the burns and cuts on her arms, understanding that these injuries were what she was referring to.

The thought of what Sikander's men must have done to her sickened me. And then I considered what they might have done to me. "Is there . . . anything I could have done to stop it from happening?"

Thala thought for a moment. "Some things are fixed, others are changeable. You can't change what's fixed or fix what's changeable. That's what my mother always said."

"But you warned me about it. Wasn't it so that I could actually do something about it?"

"I wanted to earn your trust . . . so you would free me. I needed you to understand that I . . . have value."

I looked away, uncertain of how I felt. I reminded myself she had no choice. She wasn't capable of lies, and the fear of being physically hurt loomed over her every day. I couldn't even imagine what her life had been like for all those years.

I looked around the square, wondering what Shalingar would become if Sikander ruled. Instead of the sound of Shalingarsh in the cafés surrounding us, would everyone one day be forced to speak Macedon? Would people keep slaves? Would women have no option but to stay indoors while men roamed the streets without a care in the world? Would there be dowries, discrimination toward the tribes in the west? And what would happen to the Sybillines? Would he manage to find them? To take them prisoner?

"They're going to come looking for you," Thala said. "Sikander's strategy is that he hunts down every member of a royal family, killing them one by one. He takes the women as his consorts. Then he instates his own satraps to administer his rule."

"I don't know anyone who would agree to report to Sikander."

"Someone will," she said. "Someone always does."

"Can you see whom it might be?"

"I can't see everything," she said. "Only what I'm meant to see. And sometimes it changes." Thala continued, "Sikander and his men—they don't understand anything about visions, about magic. Reading the future is like reading nature; the patterns of the rain and the sun and the wind. It moves and recedes. But they want to know everything about the future. And that isn't possible. Even the vetalas couldn't tell you that, and they're the most knowledgeable beings who ever walked the Earth."

"I could use the help of a vetala now," I whispered. "Or my father . . . I wish my father were here with me now."

"I told you. You can undo what happened."

I turned to her. "Sounds like magic."

She hesitated before turning to me. "Have you ever heard of the Library of All Things?"

I shook my head, but a line of goose bumps crept over my arms. "A *library*?"

She lowered her voice. "It's a place my aunts told me about," she said. "We have a tale about it in Macedon. Every person who has ever walked the Earth has a book that tells the story of their life. These books are kept in the Library of All Things. There's a Keeper of the Library—a vetala—and if you find him and ask him permission, he'll allow you entry into the Library. But only for a short period of time. It's where I plan on going next, so I can undo my own past. All we have to do is find the Keeper of the Library, urge him to give us entry, and once he does, you can find your father's book, tear out the pages where your father was killed, and then—"

I stood up, startled and angry. "Are you crazy?" I asked her.

Thala shook her head at me, confused.

"That's the most ridiculous thing I've ever heard. You expect me to find some magical library guarded by some creature who doesn't exist and *that's* the way I can have my father back?"

"Well, what did you think? That it was going to be easy?" she asked, her voice gruff again.

I balked at Thala, baffled, furious. I opened my mouth to say something, but just then, out of the corner of my eye, I saw a familiar face—sharp features, hazel eyes. Walking the town square in plainclothes was Nico, flanked by a handful of Sikander's men.

Terror flashed across Thala's face. She grabbed my arm and pulled me away from the well, her hands trembling.

"If we don't get out of here now, it'll be even more impossible."

Thirteen

"WHERE DO WE GO?" I glanced to my left and then to my right. The town square was busy, but there was no place to hide.

Just then, Nico's eyes met mine. I shuddered. He pointed at us, a salacious grin spreading across his face. I was wearing a scarf across my face and so was Thala, but we stood out, from the dirt and grit on our clothes. He turned and yelled something to his men.

We didn't wait to hear what it was. We were already barreling across the square, heads turning to glance our way.

"The alley where we came from!" Thala yelled.

"No! It's completely empty." I turned to her. "We need to find a crowd." I thought for a moment. "Follow the monks!" I pointed to the clusters of men and women in orange robes making their way through the narrow lanes of Ananta. There

was a pattern in their collective movements, a procession.
They were on a pilgrimage, and their destination was a small
shrine on the top of a hill.

"Let's go!" Thala cried.

We pushed past the monks as we ran up the narrow and
winding cobblestone streets that led up the hill. In the distance, I could see an ornate white building with a turquoise
and silver minaret. I remembered seeing it from my window
at the palace.

I grabbed Thala's hand, my feet moving as though they
were separate from my body.

We ran as fast as we could, weaving between packed
bodies, darting around wayward neem trees growing verti-
cally up the terrain, clinging onto structures as though for
dear life. We dodged street vendors pushing carts full of
tomatoes and peppers and limes through the narrow streets.

It had never occurred to me when I looked out my window that this precarious promontory was a miniature city
itself, lined with colorful homes that dotted the steep hillside like multicolored blocks tumbling off one another, pink
and ochre, pale blue and sea green. Lone palm or banana
trees grew from tiny squares of earth, wrapping themselves
around the vibrant structures and ornate metal grills that
muzzled doors and windows. Small children played with
toys or dolls on the front stoops of their homes, stopping to
glance up at us as we pushed our way past them.

I turned to look back. Nico and his men were behind us,
shoving people in their path to get to us.

"Faster!" I urged Thala. "They're close!"

"Every path on this hill seems to lead to the shrine. We need to lose them, or they'll eventually get to us."

She was right.

I took it all in, frantically searching for a place to hide. Now we were only about a hundred paces from the temple. On either side of the cobblestone path, in between the homes, vendors sold garlands of brilliantly ochroid marigolds, clay figurines of the gods. A mithai vendor was frying gold and scarlet rings of syrupy jalebi in a massive iron pot, bubbles of heat sputtering across the surface of the glistening slick. Even in my terrorized state, just the smell of it made my mouth water, and I realized that I hadn't eaten since yesterday.

We mounted a flight of stairs and turned around the bend.

"Hey! Careful, you!" yelled the vendor of a spice store as Thala almost knocked over a pyramid of glass vessels. I looked at the rows and rows of shelves, lined with jars of fragrant spices — cinnamon sticks and crimson chili, canary-colored turmeric, grassy coriander.

"Sorry!" I cried as we turned under an ivy-covered archway into a quaint café where men and women ate rice out of small clay bowls. They all glanced up at us as we ran past.

And then I felt someone grabbing for my sleeve. I turned to see Nico's eyes fixed on mine, his face inches away. I quickly yanked my arm back, ripping the fabric of my blouse. Nico lost his balance and tripped, stumbling into a table before him. The crowd at the restaurant scattered.

"Get them!" he yelled at his men, and Thala and I raced up the narrow streets, Nico's men on our tail.

"Where do we go?" Thala cried, and I heard the hushed desperation in her voice.

There were five of them and only two of us, and they were getting closer and closer.

I gasped. Before us was a logjam of bodies. The movement up the hill had stalled, and there was no place we could go.

Nico's men were right behind us, shoving bodies out of their way, gaining on us. My heart raced with terror; my mind was blank.

All I could think was that perhaps this is where the story of my escape from Sikander would end. Maybe this was where we would be caught, both of us thrown into boxes and carted back to Macedon.

And yet, some stalwart part of me refused to accept our capture. Some sense of justice within me screamed in rage at the idea of being married off to the man who had killed my father and Mala, plundered the palace, invaded my home, taken my beloved Arjun prisoner.

And Thala. I couldn't let her be taken into Sikander's custody again.

My eyes met those of a small boy playing with a toy horse in a tiny square patch of grass next to us. Thala noticed him too. She crouched down beside him.

"Hello. My name is Thala. My friend and I . . . we need a place to hide. Could you help us?" she asked him, an urgency in her voice that made him shrink away from her. But she continued to plead. "It would just be for a minute.

We could . . . hide in your house," she said, gesturing to his front door.

But the boy shook his head. "My mama doesn't like me to play with strangers."

"We're not strangers." Thala forced a smile at him. "We're friends. Can't you just let us in . . . for a moment?" She continued to beg him as I reached into my satchel and pulled out the dagger Mala had given me. It fit perfectly into my hand. I could see Nico approaching now, and I knew that I would have to kill him or be killed myself. All I knew was that I'd rather die than be Sikander's slave. I'd rather kill.

I turned to look at the boy, realizing that he would have to witness me stab someone. He was watching me carefully, and I realized that my scarf had loosened and that my face was exposed. I tried to cover myself back up but wondered if there was even any use.

Just then, the boy smiled and stood up, opening the door to his home, nodding at me.

Thala and I glanced at each other, and we bounded through the door.

"Thank you!" I yelled at him. I reached into my bag to pull out a handful of coins, but he shook his head, refusing my money.

"It is my duty, Devi," he said, quietly closing the door behind him.

I stood before him, stunned by his kindness, wondering at his calling me Devi, but Thala grabbed my hand before I had a chance to say anything more. We ran through the small house till we arrived on the other side. A back doorway led us to another cobblestone lane on the far side of the slope. It was quieter here, almost as though we had arrived in another land. I turned to look back at the boy just as we rounded the corner, and he was still standing there, frozen, watching us with a look of wonder across his face.

"Come on, we have to keep moving," Thala insisted. "We're safe for now, but we have to come up with a plan."

"Okay. I just need a minute to breathe," I said, carefully tucking the dagger back into my satchel and closing my eyes.

When I opened them, Thala was looking straight ahead, pointing to something, silently laughing.

"What is it?" I followed her gaze.

She was pointing to a tiny storefront, barely discernible. I might have easily walked by without noticing it, as a handful of people quietly wandering the hilltop did.

In the front was a small sign: "Meena Amba, Cartographer."

"The cartographer Mala was talking about . . . do you think that could be it?"

"Doesn't hurt to ask." Thala shrugged.

We dodged through the front door, slamming it shut behind us, both of us hiding behind a bookshelf. I glanced out the window as Nico's men hastily ran by.

I sat down next to her, a wave of relief washing over me, grateful that we were out of harm's way, if even for a moment.

"Can I help you?" a sharp voice asked, snapping me back into attention.

Fourteen

I LOOKED AROUND THE SMALL, well-appointed room. The walls were made of wood, and timber beams ran across the ceiling. Carved into the mahogany walls were shelves filled with large leatherbound books. It took me a second to realize that we were inside a tree, branches poking out of the walls to hold up lanterns lending an orange glow to the dim space.

Every surface was covered with maps—blue maps and brown maps and green maps. Maps tumbling off tables and mounted on walls, falling out of half-opened trunks, loose rolls of maps lined up against the door, stacks of atlases, and every type of globe I had ever seen. There were glass orbs, spheroids made of wood, black and blue marbles of the constellations in the sky. I was mesmerized by it, this room brimming with order and topography: a chamber of answers.

"We're not open to the public today." Her voice was sharp, and she wore fitted black trousers and black leather boots. Her shirt, too, was tailored like a man's shirt. Her dark hair was tied neatly into a bun, and she had a face that radiated intelligence. It was hard to tell how old she was, but there was an air of sophistication about her that made me stand up straight.

I was still entranced by my surroundings when I answered her. "I'm . . . I'm so sorry, but we're in trouble, and I think you know my friend . . ."

She glanced at me, confused. "And what friend would that be?" she said, putting on her glasses and looking me up and down.

"Mala," I said, tugging at the scarf that covered my face.

She started. "How do you know Mala?"

"She's my lady-in-waiting . . . she *was* my lady-in-waiting." I hesitated a minute, thinking about the last time I had seen Mala and trying not to cry. "She told us to come find you."

"This is Amrita, princess of Shalingar," Thala interjected, "and my name is Thala. This is going to sound unusual, but the palace is under siege—"

But the woman stood up. "I don't know who you are or what kind of joke this is, but you must leave now."

"Please," I said, glancing down at my filthy clothes, the half moons of my fingernails filled with dirt, my hair crusted with sand. No wonder she didn't believe me. "I know what you must think. Two girls looking lost and disheveled arrive at your doorstep claiming to be royalty. But I really am

Princess Amrita. I have no place to go, and the kingdom is in grave danger. Mala mentioned a cartographer, and—how many cartographers are there in the kingdom anyway?"

"I'm the only cartographer in Shalingar," she said.

"What can I say to you that would make you believe me?"

"I need proof."

I thought for a moment before I showed her the ring Arjun had given me. "My friend Arjun gave me this. He's the son of Bandaka and Shree, my father's advisors. He used to come into Shalingar quite a bit. You must have met him."

She looked at me with suspicion in her eyes, and I sensed that she knew Arjun, but she eventually shook her head. "You could have stolen that."

I took a deep breath. "What about this?" I pulled a diamond-studded shoe from my satchel, and even though her eyes widened, she shook her head again, this time vehemently.

"I don't even want to know where that came from, but I'll pretend I didn't see it. I'm sorry. I wish I could help you, but I can't."

I felt a wave of resignation and stood up, brushing myself off. "Come on," I said to Thala.

"You're sure you want to leave?" she asked, her eyes downcast with worry.

"We'll figure it out." I turned on my heel and walked to the door, pulling the golden dagger out of my satchel as I reached for the doorknob with my other hand.

"Wait," Meena said, her voice trembling.

I turned around to look at her. She was eyeing the golden dagger in my hand. "Where did you get that from?" she asked, pointing at it.

I stood up straight. "Mala gave it to me."

She hesitated for a moment before she quickly turned and cleared the maps from a chair. "Please," she said, gesturing at me. "You must sit down. And you too." She nodded at Thala before she removed an armload of maps from an old trunk. She walked gracefully toward the windows of the shop and pulled the drapes. She lifted a steel carafe and poured two tumblers of water before she placed them before us. "Your Majesty. Forgive me. I simply never believed this moment would come, but if you're here, we must be in grave danger. I should introduce myself. I'm Meena Amba, the royal cartographer." She reached out her hand to shake mine. It was an unusual greeting, one I wasn't used to, but it put me at ease. "I'm acquainted with your father. May he live a long and healthy—" She stopped herself before she could finish the sentence, sensing that her words came too late.

It was what people said, what they were supposed to say. I opened my mouth, but I couldn't speak. Tears pierced my eyes. I forced myself to pull it together. "Meena, we need help. The palace is under siege. Arjun has been taken prisoner. Bandaka and Shree too. My father and Mala are . . . gone. And Emperor Sikander's men are after us."

"They chased us into your shop, practically," Thala said.

"We don't know where to go, but Mala mentioned that I should warn someone. Would you know what she was—"

But before I could finish, Meena got up and went to a desk. She opened the top drawer and took out a small key. She then walked to the wall behind us and very carefully slid the key into a small keyhole in the tree.

"We've been in the map business for generations. Everyone in my family learns the trade—how to draw maps, care for them, preserve them, how to read them, how to let them speak to us." She turned to me. "I've worked with your father, Bandaka, and Shree, even Arjun. I know them all well. Many, many years ago, my family was approached by . . . an associate of the Sybillines."

Thala and I glanced at each other as Meena carefully turned the key.

"He asked us to draw this map . . . based on his descriptions. And so we did. And then he asked us to keep it safely."

She tugged at the key, and the wall opened like a door. I gasped as Meena stepped aside to reveal an iron box—a safe.

"He handed my ancestors a dagger. Not just any dagger—a golden dagger with three rubies on the handle. We were told to give the dagger to the royal family with careful instructions: If any member of the royals was ever in danger, they needed to find a way to come here with the dagger in hand. He told us to be on the lookout." She bowed before me. "This part, I can't do without you," she said.

I stared at the dagger and then back at her. Slowly, I stood up and walked toward the safe, inspecting it carefully. On the side of the box were three large rubies in a triangle, identical to the arrangement of rubies on the dagger.

"Go ahead, Your Majesty," Meena said.

I noticed a small crevice on the side of the safe and slipped the blade of the dagger into it. It moved easily into the fold, then the rubies lit up and something clicked. I glanced at Meena, who simply nodded. Slowly, I turned the dagger to the right, and as I did, the safe opened.

"It's a key," I said.

Meena reached inside and pulled out a piece of parchment with her long fingers.

"This map—it's been kept here for you," she said, unfolding it.

"For me?"

"We've safeguarded this map under lock and key for generations. It'll take you to the Janaka Caves."

"Where the Sybillines are?" I was stunned. "I thought there was no way to access the Janaka Caves."

"There is one way. And this is the only map in the world that can get you there. You must warn them that Shalingar has been attacked. They'll offer you protection."

I glanced at the complex ancient calligraphy before me.

"It's very old, but well-preserved. It's been kept in this safe for hundreds of years. You have a small window of time to get to the Janaka Caves and warn the Sybillines that their way of life is in peril."

"But what about the Library?" Thala muttered under her breath as she nudged me.

I shook my head. "This is my duty. And this is something we can actually *do*. Where's your map to the Library of All

Things?" It came out a taunt, and I regretted it the moment
I saw a flash of hurt in Thala's eyes. She recovered quickly,
turning away from me.

Meena traced her fingers along the map. "Can I offer you
a piece of advice?"

"Of course."

"Mount Moutza is on the way to the Janaka Caves.
You'll want to make a pilgrimage to the temple there."

"What for? There are men out there who want to capture us . . ."

"It can never hurt to please the spirits." She hesitated. "I
think you'll understand when you get there."

"A superstition, then?" I asked.

She watched me for a moment before she turned her
attention back to the map. "From there, you can buy your-
selves horses and ride through the desert all the way to the
caves. Three fortnights to the edge of the desert."

"That's a long journey."

"It is. But all you have to do is follow the map," she said. "I
can give you some clean clothes, refill your skin . . . I only wish
there were more I could do to help you. But the Sybillines
will know what to do. There must be a reason they had an
intermediary leave the map with instructions, and the dagger
too—it's a key to many things. Make sure you keep it safe."

She got up and opened a drawer in the wall, pulling out
simple salvars and kurtas. "You'll be relatively inconspicuous
wearing these. People will think you're pilgrims. Be careful
to keep your identities hidden."

I nodded, collecting the clothes from her. Thala and I took turns cleaning up and changing in her dressing room.

"It should be safe to head out by now, I think," I said, peeking out the window. "I'm guessing it's been enough time for Nico and his men to scour the area and head back."

Meena nodded wistfully. I could tell she was worried about us.

"Can you hold on to this for me?" I asked her, removing the ring Arjun had given me and handing it to her. "In case Arjun ever comes looking for me. You can tell him where I went." It pained me to part with it, but I wanted to make sure that if he was ever able to escape Sikander's clutches, Meena could give him evidence that I had come here and that I was headed to the caves.

"I have one more question." I turned to Meena.

"Of course."

"The intermediary . . . who was he?"

Meena cocked her head to one side. "It was many, many years ago, but we have a story about it in my family. My great-great-great-great-grandmother opened the door to the map store one day, and there he was, this young handsome man with a satchel in his hand. He had her draw the map, paid her, and left the dagger with clear instructions."

"Then what happened?"

"He told her that one day a young woman would come. She would bring with her an oracle. It was her fate to find the Sybillines and warn them."

"She?"

"Yes. He also told her that it was her duty to keep all this in confidence. To tell her daughter and have her tell her daughter and so on. She was intrigued, as you can imagine."

"And so she agreed?"

"She did . . . but there's a part of the story that I always thought had been made up, inflated and exaggerated with time the way myths are." Meena took a deep breath and looked at me. "You see, just as he turned to leave, my great-great-great-great-grandmother asked the man, 'Who are you?' and he replied, 'I am the Keeper of the Library of All Things. And I will wait for her as long as I have to.'"

At this, Thala's eyes widened. She squeezed my wrist so hard that I had to turn and look at her, vindication on her face.

"Then he stepped out the door, and my grandmother watched him fly away."

"*Fly* away?"

"He was a vetala. Vetalas can fly," Thala whispered.

"Not *was*," Meena corrected her. "If he was a vetala, and if the story is true, then he's still out there somewhere. He still *is* a vetala, an immortal. And he left the map behind for *you*," she said, looking at me.

Fifteen

"IT'S *REAL*. Why aren't her words proof enough for you?"

I glanced around the empty cobblestone alley, small yellow and pink cottages on either side of us. We were on the quiet side of the hill outside Meena Amba's store. The air was still and the street devoid of human traffic, but I wondered if we would ever truly be safe again. I turned to Thala. "She said herself she thought the story had been exaggerated."

"But she doesn't believe that now!"

"So what do you suggest we do?"

"We have to find him! I could change my history. It could be like I was never separated from my family. And you could undo what just happened. Don't you want your father back?"

I felt a pang in my chest that was so painful, I could barely breathe. "Of course I do! But I just don't believe people can go back in time and change all the horrible things that ever happened to them! Don't you think if that was the case, everyone would be seeking this Library? Everyone would be changing their fate?"

"But they don't, because they don't know how to find the Keeper of the Library . . ."

"Thala, do you know how ridiculous you sound?" I could hear the edge in my voice. "Even if I did believe you, and I don't . . . how would we ever locate this vetala of yours?"

"Based on what Meena said, it sounds like the vetala is looking for *you*. We may not even have to find him — he could come to us."

"Let's get clear here." I stopped in the middle of the road to make sure what I was going to say next registered. "You tricked me so I would release you from that cell. I don't blame you. You wanted to be free. You're free now, so there's no need to carry on this charade about the Library of All Things and some magical vetala who can change the past." Even as I said the words, I wondered if it was just a coincidence that both she and Meena had mentioned the Keeper of the Library. But I pressed on: "I have a duty to warn the Sybillines, and I won't be distracted from it."

Thala narrowed her eyes at me. "I didn't trick you, and I didn't lie. Oracles don't lie, I told you that. I know you're upset because you lost your father and Mala and Arjun, but I'm not the reason all of that happened."

I angrily tugged at the scarf that covered my face, making sure it was secure. "Actually, you *are* the reason Arjun isn't with me right now." My voice was sharp. I couldn't help it; the cruel words simply tumbled out of my mouth without any thought. I just missed Arjun, horribly. The truth was, I didn't blame Thala for his capture. I blamed myself. I hoped he was all right.

Meena Amba's words had given me some comfort, but more than that, they had given me direction, a mission. Thala's obsession was clouding her judgment, and I couldn't rely on her help. But I needed to take the matter of my kingdom into my own hands. The only thing that mattered to me right now was getting to the Sybillines. Once I got there, I could figure out a plan, maybe even find a way to communicate with Arjun and rescue him from Sikander. And then the two of us would devise a plan to take the throne back. After everything that had happened, I couldn't let Sikander simply seize what he wanted.

If Thala was right about one thing, it was this: As long as I was alive, there was a chance that my people would remain safe.

I looked away from Thala's piercing eyes, too angry to say anything.

"Fine, don't believe me then." She simply turned on her heel and walked ahead of me.

"I don't," I scoffed, but I made sure I was a few paces behind her so I didn't lose her.

I felt a lump in my throat that I couldn't swallow. *What if she was right?* The idea of never seeing my father again was unthinkable, and it made every ounce of my heart ache.

Every time I thought about what had happened, the way I had simply left him, I had to fight the urge to stop in my tracks, get down on my hands and knees, curl myself up into a ball, and cry.

But I willed my feet to keep walking. I thought about the way Thala had cleaned them for me by the well, the way she had carefully reached her hands down into the tunnel to retrieve me, the things that she had confided in me.

I thought about how she must have felt when she was ripped away from her family and taken into slavery. I wondered again about the cuts and bruises on her body, and my heart ached for her too, for an entire world of suffering I had never before encountered or experienced. Before today, I hadn't even known this kind of pain could exist.

I walked faster till I was just behind Thala. She turned to me, her face a mask of stone. "I'll go to the temple with you, but we're going to the Library of All Things," she insisted. She hesitated before she added, without emotion in her voice, "Otherwise, we should consider parting ways." She quickly cut ahead of me again.

I was too hurt to respond. The prospect of a lone three-fortnight expedition on horseback through the desert to a place that no one had been able to access for centuries terrified me, but I would simply have to find a way to do it. I wondered about my own will. Thala had pushed me past my own limit in that tunnel. What would happen when there was no one there to tell me I had to go on when I didn't have it in me?

◻

The stone road to Mount Moutza was filled with people from all walks of life. There was the occasional procession of monks, some of them with shaved heads, others with long hair and beards, all of them draped in red and orange robes. They walked quietly, wordlessly, carrying nothing but the wooden bowls in their hands, with which they begged for their morning rice.

Every now and then, a merchant caravan traveled down the road too, drawn by horses and camels, large burlap satchels hanging off their flanks. The ones leaving Ananta carried bags of tea, indigo, spices. Those coming in toward Ananta held reams of colorful silk shining in the sun—reds and indigos, oranges and greens. The men and women on these caravans wore beautiful robes made of the same silk.

Bedouins carrying all of their belongings on mules marched past us, their faces weathered and creased like stories told again and again. In their hands, they held mirrored patchwork bindles.

Entire families walked together on foot—children chasing one another down the road, their carefree voices pitched into the air above us like kites, fathers holding babies in their arms, speaking to them in soft voices, coaxing them to sleep.

They were headed east toward the sunrise, toward lands that my father had told me about, places that Mala had woven into the fairy tales she recited to me and Arjun when we were children.

There was a time when the whole world had come to me through their voices, through their words and experiences, and now I was walking that very world with my own feet, and all I could do was wonder where they had gone, where people go when they depart this life, this plane. I had never before even considered that question.

Before long Thala was many paces ahead. The tension between us was thick and heavy. She was one of the few people in the world who could understand how I felt right now, and yet I had driven her away.

I tried to distract myself. A cool breeze caressed my face and rustled the leaves on palm fronds. I walked under the blue tile archways that lined the road every few hundred paces. Along the stone road was a whitewashed wall with pink vines crawling across it, more bloom than wall. Colorful prayer flags flapped in the soft breeze, and the smell of jasmine permeated the air.

"Looks like you're having a rough day," I heard someone behind me say and snapped around, my heart racing, half-expecting to see one of Sikander's men.

But instead, my eyes met those of a boy about my age, maybe a little older, wearing a white tunic and blue pants. The very sight of him made something in my stomach tense and then flutter violently. His dark, wavy hair curled at the edges from the humidity in the air. He was gazing at me with bright blue eyes that were hard to look away from. He smiled, and I wondered if he was taunting me. There was something beautiful about him—actually, *everything* about him was beautiful: his squared shoulders, his lean hips, his clear blue eyes, and his full lips, and I realized that many of the young women and men walking by turned to get a second glance at him.

"Are you . . . speaking to me?" I asked, both irritated and confused.

Even though I wasn't accustomed to strangers and was overwhelmed with paranoia that Sikander's men had somehow sent him, his seductive smile made me impulsively curious.

"You're the only one here, aren't you?" I noticed his confident gait, his strong arms.

"Technically, there are thousands of people walking this path today."

"Technically, there are millions of people in the world. But it's you I'd like to speak with." His eyes looked back at me like a question as he cocked his head to the side, watching me.

I stiffened, feeling self-conscious all of a sudden. "What for?" I realized that he intimidated me and simultaneously drew me in while putting me on the defensive.

Suddenly, he grabbed my waist with his strong hands, pulling me to the side of the road as a camel carrying a pair of newlyweds sidestepped me. They were waving to the people along the road, tossing handfuls of sugar candy to children and pilgrims. I breathed a sigh of relief as I watched the camel thump by, golden bells on his ankles, a red and gold patchwork quilt hanging off his flanks, a thread of red pom-poms tied around his ears.

"That would have been a tragedy, if that camel dressed in wedding regalia killed a beautiful young girl on their wedding day," he said, laughing, as he waved to the couple.

He continued to hold my waist, and I felt an electric charge where his fingers touched my back, the roughness of his palms against my bare skin, the heat of his body against mine.

"Aren't you going to thank me?" he asked, and I turned my head to look at him.

He grinned, and his smile made him appear more approachable for a moment. Something about him seemed oddly familiar. I could have sworn I had seen him before, but I wasn't sure where.

"And why would I do that?" I looked at him defiantly.

"I just saved your life. You owe me one." His voice was a whisper, and he continued to hold me close.

"Do I now?" Pulling away, my body felt cold where his hands had once been.

"Here's how you can make it up to me," he said, somehow sensing that I wasn't about to walk away from him. "You can keep me company on this journey."

"I don't think so," I told him, stepping back, but it was as though we had a string connecting us. I could step only so far from him before I felt the urge to be close to him again.

"Why not?" He was grinning again, but I held strong.

"I don't know you. You could be a murderer. Or a thief. A criminal . . ."

"Or simply a nice guy who would love to accompany you to Mount Moutza."

"How do you know I'm going to Mount Moutza?" I said, alarm in my voice.

"I overheard an argument you were having with your friend."

I immediately regretted that Thala and I had failed to be discreet. But I was also annoyed that this stranger would rudely admit to listening in on us.

"And that's why you're wasting my time?" I snapped.

"That's why I'd love to keep you company. Your friend's obviously not in the mood."

I was irritated at his presumptuousness. He was probably accustomed to getting whatever he wanted on account of his good looks and felt it was appropriate to intrude on our business. "No, thank you. I'd prefer to be on my own."

He wasn't deterred by my tart response.

"It's a shame you two plan on parting ways after you get to the temple." He was watching me with such intensity in his eyes that I had to look away.

A pang of loneliness shot through my belly as I watched Thala walking ahead of me. "And why is that?"

"The temple is a good place for reconciliation. You two should reconsider your friendship once you get there."

"Perhaps you should reconsider your patronizing and entirely unsolicited advice to strangers."

This time, he laughed out loud. "So why are you headed to Mount Moutza? What are you asking for?"

"Do I need to be asking for something?"

"That's typically why people make the pilgrimage."

I didn't respond.

"I take this walk fairly often. I can tell you more about Mount Moutza, if you'd like."

"I don't have any money to pay you . . . ," I said, understanding now that this was probably some sort of scheme. Perhaps he was a guide and this was how he made a living.

He laughed. "Truly, there's nothing I want from you. I promise."

"You just want . . ."

"Your company," he said, his voice quiet but persistent. Then he glanced at me carefully. "Why does that surprise you so much?"

I held his question in my mind for a few moments, considering it carefully. I noted the kindness in his voice.

Softly, he added, "Company is sometimes the best thing we can give each other." I looked toward Thala, still several paces ahead. "It can be a balm for all the fear, loss, and anguish in the world," he said, looking at me as though he knew that I carried all of these emotions with me.

I did feel all those things, but mostly, I was afraid that this was only the beginning. We were still alone in the world, Thala and I, navigating unknown terrain, barely speaking to each other, and I felt exposed to the elements, stripped bare in the face of terrifying unknowns that could befall us at any minute.

"My name is Varun, by the way. You don't have to tell me yours if you don't want to."

Maybe I was taking a risk, but I also didn't want to believe that the world was filled with evil people like Sikander. I wanted to hope that there was kindness too.

"Amrita."

Sixteen

VARUN WAS TOO OLD to be in school, but certainly too young to be a monk. Besides, he wasn't dressed in the traditional orange robes that monks wore.

"Why would you make this pilgrimage every day?" I asked him. "Don't you have a job?" As I watched him, I realized I wanted to know everything about him: where he was from, what his life was like, and yet I struggled against the poise and decorum that Mala had always instructed me to maintain, especially with strangers. It was a barrier, and for some reason, I didn't want any barriers between myself and this stranger I had just met, something that baffled and surprised me.

He didn't seem offended by my questions. "I do. I'm a caretaker. But I'm also a devotee of the Goddess."

"The Goddess? Which one?"

He raised an eyebrow. "You don't know anything about the temple, do you?" He was teasing me again.

"Some." I held my chin high, attempting to maintain my pride. "It's the Mountain of Miracles, where the Diviners made a pact with the vetalas."

"That's it?"

"There's more?" I looked at him. "I mean, it's just some old fable. How complicated could the story be?"

"Is this your first time there?"

I nodded.

"You must know the story of Makara the Spider."

"He creates, sustains, and destroys the world."

"Right, and after he created this world, he conjured up two groups to care for it."

"The Diviners and the vetalas."

"Exactly. The vetalas were immortal. They kept meticulous records of time. Some had powers to heal any wound, any illness. They were logical beings, methodical. They believed in order and fairness. But they were spirits, lacking bodies, and so their ability to influence the world was limited—that is, unless they were able to inhabit a human body."

"That's why people are so scared of them. They devour humans."

"*Devour* is a little sensational," he said as he reached for my shoulder and directed me to a part of the path where there was less foot traffic. "They find uninhabited bodies of the dead to animate."

"Not much difference," I said, feeling a pang of regret as he removed his hand from my shoulder.

Varun shook his head, grinning at me. "They're not as scary as people think. The Diviners, on the other hand, were the first humans. They couldn't see the future, and they had a tendency to forget the past, but they had courage and will. They had the means to shape their future, something that the vetalas couldn't fathom. The Diviners were emotional beings, capable of great love and great pain. Makara created these beings hoping that they'd work together to care for the Earth, but that's not what happened. At first, humans and vetalas worked together—vetalas even taught the Diviners how to look into the future."

"Is that how oracles learned to see the future?" I said, looking ahead at Thala. She seemed to be limping, her body sagging to one side.

Varun nodded. "It's an age-old practice. Vetalas also taught the Diviners how to communicate with the Earth. But ultimately their differences cleaved them apart."

"What differences? Aside from the stealing-bodies stuff . . ."

"That was actually it. Vetalas don't procreate; the early world contained only a finite number of them. Vetalas could communicate with humans only if they inhabited a human body, so they spent their time in cemeteries, trying to find newly deceased bodies to reanimate. And when humans learned of this practice, they thought it grotesque, a violation they couldn't tolerate. A feud developed between the Diviners and the vetalas. Humans began to cremate the bodies of the dead so that spirits couldn't get to them first. And soon, there was no communication between the vetalas and the humans. That's why you barely hear anything about vetalas anymore."

"So wait—you believe vetalas really existed once upon a time?"

He laughed, and I noted the sound of it—open and kind. "They still do. They live in hidden places. And they no longer reside within clans. Most of them wander the Earth, alone."

"If they really live among us, wouldn't I have met one by now?"

"Maybe you have." He shrugged. "They exist; that's all I know. And they still understand the wisdom of the early world."

"What kind of wisdom?"

"The wisdom that the descendants of the Diviners lost . . . the ability to speak with the sky, with the ocean, with the trees. Those who broke from the Diviners lost their old ways. Humans no longer saw themselves as protectors of the Earth, connected to it, but they believed that they owned it. Their greed led to wars that destroyed the lakes, the forests, the oceans."

"Like the Land of Trees," I murmured.

Varun nodded. His long fingers pointed to the ground, his voice forceful and passionate as he watched me with his intense eyes, his gaze burning into me. "This is where it existed, the Land of Trees," he said, indicating the ground on which we walked.

My mouth dropped open. "*Shalingar* was the Land of Trees?"

"Very long ago. The Diviners lived within the Land of Trees. It was their home. Anyway, you know the story. People . . . wanted to turn it into a carnival ground. Maya, the leader of the Diviners, couldn't stand for this. The conflict escalated; they were on the brink of war. But the Diviners didn't believe in war as a solution to conflict. So Maya broke with her people and hiked up to Mount Moutza to enlist the help of the vetalas."

"But you told me the vetalas and humans didn't speak."

"You're an excellent listener." He grinned. "Maya took a risk when she climbed Mount Moutza—she was flouting an unspoken rule that humans did not enter vetala territory. Maya begged them for help, and help they did."

"What did they do?" I felt invested in the story now.

"Vetalas have great strength. And the ability to fly. So they transported the Diviners—or at least some of them—to a sanctuary."

"The Janaka Caves?"

He nodded. "Sadly, they weren't able to save the forest. And so humans eventually destroyed the Land of Trees."

"So what good was all that work?" I said, annoyed at his story.

"You assume that's the end to the story . . ."

"Okay, so what's the end?"

He glanced at me intensely, and once again, I had to look away from his gaze. "The Diviners spread out all over the Earth. One group went to Macedon. They became the oracles. Another group stayed in the caves—the sanctuary the vetalas helped them find. They became the Sybillines . . . guardians of the most precious material the Earth produces."

"Chamak."

"Exactly. The other chapter of the story has to do with the temple at the top of Mount Moutza. When Maya climbed the mount, asking for help, a vetala fell in love with her—a divine love growing between the two of them. They spent the rest of her life together. But he was immortal, and she was human."

"I know this story! About the vetala that wanders the Earth looking for his beloved." I thought about Arjun then, about how we had spoken about this very part of the tale one of the last times I saw him.

Varun nodded. "Do you know why he does that?"

"I assume because he's heartbroken."

"Yes and no. Of course he's heartbroken, but before she died, she made a promise to him: that if the people of her land ever needed her aid, she would return to the Earth in another incarnation. Mount Moutza itself is a temple devoted to the bond between Maya and her beloved . . . a place where miracles happen. Where vetalas and humans come together. Where any desire can be expressed and fulfilled."

"Yeah, I don't believe in stuff like that."

Varun shrugged. "You don't have to. But many do. You know, the king of Shalingar comes to the temple once a year too. He is a great devotee of Maya."

My heart dropped into my stomach, and I felt my hand instinctively press against my rib cage. I couldn't speak for several seconds, and Varun waited me out.

"Are you all right?" he asked.

Finally, I took a deep breath. "The king of Shalingar?"

Varun nodded. "There's a reason people come from all over the world to offer prayers to Maya. She's our most beloved deity. She gives people courage to stand up for what they believe in."

In the distance, I could see Mount Moutza, and if I squinted my eyes, at the very top, I could just barely make out a structure cut out of red rocks.

Was it possible that Maya the Diviner would actually descend to Earth now that we really were in trouble? I was too old for fantasies, had never believed in magic, but I desperately wanted to trust that someone would come and save us, or at the very least, someone would come and tell me what to do—how to reclaim my kingdom, how to save Arjun, and maybe, if it was even possible, how to go back in time and save my father and Mala.

I felt a hollowness in the pit of my stomach when I thought of my father making this very pilgrimage to the temple at the top of Mount Moutza. I wondered what he thought about when he went there. I wondered what he asked for. I wondered why he never brought me with him. My heart ached to speak with him again, to laugh with him.

"I wish there were something I could tell you to convince you that the story is true. But . . . you'll have to go to the temple, see for yourself," Varun interrupted my thoughts. I looked down at my shoes. I was wearing the white sandals that Thala had purchased in the town square, and my feet were horribly cut up and blistered. They ached with every step to Mount Moutza, but I didn't even care. The ache in my heart hurt far worse.

I wondered how many people made this journey despite themselves, handicapped by grief, by pain, by injury — all the things I had never been exposed to before today.

I noticed Thala far ahead of us, stumbling on a jagged cobblestone. My impulse was to run to her, but she caught hold of the wall next to her, stabilized herself, and continued to slowly walk ahead.

Varun watched Thala with concern in his eyes before he turned back to me. "People say that you can ask for anything on the top of Mount Moutza. It doesn't matter where you come from, what you believe, what faith you adhere to."

"What do you ask for — since you make the journey there all the time?"

Varun hesitated. "I lost someone I loved too. Long ago. I hope one day she'll come back to me."

I wasn't sure why I felt a hint of jealousy when he said this, but I put it aside, reminding myself that he was a stranger, free to love whomever he wanted.

I thought about Sikander, realizing that it wasn't the first time this very land was in crisis. "Except we don't have Maya the Diviner to help us this time," I said wistfully.

"But we do." Varun turned to me. He grinned that

alluring grin and watched me carefully. "It's a very special place. You'll understand when you get there," he said.

I paused, struck by the similarity of his words and Meena's. But before I could question him, I heard a thud and looked ahead of me.

Her hissed whisper cut through the ambient sounds around us. "I can't," it said, and there was Thala, crumpled into a ball on the earth.

Seventeen

I RAN TO HER, collapsing to the ground next to her. "Thala! Thala, are you all right?"

I reached for the skin of water, handed it to her, but she could barely lift her head. I tilted her face back to look at her. She had a smile across her lips, but her eyes were closed. "Feeling so strange . . ." she mumbled. "Out of sorts. Dizzy."

"It must be the heat," I said.

Varun reached down, pressing his palm against her forehead, a hint of uncertainty crossing his face. We helped her up, guiding her to the nearest fountain. The way her body slumped against it when we carefully sat her down frightened me.

"Thala, Thala!" The pitch of my own voice was enough to induce a terror in me. She was practically the only person I knew in this world. If something happened to her, I would be completely adrift. I forced myself to maintain my composure, but my heart was already racing with fear.

"Thala, I know you're tired. We can rest here for a bit. And when you feel better, we'll start walking again," I whispered to her, and she merely nodded.

I turned back to Varun. "She's been through quite a bit today," I said to him. "I think it's probably just exhaustion. Maybe if we rest here—"

Varun shook his head. "No, that's not it," he said. His voice was coated in worry, his brow furrowed as he carefully examined Thala.

"What do you mean?"

"Her eyes . . ." He gestured to her, and some sort of recognition registered on his face. "I've seen this before. Your friend—she needs chamak."

"She *needs* chamak?"

"Look at her eyes, her skin . . ."

I carefully inspected Thala's face. Her skin was paler than I remembered it, beads of sweat glistening across her forehead. But it was her eyes that terrified me. Her irises were large and black. I placed two fingers on the hollow of her throat, as Mala had once instructed me to do to measure out my own heartbeat, and the swift pounding of Thala's pulse, beating like a war drum, terrified me.

Varun reached for my arm, touching it gently as though to brace me for a jolt. "She's been taking chamak—a lot of it—and from the look of her, she hasn't been properly weaned off it. Look at the goose bumps on her arms, the way her teeth are chattering. She's very sick, your friend," he quietly said.

I anxiously watched Thala again, and I knew he was right.

"What can I do?" I asked.

"There are two options. We could give her more chamak to stabilize her, but the results would be temporary, and we'd have to keep giving her more and more. Taking risks with chamak can do severe damage to her body's natural balance. Besides, it looks like it's already too late for that, given her symptoms. At this stage, if you give her chamak, she might stay in this state indefinitely—hallucinating, her mind still active but her body unable to function. The best thing would be simply to wait until it's out of her system, but I should warn you—"

My head snapped back in his direction. "Warn me of what?"

"It's very difficult to wean one's body off chamak. It can sometimes be deadly. And even if she does survive, it'll get worse before it gets better."

"You mean she could—"

"She could die."

His words hit me like a slap, blood draining from my face, terror filtering through my body. I opened my mouth, but I couldn't speak.

"She's cold now, but soon her body will burn up from the inside. It's excruciatingly painful. A medicine man can help with the pain, maybe give her some herbs to help boost her immunity, but there's no way of knowing whether she'll—"

I didn't want to listen. I couldn't bear to hear those words again: *She could die.* "Where can we find one—a medicine man?" I asked, desperation in my voice. Thala's head fell against my shoulder, her eyes closed. I tried to shake her awake.

"Thala." I squeezed her hand. "Stay with me, please! I can't lose you too," I whispered. I unwrapped my scarf from my face, dabbed the sweat away from Thala's forehead before I turned back to look at Varun.

He did a double take when he saw my face, and for a second, our eyes locked. I knew he felt it too, that strange electricity between us, a familiarity that neither of us could explain. I felt myself redden and turned my attention back to Thala.

"She's going to be all right. We just need to get help," I said with determination in my voice.

When I turned back to Varun, I noticed that his gaze was still fixed on me, as though he couldn't look away. A series of emotions registered across his countenance: shock, morphing into tenderness. I wondered if he knew who I was.

"Not . . . a lot of medicine men in these parts," he said softly, crouching down next to me, so close that I could feel his breath in my hair. There was hesitation in his voice, and the look on his face suggested that he couldn't bear to give me bad news.

I looked up and down the path as I quickly wrapped my scarf around my head again. Varun reached to help me, his hand carefully tucking back a stray hair.

I tried to speak, but I was distracted by the way he looked at me and scared of the condition that Thala was in, too overwhelmed to think straight. Finally, I found my voice.

"We're still hours away from Mount Moutza, and it's a few hours back to Ananta," I said to him.

I considered walking back toward Ananta, but I was afraid to leave Thala on her own in this state. What if Sikander's men were making this very journey right now? What if they found her? In the condition she was in, there was no way she could defend herself. My hands were trembling, my heart racing with uncontrollable terror.

"Why don't you stay with your friend? I can walk back toward the city," he offered, gesturing down the road. "I'll find a medicine man on my way. Perhaps there's one making the journey to Mount Moutza right now."

A wave of gratitude washed over me. "How could I ever repay you?" I asked.

He hesitated, but his eyes stayed on me. Finally, he smiled. "It's my pleasure to help you, just as it's my pleasure to have met you." He pointed to the road ahead of us, toward Mount Moutza. "This road . . . it's going to be filled with people all day. She needs a safe and quiet place to stay the night."

"Where can we go?" I asked.

"Fifty paces ahead, you'll see a break in the wall, a fork in the road, and from there, if you walk another fifty paces, you'll see a forest. Look carefully and you'll find a banyan tree as wide as an elephant."

An uncontrolled laugh escaped Thala's lips. "An elephant," she repeated in a hollow voice that terrified me. Then her tone became serious. "I've never even seen an elephant," she quietly added. "There's so much I haven't seen."

Varun turned back to me, compassion in his eyes. "You'll recognize it. Wait for me under the tree," he softly said.

I nodded, lifting Thala up and wrapping an arm around her waist. My heart raced in panic as she fell against me like a rag doll. I grabbed her arm and threw it around my neck. "Your pilgrimage . . . ," I said to Varun, realizing that there was no way he would make it to Mount Moutza by sunset now.

"It's all right," he said, touching my hand, sparking off an electric desire within me again. "Helping you is as good as making an offering to the Goddess," he said. His eyes lingered on me for a moment as though there was something more he wanted to say. But instead, he turned and quickly took off. I watched him, overwhelmed by his kindness.

I turned my attention back to Thala, reaching for the end of her scarf, making sure it was securely wrapped around her face, covering her indiscreet hair.

"It was so short, my time. I wish I could have spent it all with my family instead of with those brutes," she slurred.

"We'll find your family, Thala." There was urgency in my voice. I remembered Shree once telling me hope could literally keep a dying person alive. "Once you're recovered, we'll travel to Macedon. To your mother and your aunts."

What I really wanted to say was: *Don't die. Please don't die*

on me. If you die, I don't know what I'll do. I'll be alone in the world.
Instead, I held my breath and walked us to the edge of the forest, where I could make out a dirt path cutting into the trees.

"Promise me." Thala's voice was firm. She looked at me
with clear eyes. She was lucid in that moment, as though
something in my words had awoken her from her trance.
"Promise me that if I live, you'll come with me to Macedon."

I swallowed hard. "I promise," I whispered.

She smiled. "I can't possibly die now, can I?" she said,
but the way she slumped into my side made me shudder.

Eighteen

THALA SLIPPED IN AND OUT of consciousness. There were moments when she was incredibly lucid, and others when her eyelids began to droop, and I had to shake her awake, sometimes violently. My whole body was alert, looking for strangers, predators, Sikander's men.

It was getting dark. I wondered when Varun would return. Something rustled in the distance and I jumped, my eyes scanning the woods. My heart raced, throbbing like fire in my ears. A small creature sprang from the brush, running toward us. I braced myself, swiftly grabbing a stick with my hands and getting back on my feet.

I squinted my eyes. A rabbit. I breathed a sigh of relief.

"I'm so cold," Thala groaned.

"I know," I said, trying to hide the panic in my voice. It was cooling down, but it was still summer, balmy and warm.

I made Thala a nest of leaves and twigs. With a handful of grass, I crafted her a pillow. Since there was no one nearby, I removed the scarf from around her face and covered her with it. Then I took off my own scarf and layered it over the first one. I sat beside her, keeping watch. I was determined to keep her unharmed.

"If I go—" Thala started.

"You're not going anywhere," I told her, my voice firm. "We have a deal. You'll be fine. We'll go to Macedon and find your family." I said it as though I believed it. I had to. "Varun will be here soon, with a medicine man. He's probably on his way back by now." I wondered if my words actually made a difference. If they gave her peace of mind.

Thala paused for a moment and gasped for breath. "This is why," she said.

"What is why? What do you mean?"

"Why I'm desperate to go to the Library. This is why. I don't just want to change the part about my being kidnapped by Sikander's men, about being a slave. They started giving me chamak when I was nine. Now I'm sixteen. I don't even know if I can live without it. Don't you understand? If I don't change my fate, I'll never be normal."

Her words caused all the air to escape from my lungs, as hot tears streamed from my eyes. "I'm so sorry, Thala. I'm sorry for what you've been through. I'm sorry I didn't understand."

She reached for my hand. "You can't let him get control of the chamak. You're right to go to the Sybillines. You're right to warn them. It's in Sikander's interest to breed addicts like me. The sicker people like me become, the more power-ful he is."

It was horrific, what she was suggesting, and I felt an uncontrollable outrage toward Sikander. Everything bad that had ever happened in my life was because of him. And I imagined that it was the same for so many others.

"It's hot. I feel like my hands and feet are on fire."

I remembered what Varun had said about Thala's body burning up from the inside out. How he had told me it would get worse before it got better. I needed to distract her. "Tell me about your mother," I urged her.

Her breathing was rapid, her entire body drenched in sweat. I fanned her with a large leaf.

"She has red hair," she said.

"Like yours."

"And kind eyes . . . the best seer I ever knew. Maybe she can even see me now."

"Thala, we'll find that Library. I promise you. I don't know how, but we have to."

"I know we will," she said. "I've known that from the very beginning. I just hope we find it before it's too late."

"What do you mean?"

"It was the very first vision I had when I saw you," she said, and her eyes turned a clear green, the color of algae. "You were there. You're the only one who can find it. He'll let you in, I know it. But I don't know if you'll be able to get there in time to change *my* fate. I don't know if it will be too late for me. If there's a chance for me to change this one life . . ."

She didn't finish. Instead, she closed her eyes, slumping back against the tree. I didn't know whether she was hallucinating or if what she was saying was true, but I understood now why the Library was so important to Thala.

And I was afraid. Thala was shaking violently now, her whole body seizing with tremors. Small cries escaped her lips.

"It hurts," she whimpered. "It burns!"

I grabbed the skin of water, poured some on my scarf, and tried to cool her down, but by now she could barely even speak. My heart raced with terror. I watched her eyes roll back into her head, leaving behind an ocean of white.

"Thala, it's all right, just stay with me. He'll be here soon, he'll—" My voice was frantic, desperate, but it was no use. I wasn't a healer. I dabbed the cloth on her forehead, panicked tears streaming down my face. "Just stay with me. *Please*," I cried.

I wish I had somehow been prepared for the turn that took place then. I wish I didn't remember her screams, her body convulsing in agony, as though she was literally on fire. Her cries were desperate, as if her skin was being lacerated by hot knives. Her hands shook. When her wails became so loud that they pierced the quiet of the forest, I had to cover her mouth, for fear that someone on the trail—possibly Sikander's men—would hear us and find us.

I wondered, as I spoke to Thala in a soothing voice, trying to cool her down, if Varun had duped me, if I had been seduced by his attractiveness. Perhaps there was no medicine man; perhaps he simply fled at the sight of a messy situation involving two young girls he didn't know. Maybe I had been wrong to trust him after all. What did I know of him? He was a stranger I had met on the path to Mount Moutza.

Desperate, I held Thala's hands, begged the trees, the sky, anything, for some sort of help, any kind of aid. But no aid came. Tears fell from my eyes as though some dam had been breached.

My mind turned to an even darker place: I had told Varun my name. I had accidentally shown him my face. I had essentially given him everything he needed to turn me in to Sikander. I had even taken his advice to wait in the woods.

My fears consumed me: terror of being caught, horror at Thala's plight, but the Unknown was my greatest source of trepidation. We were alone and adrift, two girls who had lost everything, and I couldn't bear to see Thala die or to be caught because of my own stupidity.

I had believed till then that what had happened to Mala and my father, or even Arjun's capture, or crawling through that tunnel in a state of panic, was the worst thing I had ever observed, the worst things that had ever happened to me. But Thala's cries of agony were like nothing I had ever known.

All of a sudden, her body went completely still. I froze, unable to speak or do anything, till my stomach lurched, propelling me into action. I reached for her, trying to find her pulse, some semblance of a heartbeat, some evidence that Thala, my friend, was still with me.

"Thala?" I touched her wrist, her throat. Nothing. "Thala!" I tried to slap her awake, shake her. My breath quickened in my chest, terror poisoning my blood.

And then I heard a sound that made me whip my head around, scanning the woods. A rustling, a flapping.

I saw it coming straight for me, hurtling through the sky.

My eyes desperately peered at the dark horizon as it approached, closer and closer, making my heart race.

It landed with a thud just paces from me, and I had to fight the urge to scream.

I braced myself, blocking Thala's body with my own. In my hand, the dagger. This time I was ready to strike.

Nineteen

THE WHITE BIRD waddled toward me, squawking as it approached. It was massive, almost my size.

I gripped my dagger tightly, and we stared at each other, unblinking, for a few moments before I noticed that there was something tied to its foot. Slowly, I approached it, reluctantly putting my hand out to pet it, worried that it might bite me. But it didn't. It simply nuzzled my palm and made a contented noise. I tentatively reached for its foot and untied a small package that I sensed was for me. In it, a glass vial, attached to a note.

I held the vial in front of me. It was filled with a thick, clear green liquid that shimmered in the moonlight. I unfolded the parchment and squinted my eyes to read it:

> *Amrita,*
>
> *I'm sorry I wasn't able to return to you. This is part of the antidote that your friend must take, but*

there's something you have to do first: Find a tree
that sparkles silver in the moonlight. Scrape off a
piece of its bark. Add a pinch of the bark to the vial.
It's a potent drug. It will help her sleep. Before the
sun rises, find the earliest morning dew. A few drops
should do. Add them to the mixture too. Then ask all
the forces of nature to help you: the earth, the sky,
the wind, the rain, the sun. You will bring her back, I
know it.

Varun

"Bring her back?" I said aloud to the bird before I turned back to Thala. I felt for her pulse and feared the worst. It was weak and slow, barely audible, but I knew I couldn't give up. I had the antidote. Or at least part of it.

"Are you coming with me?" I asked the bird. It watched me, turning its head to one side. "I'm going to call you Saaras," I said to it, remembering a story Mala used to tell me about a bird named Saaras.

I took off in search of the silver tree, scouring the woods, Saaras following me as I dodged between massive tree trunks.

"Silver in the moonlight, silver in the moonlight," I kept repeating to myself.

I wondered why Varun hadn't returned. I buried my feelings of disappointment and reminded myself that I had more important things to worry about. I was also simultaneously relieved that my instincts about him hadn't been wrong: He *did* want to help us. He wasn't trying to harm us.

Saaras and I wandered the forest for some time before

I saw it. We were deep in the woods, and it was dark, but the tree was unmistakable—it practically glowed silver in the moonlight.

"There it is!" I whispered. I pulled my dagger from the waistband of my salvar, but as I approached the tree, my hand hit an invisible wall, sending a slight electric shock down my arm.

"What the—" I pressed my palm against the wall, and this time, it sparked at my touch, frightening me. "What is this?" I asked as I slowly circled the tree, realizing that there was some strange sort of unseen shield around it that prevented me from accessing it. "I've never seen anything like this before." I turned to Saaras, as though he might have some suggestions. He simply stared back at me, mute.

I thrust my dagger at the invisible wall, but it clanged against nothing and rebounded back toward me. My heart was beginning to race with panic. I got down on my knees, trying to find the roots of the tree, to no avail. They were protected under the strange invisible field too.

I stood up on my toes and tried to reach for a branch, but once again, I was stumped. The tree was somehow protected by a force that was out of my control.

I wondered if there was another silver tree before I collected myself and went in search of it, wandering the forest till the white wedge of the moon began to sink into the horizon. I was frantic by now, tripping over roots and dodging under low branches, the smell of eucalyptus the only thing helping to calm my frayed nerves. But it was clear that there was only one silver tree.

We circled back to it, and I must have spent another hour trying to drive my dagger into the wall, throwing my body against it. Still nothing. Finally, I collapsed to the ground in frustration, tears streaming down my cheeks, my palms covered with dirt.

"Please!" I said to the tree. "My friend is sick. She might even be dead. All I want is to help her. Don't you understand? I need to help her!" I was sobbing by now at the thought of Thala dying, all because I couldn't procure the antidote she needed.

Slowly, I pulled myself together and stood up, reaching my hand against the wall to catch my balance, and what happened next stunned me. The wall had disappeared, and I stumbled against the tree itself.

"How did that—" But it didn't matter. With my dagger, I peeled off the tiniest bit of bark, and as I did, I noticed a drop of red rolling down the trunk of the tree.

"Is it . . . blood?" I asked Saaras.

I wondered if I was hallucinating as I added a pinch of the bark of the silver tree to the vial. It fizzed before it turned silver in the moonlight.

I still had a piece of bark in my hand. I tucked it into my blouse, in case I needed it later.

I looked at the tree. I felt the need to acknowledge its aid in some way. "Thank you," I said, and its branches appeared to bow down before me, causing me to jump. I turned and ran all the way back to Thala.

There was dew on the grass by Thala's feet, and I collected a couple of drops on my fingers, adding them to the mixture. This time, it gurgled. I opened Thala's mouth, tipped her head back, and poured the contents of the vial down her throat.

"Please work," I said to it, and then I remembered Varun's note.

"Please, earth, sky, sun, rain, wind. Whoever is listening, whoever has the power to help. Help my friend stay alive," I whispered. I couldn't believe I was asking these forces to help me. It sounded like . . . magic, and yet, I was willing to do anything to make Thala better. "She's been through too much." I wiped my tears on the back of my hand as Saaras looked on.

I turned to him. "She'll be all right, won't she?"

I was drenched in sweat, stretched taut with a panic I had never before experienced, but I still had hope.

Saaras watched me carefully, and I couldn't help but think that he knew what I was asking, that he understood. And for that moment, it was enough.

Twenty

I ROSE WITH THE SUN, questions burning on my lips, the journey ahead already unspooling within me.

"Thala," I said aloud, remembering yesterday's ordeal, her suffering, and my terror, and then in the same breath, I admonished myself. I couldn't believe I had fallen asleep. I jumped up. Thala wasn't under the base of the tree where I had left her.

"Thala?" I cried out. I circled the tree, finding her cross-legged on the other side of its trunk, petting Saaras.

She turned to face me. "Morning," she said. "How did you sleep?" There were dark rings under her eyes, and her lips were cracked. But she was alive.

I exhaled slowly, the tightness within me finally loosening into relief.

"I wanted to let you rest," she said, her forehead filled

with concerned creases. "I think I'm . . . all right. Did you see this?" she asked me, holding up a satchel so small, it fit perfectly into her palm. "It's herbs, for your feet. He had it tied to his collar."

So Varun had noticed my feet too. I wasn't sure what to make of the fact that he had saved us, sending us some sort of magical potion that had brought Thala back from the edge of death.

All I knew was that I wanted to see him again. It was as though I could feel some sort of magnetic pull toward him. I shook away the thought, remembering that just a few days ago, I was professing my love to Arjun.

I took a deep breath, and the strong scent of eucalyptus saturated my lungs. I looked around. For the first time, I really *saw* the forest. The entire day and night before, I had been so consumed by Thala's state, I didn't even see how beautiful it was. Tall, stately trees, their branches reaching toward the sky, their leaves delicate and long and papery. And the tree that had given us refuge—it was a special one, a banyan. I returned to it, running my hands over its long limbs—branches turning to roots, and roots reaching up to the branches. My hand stopped at the tree trunk, just above the ground. Someone had carved three equidistant circles, painted them red. They matched the symbol on my dagger. I traced the symbol with my finger.

"Let me put this medicine on your feet," Thala said. "You should thank him, the boy who helped us," she added, handing me the bit of parchment that was attached to the vial I had given her. I searched though my satchel, found a quill, and began to write.

> *Varun,*
>
> *I don't know how to thank you. Thala is alive and well. We're headed to Mount Moutza and then beyond. I hope I see you again. You came to our aid when we most needed it, and I can never repay you.*

I hesitated.

"What are you thinking?" Thala asked. She had covered my feet with leaves that she had moistened with the medicine from the vial. As she removed them, I gasped. All my cuts and scrapes were gone. But my attention turned back to the note in my hand.

"I . . . don't know how much I can tell him."

"Then send him this," Thala said, pulling my diamond shoe from my satchel. "Tell him to get it to your Arjun."

"I don't want to put him in danger," I told her. "He helped us."

"He wanted to," Thala said.

"He's just a boy, our age. How would he sneak into the palace? We're under siege."

Thala pointed to Saaras. "That's how," she said. "Tell Varun you're headed to the Janaka Caves and stopping at the temple on the way. Tell him to communicate with Arjun through Saaras, and that Arjun can do the same."

It was so brilliant, I threw my arms around Thala. Then I

turned my attention back to the note, scribbling my plea and a set of instructions. I finished and tied it to the bird's foot, instructing him to get it to Varun.

He nuzzled my hand before we watched him fly back toward Ananta, and I couldn't help but feel a little wistful at his departure. I turned to Thala.

"Ready?" she asked me.

"You're sure you can make it?"

"I've never been more certain in my life."

It was clear now, what we needed to do: take the path to Mount Moutza, warn the Sybillines, find the Library of All Things.

Twenty-One

CUT OUT OF THE RED MOUNTAIN ROCKS, it stood, majestic and stately against the bluest sky I had ever seen. Pillared colonnades buttressed a high roof that curved like a rust-colored sail over the lofty complex. The entry to the temple was a square opening in the rock.

Across the hilltop, lines of prayer flags flapped in the wind. And in between the crevices in the rocks, small bits of parchment, each carrying a long-held wish, a plea, a prayer. Millions of appeals and entreaties, carefully placed into walls of the temple. I wondered if Maya the Diviner could see them, hear them, feel them. I wondered if she really had the capacity to make wishes come true.

"It's . . . amazing," I said. "Like nothing I've ever seen." I wandered toward the entrance, past a steady stream of crowds strolling in and out of the massive structure.

I looked at the elaborate carvings across the edifice of the temple, relaying a story as old as the temple itself. They reminded me of the carvings inside the Temple of Rain, etched by a skilled hand, someone who sought to record and relay old truths. I wondered if those truths had any bearing on our lives.

I understood, as I stood there, that I would petition her too, with all my prayers, all my pleas, just as people had done for hundreds of years before me, just as my father had done. I wondered what he had come here to ask for.

Varun was right. Mount Moutza wasn't just beautiful. It was otherworldy. It was befitting that we were celebrating Thala's return to us on the Mountain of Miracles. I swallowed hard at the thought that I might have lost her. I smiled at her, grateful for her company.

"Can you imagine that this place was once home for the vetalas?" I asked.

Thala glanced at me, a surprised look on her face. "Since when did you start believing in all that?"

I blushed, thinking of Varun. I didn't know what to say, so I just shrugged. "There's no way to know they aren't real," I said.

Shree had taught Arjun and me to be critical, discerning, to never take anything literally. Mala had offered us a string of myths and stories, intertwined together. What these two women had given me were two separate and distinct parts of my life: practicality, strategy, and logic from Shree. Magic from Mala. But I had always kept them separate, and yet, after Varun told me the story of Maya the Diviner, I wanted to believe it. I wanted to believe that there was magic woven into the world in which we lived, something underneath the surface of what we could see, an entire universe we didn't quite understand, but that didn't mean that it didn't exist.

I also wanted to believe in *something*. I had lost everything I had ever known. All I had now were stories, words, and hope. Those were the things I needed to hold on to tightly, or I would feel adrift in an ocean that I didn't have the skills or wherewithal to navigate.

I glanced around, making sure Sikander's men weren't following us, but I felt safe here. Besides, we continued to be well-disguised with our scarves covering our faces. We looked like Bedouins, Thala and I. Not like what we really were. A princess. An oracle.

"Let's rest here a moment," I said, glancing at Thala's tired eyes. "I'll get us something to eat." With a handful of sikkas, I bought us two fists full of bright purple figs, speck-led green oranges, and some walnuts roasted with sugarcane from a friendly-faced vendor who threw a strand of mari-golds into my hands.

I thanked him before I returned to Thala, handing her a fig. She inspected it carefully, and even though I couldn't see all of her face, I could tell from her eyes that she was smiling, delighted.

She looked up at me. "For years, they fed me slop," she said. "Look at this, how pretty it is. The perfect fruit." She took a bite of it, closing her eyes, savoring the taste.

She turned, looking out into the distance. I followed her gaze. I could see Lake Chanakya, the palace, the entire city of Ananta. The kingdom was vast, and I could make out every part of it from this vantage point—the city, a major metropolis bustling with activity and trade, tiny carriages and horses winding up and down the lanes, but also the tea plantations built like concentric amphitheaters, the purple mountains to the east, and the Silk Road, a long stone avenue cutting through it all.

"When they built this temple, none of that existed," I pointed out. "It was probably all plains and meadows and forest."

My heart sank at my own words as I thought about everything that had changed in a couple of days for me. And yet, a wisp of hope was growing within me. Returning from the worst experience of one's life was possible: Thala had taught me that.

"We'll go in, say a prayer. Then we'll get two horses and head to the Janaka Caves," I told Thala.

Thala nodded, but she looked uncertain.

"What is it?" I asked.

She shook her head. "They say human plans are opportunities for entertainment for the immortals."

"Are you trying to tell me something?" I asked.

Thala hesitated. "Maybe we shouldn't go in."

"What do you mean? Meena said we should stop here, and Varun . . ."

"It could be dangerous."

"It's a temple," I said. "It's probably the only place where we *are* safe in all of Shalingar."

She nodded her head slowly, but I could tell that she sensed something was not quite right. And yet, I felt propelled toward the temple in a way I couldn't even understand.

"I think I have to go inside," I said to her.

She nodded. "I think you do too. But I'm also afraid."

"Of what?"

She shook her head. "Something dangerous. Something I can't quite see," she said. "I'm sorry. It's like that occasionally—I told you I can't see everything."

"I know," I told her. "But we'll have to take the chance."

Heat radiated from the walls as though the rocks themselves were nursing a burning fever. Swarms of people were packed like fish caught in a net, except they weren't trapped. They wanted to be here.

They had come from so many different walks of life: the young and the old, monks and scholars, locals, some foreigners that I could recognize from their strange and unique clothes. There were wanderers, carrying their belongings on their backs. The sick and the injured with bandages on their limbs. Newlyweds at the beginning of their journey together, asking for blessings. All of them swirling toward a golden statue that I could barely glimpse because all I could see was the mash of packed bodies before me.

I reached for Thala's hand to make sure we stayed close and didn't lose each other, but also because the claustrophobia was making me nervous. Beads of sweat were forming on my upper lip, and I wanted to rip my scarf away, but I knew I couldn't. The very idea of anyone recognizing me terrified me, and yet I was struggling to breathe.

I squinted at the gold statue, her feet strewn with garlands made of marigolds and jasmine. People clamoring to touch her feet, catch a glimpse of her.

"That must be her — Maya the Diviner," I whispered to Thala, but I still couldn't see her.

I felt an urgency to touch the statue, to stand before it and make my plea, beg her to give us her blessings for our journey. I wondered if she could quell all the anxiety and fear swimming through the murky waters of my mind.

As I contemplated this, I realized that I, myself, had changed in some way. I had somehow become the kind of person who sought blessings and hope from a statue, who believed in magic. And I wasn't ashamed of this.

If so many of my father's own subjects believed that Maya the Diviner could help them, could save them, if even my father had made this journey so many times over the course of his life, who was I to turn my nose up at it?

Finally, we were close, almost before her. I squeezed my way through shoulders and elbows, and finally the crowds parted and there she was. I glanced at her gilded feet, the fabric draped over her auric legs. Her exposed shoulders, shimmering in the light, and in her hand, a dagger with three rubies on its side — exactly like the one Mala had given me.

I looked up at her face, and my heart stopped.

The face I was looking into was my own.

Twenty-Two

"THERE! THERE THEY ARE! Get them, now!" My head snapped back as though it were on a string. I wasn't the only one. All around me, people halted their prayers and their pleas, pieces of parchment hovering midair between their fingers as they turned to look at him.

Nico was mere paces away from us, his men flanking him. My eyes met his as I realized we were the only ones in the entire temple whose faces were covered with scarves. I hadn't thought that our attempt at hiding, at disguising ourselves, would be the very thing that gave us away.

My mind went blank, but my reflexes were quick. I grabbed Thala's arm and tugged her through the crowds, pushing past a wall of bodies, terror lunging at my heart, ripping violently at my nerves. I couldn't bear to look back.

"We need to get out of here!"

Thala's reflexes were quick too. She dodged away from

Nico's henchmen, but Nico's hands grabbed for me. I ducked, squeezing myself between two monks, dragging Thala along with me.

"Oh no, not this again!" Thala cried. We pushed through the bustle and jolt of bodies, a mess of arms and legs all around us, elbows digging into my flesh, sweaty palms on my back. Dozens of curious eyes turned to look at us. We were inadvertently starting a commotion, advancing in the wrong direction, pushing against the crowds instead of moving with them, and Nico's leering voice was drawing attention to us.

"You troublemakers!" he cried in Shalingarsh. "You can't run forever!"

"Watch yourself!" a woman snapped when I accidentally stepped on her foot. The rush of bodies and the heat was making me panic. I couldn't breathe. I couldn't think straight.

"Stay with me," Thala yelled.

But Nico's rage competed with Thala's desperation. "They're criminals!" he cried. "Pickpockets! Thieves! Don't let them escape!"

His voice was a bellow, echoing around us, bouncing against the walls of the temple, and even if it wasn't true, I could see his words registering within people's hearts from the way they looked at us.

I noticed it in the eyes of everyone we passed: terror, anger, rage. And it was directed at us. My legs shook with nervousness. We had seconds to get out of here, before someone blocked us or grabbed us, but how? In the distance, I could make out the doorway to the temple, but the crowds were so dense that getting out of here quickly wasn't an option.

"We'll never be able to just walk out of here," Thala said. "Look at these crowds." She gestured to them. "Any minute now, we've got an angry mob on our hands, and they don't even know why they're angry, or whom exactly they're angry at . . . and what happens when they get to you and rip your scarf off your face and see that—"

She lowered her voice. "She looks exactly like you. Or you look like her—you *are* her. That's why Meena sent us here. She wanted you to know who you are."

Her words rang through me, echoing deep within me. I was trying to piece it together through my panic, but it was all a nonsensical blur.

"There's no time for this," I told Thala before I grabbed her hand, trying once again to squeeze through the throngs of bodies before me, to no avail.

She shook her head. "No. That's not going to work," she said.

"What can we do?" I asked her.

Her eyes lit up, and breathlessly, she exclaimed, "They're your devotees. They'll want to help you." She was slowly making sense of something in her head, a small smile across her lips, but I wasn't sure what.

Thala ripped the scarf away from my face, causing me to gasp.

"She's the Goddess," Thala yelled. "She requires your aid in exchange for her blessings!"

I looked at Thala, dumbfounded, as thousands of heads turned toward her voice, toward us, and audible cries filled the air around us. All of a sudden, people in the temple were dropping to their knees, and soon, a path to the exit was carved for us. For a moment, everything went still.

As Thala and I began to walk, devotees touched my feet. I tried to hide the look of astonishment on my face.

Thala pointed to Nico and his henchmen. They were the only ones who had remained standing, stunned still for the moment by what had come to pass. "Don't let them through!" she implored the crowd. "They are trying to harm our beloved Goddess!"

Concerned murmurs traveled through the crowd, and a mob descended upon Nico and his men.

"Don't look back," Thala said to me as we swooped through the exit to the temple, cool air against my exposed cheeks. Instinctively, I pulled my scarf up with my free hand as I continued to hold on to Thala. I was speechless, shaken by what we had just experienced.

I thought about the little boy on the hill calling me "Devi." *Goddess*. I thought of my father taking annual pilgrimages to the temple, while keeping me safe within the palace. I thought about Meena Amba insisting that we stop at Mount Moutza. I thought about how Varun had looked at me when I removed my scarf from my face. Even Arjun, telling me about visiting a temple on top of a hill before he became quiet. My entire body went cold. *They all knew.*

And yet an overwhelming sense of disbelief descended upon me. I had gone to the temple seeking help for myself entirely *because* I felt helpless. And if I was some sort of incarnation of Maya the Diviner, wouldn't I feel it? Wouldn't I have known it somewhere along the way? Instead, I simply felt lost and afraid. It had to be some sort of mistake, a misunderstanding.

Thala had powers. She could see the future, even the past. But what powers did I have? I was a mere mortal. I had royal blood, but on the run, with no home and no throne to return to, what did that even amount to? What could I possibly do to help my subjects, to save them from Sikander?

We rushed around the back of the temple, an empty stretch of the rocky cliffside overlooking the city.

Before I could catch my breath, I felt the cold slap of metal on my wrist. I shuddered.

"Got you." It was a Macedon tongue. His voice was gruff and gleeful. He ripped my scarf away from my face and squinted at me. I was standing eye to eye with a large, burly man. He had thick eyebrows, a full beard, and a cruel mouth.

I tried to scream, but he covered my mouth with his filthy palm before he turned to a group of men behind him and yelled, "We have the royal runaway in our custody."

"It's her, isn't it? Spiro, come here and take a look."

A young soldier with a wiry frame and hair that was so pale it was nearly white approached. He stood facing me, his visage expressionless.

"It's her," he quietly said.

"The master will be pleased," the first man said. "He sent many infantry units out looking for you. And we've found the oracle too! Today must be our lucky day!" he said.

I looked down at my wrists and ankles. They were bound in cold, heavy chains. My heart was beginning to race.

"Only one way to get these two out of here without a fuss." He gagged my mouth with a piece of cloth, and before I knew it I was being tossed in a large burlap sack. I tried to scream, desperation pulsing through my body like an electric charge.

The last thing I saw before everything went black was the shock and fear on Thala's face.

Twenty-Three

"THREE FORTNIGHTS, that's how long before we're the richest men on the Earth!" a voice boomed.

A timid voice piped in. "Sir . . . what if it's a trick?"

"Again, Spiro? A trick?"

The light was a searing white. I wiped the grit away from my lashes as I crawled out of the burlap bag. There was white sand everywhere the eye could see, and the sky was an intense, cloudless blue.

I turned slowly and saw them. Dressed in plainclothes, they sat in a line with their backs to me. A sorry-looking infantry unit of Sikander's soldiers made of a ragtag group of young boys. And just paces away from them, two men arguing: the burly man who had captured me and the pale, wiry one who had confirmed my identity.

A hand gripped mine, and I snapped to attention.

"It's all right, it's just me," Thala whispered. She was covered in sand too, but she was sitting on top of her burlap sack, her gaze fixed on the two men. Even though her hands and feet were bound in chains, there was a look of defiance in her eyes. Slowly, she raised her bound wrists and removed the gag from my mouth.

"Thala! Where are we?"

"Shhh . . . I'm trying to listen in. We're in the desert. You passed out. We've been journeying for a whole day and night. Well, more like being kidnapped, thrown into burlap sacks, and carried around by these brutes."

My heart sank as I saw my satchel in the burly man's hand. He pulled from it the map to the Janaka Caves.

"Oh no," I breathed.

"This is a cause for celebration! A good day for us, no?" the burly soldier said as he shook the map in the air, his voice filled with glee.

"But we have strict orders from Nico, coming directly from Master Sikander—"

"Boy, Nico is gone, and Sikander doesn't know. And you know what they say about the things people don't know."

"What if he finds out that we captured his bride-to-be?"

"How will he find out? We're already a day's journey out of that city. And once we find those caves, what do we need Sikander for?" He rifled through my satchel as though it were his own and pulled out my dagger.

"No, no, no!" I whispered.

Meena had insisted I keep the dagger safe, and now both

the dagger and the map to the Sybillines were in the hands
of this man with crazy eyes.

"Spiro, stop your whining. You'll thank me for taking
matters into my own hands. All you have to do is ride this
wave of good fortune that I've brought us," he said. "Your
job is to navigate, care for the horses, and cook our meals.
You do that, and you'll find yourself a very rich man in three
fortnights. My job is to rally the men."

"Yes sir."

"You can do that now, can't you?"

"Yes sir, Master Alexi."

"Good, now you hold on to this," he said, handing Spiro
the map, "and I'll take this gift that the princess brought us."
He waved the dagger in the air as he laughed heartily.

I wanted to stab him with the dagger. *My dagger. My map.*
And yet I was helpless, tied in chains, held prisoner with no
recourse.

Spiro looked back at the man, defeat on his face. "Very
well, Master Alexi. The sun will be setting soon. We should
try to get as far as we can before dark."

"Come now, men! Let us be masters of our own destiny!"
The burly man turned to his soldiers.

The soldiers stood up, but without ceremony. I
watched them closely. They were young—my age, many
of them so gaunt that it was shocking they were soldiers
at all. I thought about what Thala had told me about
Sikander's army of the unwilling soldiers, young orphans.
Just looking at this group of men made me wonder about

the unfortunate circumstances and conditions that had
brought them here.

And their silence suggested that they were afraid of Alexi,
just as I could tell Alexi was afraid of Sikander from the way
his lip quivered when he said Sikander's name. Sikander's
entire army, his entire operation was built on men fearing the
force of other men.

"What say you?" he asked his men. "Do you want to return
back to your homes in Macedon the richest men alive?"

The soldiers looked ragged, starved, and exhausted.
Some of them raised their fists in the air as though they
had no choice, but the way they lethargically slumped their
shoulders, the way their grim eyes stayed fixed on Alexi,
made me wonder what they really thought.

Only Spiro was silent, squinting into the sun. This wasn't
lost on Alexi. I watched as his eyes narrowed at Spiro.

"Any other scared fools here?" he asked.

Silence.

Spiro approached me, wordlessly checking to see that I
was still bound. He handed me a skin of water without making direct eye contact with me.

I watched him carefully, taking him in for the first time.
He was slight with pale green eyes. Too pretty to be a soldier.
And timid, from the way he spoke. But his words were measured and thoughtful. In fact, he appeared too thoughtful,
too considered to be one of Sikander's soldiers.

"You know you'll never get away with this, don't you?"
hissed Thala. "She's royalty. You can do whatever you want
with me, but there will be a price to pay."

Spiro didn't respond.

But Thala's hissing caught Alexi's attention. He approached us and grabbed Thala's jaw with his hand, making me gasp. "You keep quiet now and do as you're told, or you'll see what's coming for you and your friend."

Thala's eyes remained defiant as Alexi pulled his hand away, slowly, his leering face still looking at her.

A wave of terror coursed through my veins, and I thought about the bitterness she must have tasted right then: to be bound in chains yet again, to be held captive by the same people who had tormented her half her life. She had been so close to freedom, to the possibility of returning home.

What would happen to us now? Would they kill us? Take us captive for the rest of our lives? Would we be delivered to Sikander as gifts now, as slaves, the way Thala was once delivered to my father and me?

Before the sun descended behind the desert plains, Spiro hunted a dozen quail for our dinner. He found us a place to camp, and he was the one who built a large campfire to roast those quail and to keep us warm through the night. He tended and fed both Alexi's horse and his own. And then he carefully inspected the chains binding our wrists, making sure they weren't too loose or too tight, determining that we weren't injured, giving us water to drink. All this, wordlessly. I could see that he was the best rider, the best shooter. And he was a workhorse.

I wondered how he had ended up here.

And then I wondered how Thala and I had ended up here too.

Spiro set a piece of quail on a steel plate before me, and I hungrily scarfed it down before I lay back in the sand, thinking of Arjun. Had Varun sent him my message, informed him of my whereabouts? How would he ever find us now?

Meanwhile, Thala spoke in whispers to some of the other soldiers in Persian. I watched the shadows of her elaborate hand gestures conveying a sense of urgency and, at times, sadness.

"What are they saying to you?" I whispered to her. We were seated side-by-side in front of the campfire, the warmth it provided the only pleasure the desert, and our circumstances, could afford us.

"They were kidnapped as children. They haven't seen home in so long. They miss their families. They were forced to fight in violent battles. They've seen their friends die."

"That's awful."

"But they've also gotten to see the world. They hope to one day buy out their own freedom."

"I hope they're able to."

"I do too," she whispered to me.

"What do you think of Spiro?" I whispered.

Thala closed her eyes. "He's our age. Was taken from his family in Macedon when he was only five years old. His mother still hopes he'll return one day." She shook her head. "That's all I can see. It's harder for me now, without the chamak. Anyway, he strikes me as curious, quick, and capable, certainly more adept than that loudmouthed fool Alexi," she added underneath her breath.

"What are we going to do, Thala?"

"We're going to find our way out of this."

"How?"

"You're a goddess. Surely if these men knew—"

"What happened at the temple was different. I can't get us out of this!"

Thala was silent.

"What are you gossiping about, seer?" Alexi yelled at Thala. I could tell from the way he slurred his words that he was drunk. He pulled my dagger from his belt, holding it out so it was inches from her face. He inspected it carefully.

"It's a beauty. Not unlike you," he whispered, pressing the side of the blade against her cheek.

I froze in fear. "Don't touch her."

Alexi turned to me, a sinister grin on his face. "Are you going to *protect* her, Princess?" he jeered. He brought the blade of the dagger to my neck. "No way to get to the Sybillines, my arse. You're full of treasures," he said, stroking my neck with his thumb.

I bristled at his touch. I opened my mouth to say something, but no words came out. I looked at the dagger as it sparkled in the light of the setting sun.

"You want to know what we were talking about?" Thala asked Alexi. I could tell she was trying to distract him, and it worked. He turned toward her. "I saw something. Something in your future that you didn't anticipate." She smiled a secretive smile.

"Well? Do tell." Alexi grinned at her.

Thala closed her eyes, then opened them. They sparkled golden in the night. She looked down. Her voice was calm. "Tomorrow, a sandstorm. And you're woefully ill-prepared."

Alexi was silent for a moment. Then he vehemently shook his head. "I don't believe you. It's not the season for sandstorms," he said.

"Season or not, you'll need to build an encampment." She furrowed her brow. "Otherwise, you'll never make it to the caves."

I turned to Thala, and from the look on her face, I knew she was telling the truth.

"Your best bet is to let us go," she said.

Alexi laughed out loud. "You think I'm going to fall for that? So these imbeciles can rat me out and tell the emperor that I tried to run away with his bride-to-be and his magical seer?" He fell backward into the sand, laughing so hard that his belly shook.

"I didn't say you should return us to Sikander. Besides, Sikander's got his mind on other things. He's no longer in charge. His satrap Arjun is," she said calmly, inspecting her wrists.

My head whipped in Thala's direction. When had Arjun become Sikander's satrap? My heart raced in panic. Surely he wouldn't have taken on this position voluntarily. He must have had to, under duress.

"Seer, you must think me a fool!" Alexi roared. He turned to his men. "This seer thinks I'm a fool! What do you think I should do to her?"

I stiffened as I watched the men standing before Alexi. What *would* he do to her? What would he do to *us*?

I looked around at the faces of Alexi's men, noting the resignation in their eyes. I wondered how long they had marched with Sikander's army. If they had forgotten the tastes and smells of their homes. If they could still remember the faces of their families.

"You don't believe me, and you don't have to," Thala said. "But if I were you, I'd let us go. If you asked your master, you would know that oracles don't lie.

"The tide will turn after the storm," she told Alexi. "It would be to your benefit to shore up the courage of your men." I wondered what exactly she meant by this, but Thala's predictions were often cryptic, and Alexi simply scoffed at her. I wasn't sure whether his disaffection was mere bravado or if he actually believed her.

I turned to look at Spiro. His eyes met mine, but he shook his head slowly, like a man who had no control over his own destiny. Still, he spoke up. "If it's true," Spiro asked, his voice trembling, "what can we do about a sandstorm? We don't have supplies."

"Turn back, for God's sake," Thala said. "Free her." She gestured to me. "What kind of fool are you? Are you willing to march yourself and your men toward death?"

"You'd love that, wouldn't you?" Alexi yelled.

"Perhaps she's right, sir," Spiro quietly said.

"Right?" Alexi stood up, barreled toward Spiro, and grabbed the scruff of his shirt in his hand. "You want to believe her? Go ahead then," he said as he shook a frightened Spiro. "But you're not coming with us to those caves of magic, you understand?"

"I understand!" Spiro begged.

"No, I don't think you do," Alexi said. And then he took my dagger, the dagger Mala had given me, and sliced Spiro's throat open.

Twenty-Four

I TRIED TO QUIET MY MIND, begging the desert for help. *Even if I die, please keep my friend safe*, I asked. I knew no one was listening, but it felt better just to ask.

It had been a whole day since we had walked away from Spiro's dead body in the desert, leaving it behind like a thing and not a once-living, breathing person. I remember watching him die, choking on his own blood, falling to his knees before he fell face-first in the sand. I thought about the way my father had died. And Mala. Everywhere I looked, I saw it, again and again. Fear, blood, violence, death.

I remembered Thala's words about Spiro. I didn't even know who he was, much less where exactly he came from in Macedon. I wondered about his mother, his father. How they must have worried about him. They must have wondered how he was. Perhaps they would spend the rest of their lives waiting for him to return. Now he never would.

I took a deep breath and leaned back in the sand, feeling broken, defeated. Thala was already lying beside me.

"Stop," she said to me.

"Stop what?"

"What it is that you're doing. We're going to get out of this."

"How?"

She didn't have an answer.

"If he doesn't kill us, the sandstorm will. Either way, we're dead," I said.

I looked out into the night sky. What was Arjun doing right now, as Sikander's satrap? Were Shree and Bandaka safe? Was Sikander's army marching in the direction of the caves too? Were there search parties out scouring the kingdom for us? Would Sikander find the Sybillines and destroy them?

But every question I asked myself felt like a grain of sand let loose in the wind, merging with billions of other grains of sand, and eventually, my mind had no option but to quiet itself. I was here, in the desert, Alexi beside me, boasting of his fate.

He was the commander of a lucky unit, he told his men. They were headed toward the caves of magic. They would destroy the Sybillines. They would be rich.

I looked again at Alexi's men and wondered if they had ever felt they had a choice in life, a say in how their destinies had unfolded. All I could see were their tired eyes that looked far too old for their faces.

"Where do you think we'll go after this life ends?" I asked Thala.

The sun had set, and we were camped around a crackling blaze. The plains were naked, bare, and the moonlight dripped on them like wax from a white candle. Looking out over that endless bowl of sky full of billions of stars, billions of other worlds, I felt like we were the only living creatures left on Earth. The world felt vast, full of mysteries.

"I don't know. I wish I did. But I can't see it. There's a veil between life and death that I can't see past. You won't be gone for some time, anyway," she said.

"I think you're wrong."

"I'm the seer."

"Even so, I know in some deep part of me that my life is already over, Thala. It doesn't matter that you're the seer. I know it in my bones. Everything I once was . . . is gone. I'll never return to that life. I'll never be home again."

"Then maybe you should tell me what you'll miss."

I took a deep breath and smiled at my memories, alighting upon me like benevolent fireflies. "I'll miss laughing with my father, eating breakfast with him in the mornings. Toast with mango murabba and chai. Shree showing me how to read my first book. Running with Arjun through the orchard in the rain. The way Mala woke me up every morning, with such care. Tippu the gardener giving me a flower from the garden practically every time I passed him. Falling in love with Arjun. The view of Ananta from my window, neem trees, hot baths, cardamom kulfi, stories that Mala told me."

I was crying now, and laughing too. It had all been so . . . beautiful, despite the last part. I had lived such a rich life. I had been lucky.

"What do you regret?"

I thought for a moment. "That I never got to meet my mother. And leaving Arjun behind."

Thala nodded. "You've lived a wonderful life, Amrita."

"I know."

"You're right," she said to me after a moment. "You'll never return to Shalingar. You'll never rule your kingdom, the way you hoped you would one day. You have to accept it. That life is gone."

Even though I knew this, hearing Thala confirm it stunned me. I felt a deep panic welling inside me. It was one thing to feel resigned, to feel as though that particular life had ended, but it was an entirely different thing to relinquish my identity altogether. I felt like I couldn't breathe.

"Look at these men around you," Thala whispered. "Look at me. We all had to give up who we were once. The only advice I have for you is that your identity means nothing to Alexi, to these men, to the sandstorm that's coming our way."

I shook my head. I might have been ready for death, but if I wasn't Amrita, who was I? If I wasn't the collection of my experiences, then what was left of me?

"You're not Amrita anymore," Thala told me, her voice soothing. "You're Maya."

But every molecule in my body rejected her words. "I don't even know who Maya is! To me, she's just some statue in a temple."

Thala had no words for me then. She simply rested her shackled hands over mine.

In the distance, the wind howled. *Please*, I asked the vast landscape, pitching my desperate wish across its surface like I was throwing a stone. *Please keep my friend safe. Please get her to the Janaka Caves.* It had become an hourly prayer. Something I did simply to pass the time, to make myself feel better.

Thala lifted her head, turned to look out toward the sunset. "It's coming," she said. I expected to hear dread in her voice, but instead, I heard a crackle of excitement.

The sandstorm hit well into the night, just when Thala predicted it would. All of a sudden, a wall of dust engulfed the stars. The horses began to whinny, and fear radiated from Alexi's face. I knew there was no way we would survive a sandstorm out here without supplies. And yet, there was nothing we could do tied up in chains.

"Make a barricade with the horses," Alexi yelled over the terrifying hiss of the wind. "We'll stay in the middle."

"That won't work." One of the soldiers shook his head. His voice was surprisingly calm. "We'll be buried alive. All of us."

"You have a better idea?" Alexi shouted over the wind.

Two soldiers approached Thala and me, lifting us up to carry us to higher ground.

"Thank you," Thala said, touching the arm of the soldier who carried her.

I watched Alexi frantically yelling at his soldiers as he

gesticulated at the wind. But it was obvious to the rest of us: We had no chance of surviving this sandstorm.

I turned back to Thala, who was speaking loudly over the howl of the wind to the two soldiers who carried us. She spoke quickly in Persian, and after she finished, the soldiers glanced at one another. They ran in the other direction, mounted their horses, and took off. I watched them ride away from the storm.

"What did you say to them?" I shouted.

"I told them that I predicted this storm. And I can make another prediction that might be of use to them. There are a few outcomes to their fate. Had they made it to the caves, Alexi would have killed them so he could keep the loot for himself. Lucky for them, he'll never get there. If they stay here, they'll die in the sandstorm. If they go back to Sikander, he'll kill them. Sikander is going to see them as deserters. It wasn't their fault, but they abandoned their post, kidnapped the princess."

"Those are all terrible outcomes," I said.

"Yes, but they have one good option."

"What?" I asked.

"Run," she said. "I told them to get ahead of the storm. They can still make it. Ride back where we came from. Hide in the forest. When they emerge, they can make their way back to Persia, taking the Silk Road all the way west. They can return to their families alive. They can fight to have their lives back. It's not going to be easy. But it's possible. And worth trying for."

I glanced in the direction of the storm. It was getting

closer. My stomach twisted into a knot. I imagined sand in my eyes, in my mouth, my ears. I imagined being buried alive. I had never considered that I would die this way, but now it was looking like a distinct possibility.

I turned to look at Alexi, who was watching in horror as all of his men took off on their horses, leaving him alone in the sand.

"Think they'll make it home alive?" I asked.

Thala looked at me. "That I can't see," she said. "Like I told you before, without chamak I'm not able to see things as sharply. I can still make out some things, but not others." She smiled. "But this moment, right now, what they're feeling? It's the greatest feeling of their lives."

I could barely make out her words over the howl of the wind now.

Alexi approached us, unshackling us quietly, without ceremony, without words. He did it because he knew he had no choice. He looked at me with fear in his eyes before he turned and mounted his horse, bolting away from the storm.

I watched him ride away.

"Coward," I said over the howling wind.

"But look what he left behind in his panic," Thala said.

I followed her eyes to a spot in the sand where my satchel sat waiting for me. I grabbed it, eagerly opening it. The map, the dagger, it was all still there. I held the satchel tightly to my chest as I looked back up.

It was closer now, the storm. I could see it coming for us, like a bulwark of dust. It looked like a solid mass.

"So . . . what now?" I yelled.

"I don't know what happens now," Thala said.

I reached for Thala's hand and closed my eyes. We stood there, the wind screaming into our ears, cold sand whipping our faces. I braced myself for whatever was to come. I opened my eyes to see objects flying through the air: palm leafs and entire tree stumps, pieces of fabric, flags, all violently cycling around us. Soon that would be us, I imagined, the storm chewing us up and spitting us out. My grip tightened around Thala's hand, and my stomach plummeted.

Please, I pleaded with whatever force might listen. *Please don't harm us. Please deliver us to safety.* I realized I was speaking with the storm itself. *Please*, I asked again. *If you can hear me, please know that all I would like is for my friend and me to make it to the edge of the desert, to the Janaka Caves, unharmed. We want to live. You owe us nothing. But I ask you, humbly, to deliver us to safety.*

I no longer have a father. I don't know my mother. Everything I've ever had is lost, gone. I am no longer a princess.

I am nothing, nobody.

I come to you with nothing but a plea. Please help us.

The wind continued to howl, louder and louder, whipping my hair across my face, the taste of sand in my mouth. And then a voice emerged from the roar of the wind.

We have heard what you have to say. We will grant you our aid, I heard. My eyes snapped open.

I gazed up at the stars, and as I did, we were lifted into the heavens by a bump of air, and we were flying higher than the storm, looking down into a funnel of sand, shifting, twisting, like those palm leaves. I tensed for a moment before I closed my eyes and gave in to it.

Before I had a chance to make sense of those words, we were within it, engulfed. We found ourselves floating in the eye of the storm, watching as sand and debris spun around us.

I was surprised at how quiet and still it was. Peaceful, almost.

"It's already happening," Thala said, her eyes full of amazement. "You're becoming her. Maya."

I couldn't even bring myself to respond. I had always thought of storms as violent, but this was majestic, a force of nature that commanded respect, not fear. I would remember it always. A storm protecting us from itself.

Finally, I spoke. "I don't even understand what that really means," I said to her.

"Just keep watching and listening and asking. You'll find out," Thala replied.

I don't know how long we were inside the storm. Maybe it was a few hours, maybe it was days, or weeks.

All at once, we landed gently on our feet.

It was almost dawn, and the sky emerged a clear, pale pink where the storm had been. It was as though the winds had scrubbed the desert clean, or rearranged it to their liking. We stood quietly, watching the cyclone as it went on its way. I was stunned at how I felt: Sad to see it go, as though it was yet another family member I was saying goodbye to. Amazed at what we had just witnessed. It *was* majestic, but it was also whimsical, lovely. I had seen another side of something that I had previously considered only dangerous and destructive. How limited my perception had been before this moment.

Thala's laughter snapped me out of my thoughts. "Look where we are!" she said. "It deposited us at the edge of the desert. A day's walk from the Janaka Caves. It's as though it *knew*."

I felt a sense of amazement at her words.

"I've heard that the Diviners knew how to do that—how to speak to the sand, call to the wind, ask for their aid. And they offered it to us. To you."

I couldn't help but think about the voice I had heard when we were in the eye of the storm.

Thala smiled a rare smile. "We're going to make it to the caves," she said. "I knew it."

We began to hike up the trail.

"Did you hear that voice?" I asked Thala.

"What voice?" she asked.

"Earlier . . ." But from the way she looked at me, I knew that I was the only one who had heard it. And then I knew she was right—I had spoken to the wind and the sand. I had spoken to the storm. And it had offered me what I had asked for.

Twenty-Five

PEBBLES SCATTERED, tumbling down the edge of the mountain.

I leaned over the vertical drop beside the trail to see where they would land, but gazing down the purple and green ravine made me dizzy.

"Careful!" Thala pulled me toward her.

The sun was rising over the bare golden dunes, and we were filled to the brim with an unexpected euphoria. We were alive. And only a day away from our destination. A sense of possibility loomed over us. I could see it in Thala's smile, her graceful movements: We were free.

We had been hiking up and around the hills and valleys the entire day, each turn revealing something unexpected. After miles and miles of desolate rock face, a verdant meadow, sheep grazing at our ankles. On a particularly narrow path, a boulder that we each took turns hanging on to as we scuttled around it, a terrifying drop just beneath our feet.

There were no people here, and so many different paths cutting into the hillside—some going up, others going down—that without a map, we might have been hiking for years before we found what we were looking for.

Luckily, we were able to find sustenance just when we needed it, almost as though someone had planned for our visit. On the top of a particularly steep hillside, an aquamarine lake that we dipped our toes into for a brief respite.

"We're lucky. I'm almost out of water," I said to Thala, refilling my skin.

And farther up a hill, brambles full of berries I had never before seen—pink and white, the shape of hearts, iridescent in the sun.

We sat down for a moment, resting in a patch of grass. "Thala, do you know what happens when we get there?"

"All I can see is Macedon."

"Do you think Sikander will make it to the caves?"

"I don't know." Thala shook her head. "Maybe it's because I haven't taken chamak in some time, but I feel . . . like a normal person. You have no idea how difficult it can be, seeing the future all the time. And people don't even believe what you tell them. Only the Library knows everything. Whether you believe in it or not." She smiled.

"I do believe."

Thala turned to me sharply. "Since when?"

I thought about the storm again. "Since this journey taught me how little I know about everything," I said to her.

We got back on the trail, and as we climbed, my mind drifted to Arjun. I thought about how he had kissed me that first time, out in the mango grove. I thought of us lying in the hammock together, laughing. My heart longed to hear his voice again. Then I thought about Varun's hands on my waist, the way he looked at me, the intensity in his eyes as he told me about Mount Moutza and Maya.

"Don't get distracted," Thala said, picking up on my mental state. "We're close. Right now, your only focus should be on the next ten feet ahead of you."

We were hiking up a pebbly path that laced the edge of a mountain. I was grateful for my healed feet, for the comfortable sandals Thala had selected for me. Every hairpin turn, every time we had to lean into the rock face in order to progress up the trail, my heart raced.

"How much longer till we get there?" Thala asked. She was ahead of me, and before her, I saw nothing but a drop as the trail turned, twisting around the mountain. I pulled the map from my satchel, opened it, and looked at the X that marked the Janaka Caves.

"They should be right here," I said as I came up behind her.

I followed her to the edge of the mountain and turned my head to see the path curving around the bend. But there it stopped.

I gasped.

Before us was a wall that stretched so high, I couldn't even see the top of it.

"What now?" Thala asked. "Did we go the wrong way?"

I shook my head. "This is where we're supposed to be. The Janaka Caves are right here, according to the map. They must be on the other side of this wall," I said, running my fingers over the smooth rock surface before us. The top of the wall seemed to disappear into the clouds.

"We can't scale that. It's too high."

I looked around. Beside us was a terrifying drop. Behind us, the path we had come on.

"Do we have any more water?" Thala asked.

I nodded, reaching into my satchel, and my hand instinctively grabbed the dagger. Suddenly, I realized it.

"The dagger! It was the key to the safe at Meena Amba's. It must be the key to this wall too."

I turned to look at the wall, inspecting it for a keyhole. But the surface of the wall was too clean. Almost glistening. There was no keyhole, at least not one I could see. I held the blade toward it, hoping it would tell me something. I poked the wall with the blade. Nothing. I pointed it up toward the sky. Still no evidence that it was the key that would open some sort of doorway to the Sybillines.

"There must be another way." Thala shook her head.

"I don't understand. Meena Amba said it was the key to many things. It *has* to be the key to the Janaka Caves!"

After a few more tries, I sighed, letting my arm drop. Then, a jolt. I looked down at the dagger. The rubies had lit up, shining bright crimson in the light of the setting sun.

"It's saying 'not up, but down.'" Thala pointed to the ground below our feet.

Slowly, I crouched, bringing the dagger to the ground with me. Gently, I stuck it into the ground. All of a sudden, the mountain appeared to tremble.

The ground gave way, and we were both falling.

Twenty-Six

WE LANDED WITH A LOUD THUD, and dust filled the air, causing a violent sneeze to escape my nose.

"Are you all right?" I asked.

"I can't see anything," Thala responded.

I palmed the floor, feeling the ground beneath me. My fingers grasped long fibrous stalks knotted into the ground. Roots. I looked up to see where we had fallen from, but the opening was gone. We were shrouded in darkness.

"Hold on a minute," Thala said. I heard a whoosh, and then a flame lit up her face. She had found a sulfur stick.

The walls instantly illuminated, and I noticed that the interior of the cave was made of bundles of fibers. I had initially thought that they were roots, but they were different shades of blue—cobalt and aquamarine and sapphire and indigo—and they appeared to be breathing.

"It's alive," Thala said as she stood up. It was a tunnel, the ceiling just barely touching the tops of our heads when we stood up. She was right. Only something alive could move in this way.

"This is incredible," I said as I ran my hand over the glowing cords, which undulated like sea hydra. "This must be the way.

"What do you think this is?" I asked Thala.

"No idea."

"You've never seen anything like this before?"

"Just because I'm a seer doesn't mean I've seen everything," she quipped.

I looked at the dagger in my hand. It was pulsing, the rubies lighting up as if in rhythm with the breathing walls.

We began to walk, carefully negotiating our every step. The tunnel moved and shifted with us, like a rope bridge, twisting and turning in concentric circles.

"I feel like we're going down, but I can't tell," Thala said.

It was disorienting walking through this thing—whatever it was—but we were descending deeper and deeper into it. We kept walking till I noticed tiny bulbous knots growing on the fibers. I stopped before them, carefully touching one with my fingers.

"Mushrooms," I said, glancing at the polka-dotted lavender toadstools before us.

Even farther on, snails with lapidary shells the color of jewels: peridot and ruby and emerald and sapphire. They moved slowly, crisscrossing the tendons of light and leaving behind dewy, iridescent trails.

"Look out!" Thala yelled. I looked up and saw something

approaching: a cloud of glitter, chirping as it made its way toward us. As it flew by us, I realized that the cloud was made up of winged insects.

"Butterflies," I whispered. They landed in the crevices of the roots, resting their sparkled wings for a moment before they flew off again.

From the spots where they had landed, tiny flowers grew before our eyes. Crimson and ochre and magenta pom-poms, shivering in the cool air.

I shook my head. "I can't believe this."

And then I heard it: from a distance, a purring sound.

"Do you hear that?" I whispered.

Thala stopped for a moment. She placed a hand on my shoulder. "Careful," she said.

"What?"

"This thing . . . whatever it is . . . it's not entirely benign."

We turned a corner and were suddenly standing before a dark blue wall.

I moved closer to it, almost pressing my face against it, trying to figure out what it was, when a yellow eye the size of a window blinked open.

It took everything in me not to scream as I recoiled violently, my mind racing to put it all together. When I stepped back, another eye opened. And then I saw it: a face as large as a wall. It moved closer to me. I realized that those roots that lined this entire cave were tentacles of some sort attached to the face. They moved with this creature.

"It's a spider," Thala said, her voice shaking.

"I've never seen a spider this size," I said.

I was too afraid to move, too afraid to speak. Thala's hands shook.

And then it hit me. "It's Makara. He who creates, sustains, destroys . . . ," I whispered.

Just then, Makara smiled, baring hundreds of glittering fangs.

I jumped back, the dagger in my hands, my heart racing at such a pitch, I was certain that the spider could hear it. He looked right at me, adjusting his head, inspecting me with curiosity.

As he did, I noticed something behind him: a silver door. On the side of the door, a crack the same size as the blade of my dagger. And just beside the crack, three rubies. The terrifying arachnid moved toward me again, blocking the only exit from this place.

I knew that on the other side of the door were the Sybillines. And this creature guarded the entrance.

"What do I do?" I whispered.

"Are you supposed to . . . kill it?" Thala asked, glancing at the dagger in my hand. I looked down at the blade, trying to decide what to do next.

The creature appeared to sense what I was thinking, because in a flash, a tentacle wrapped itself around my waist. I screamed, the sound of my terror echoing through the cavernous space. Another tentacle emerged from the wall like a rope lasso and grabbed Thala.

"Kill it, Amrita!" Thala yelled. My wrist free, I reached

for the tentacle that held me, pressing a blade against it. But something stopped me.

"I can't," I said.

"What do you mean, *you can't*? This thing is going to eat us alive!"

I turned my head and looked at the face of the creature. He was inspecting us, rotating us in his strong, cord-like limbs, but something told me he didn't want to hurt us.

Slowly, tentatively, I reached for the spider's face, placing a hand just above his eye. He closed it for a minute, and as he did, I heard something, a voice.

I just want to play, it said.

"Did you . . . did you hear that?" I asked.

Thala raised an eyebrow. "Hear what?"

"I can . . . hear him. He's not going to hurt us," I said.

"Really? Because those teeth look as though they were made expressly for that purpose," Thala said.

"He's . . . curious," I said, watching as the creature flipped us right side up and back upside down in delight. "He probably hasn't had visitors in a long time."

The creature tugged at Thala's feet and let out a sound that was a mixture of a purr and a hiss. He was chuckling.

"See? He's friendly," I said. "His body houses so many living creatures. He's an entire ecosystem. If we hurt him, we hurt everything that depends on him. And if he really is Makara the Spider, if we destroy him . . ."

"I get it," Thala said, "but we have to convince this thing to let us pass." He swept her up and swung her toward him, pressing her toward his eye.

I placed a hand back above his other eye. *Please let us go*, I thought.

No, it replied.

I felt disappointment, urgency, frustration.

All right, I thought. *How much longer do you want to play?*

The creature smiled again, his fangs so huge that we both gasped.

To me, a short time. To you, forever.

Panic filled my lungs. I looked at Thala, and she could sense my terror.

"What?" she asked. "What is he saying?"

I didn't answer her. I remembered the story. *He sustains the world while he's awake. He creates while he dreams.*

I needed to get him to fall asleep. I had an idea, but I wasn't sure whether it would work.

Makara, I called after the creature. *I'll play with you.* I thought the words instead of saying them, and he grinned that terrifying grin again.

Do you know how to play catch? I'll throw you something, and you catch it in your mouth.

Play! Play! I heard in response.

I reached into my satchel, pulling out the diamond shoe, throwing it into the air. Makara lunged for it, catching it between his fangs, swallowing it whole.

How about this? I threw him the skin of water, and once again, Makara darted toward it.

I reached back into my satchel for the thing I was looking for, holding it in my fingers. It was the leftover bark from the silver tree. I had saved it. Varun had told me it was a potent drug, that it would help Thala sleep. I didn't know if it was potent enough to work on Makara the Spider. But I had no other option.

How about this? Can you get this?

I aimed the piece of bark the best I could, throwing it at Makara's head. It struck him right between the eyes before he caught it in his mouth.

I watched as his eyelids got heavy, then closed. The tentacles loosened around my waist, and we both fell to the floor.

I let out a slow breath of relief before I turned to Thala's stunned face.

"Quick, before he wakes up!" I whispered.

We stepped over his body and squeezed together before the silver door. I placed the dagger in the crevice, turning it on its side.

The rubies lit up and the door flew open, and I breathed a sigh of relief as we crossed the threshold.

On the other side at last, the door closed behind us with a click, and hundreds of eyes turned to look at us.

Twenty-Seven

THE JANAKA CAVES were an ancient city built into the interior of a mountain. Cave dwellings embedded in the rock swirled up in an interminable spiral that touched the clouds. On every surface were reliefs that bore a striking resemblance to those in the Temple of Rain, except this was no abandoned site. It was alive with color. Murals stretched from the ground far beyond where my eyes could see. Paintings of multiarmed gods, creatures that were half-man, half-tiger, white birds with wingspans the size of elephants against bold blue backdrops.

And directly before us, a crumbling, ancient-looking mural of a young woman: Maya. I looked down at my tunic. It was the very same one Maya was wearing in the mural. And in her hand, a dagger with three rubies.

A trail of goose bumps climbed up my arm.

The mural was not only of Maya—it was of me.

The Sybillines halted their activities. A man carving a bowl out of wood put down his tools. An elderly woman in a white sari trimming and collecting flowers set down her basket and the shears in her hand. Men and women playing games on wooden boards glanced in our direction.

"They're here," some of them whispered.

"She's returned!"

Finally, the woman in the white sari approached. Her face was creased with lines, but her smile was youthful. "We've been waiting for you," she said.

I couldn't bring myself to respond right away. My eyes scanned the magnificent caves, trying to take it all in.

Trees grew like webs, climbing up the rock face, creeping over the entrances to homes. On the far edge of the mountain, a waterfall pooled into an aquamarine lagoon where people washed their clothes or bathed. On various levels of the caves, stone balconies housed gardens with exotic-looking plants in hues of lavender, pink, turquoise, and yellow, and on every surface of the mountain, a silver dust: chamak. It glistened in the sun, making the entire city sparkle.

I saw Thala taking it in too, her mouth agape, a mixture of curiosity and fear in her eyes. I reached for her hand.

"It's all right. We'll be fine," I assured her, but the very idea of Thala being surrounded by so much chamak made me anxious.

At the base of the vertical city was a bowl, a vast arena where all civic activity appeared to take place. A man watered a garden filled with varieties of fruit and vegetables I had never before seen. A woman wove white scarves from skeins of cotton thread. Children sat on swings made from the boughs of trees and linen-colored rope.

Finally, it was Thala who spoke. "It's a . . . volcano. We're inside a massive volcano."

She was right. The Janaka Caves were built inside a dormant volcano, and within that volcano was an entire civilization that maybe no one from the outside world had ever seen. No one except us.

I turned to the woman. "You've been waiting for me?"

A youthful laugh escaped her lips. "We knew that one day you'd return, Goddess Maya," she said as I glanced again at the mural behind her. "I'm Kalyani. You're the first visitor we've had in years. Welcome," she said, bowing before me.

"This place is . . ."

"Uncontaminated, exactly as it was when my people first came here hundreds of years ago," she said, gesturing behind her. "Of course, anyone is allowed to leave, and many do," she said to us. "But visitors are not very common. Oh, I forgot to mention—we received a dispatch for you yesterday. That's the other reason we knew you'd be here soon," she said, pointing to the edge of the lagoon where a flock of birds had congregated.

"Saaras!" I exclaimed, running over to him. I noticed a note tied to his foot. I hurriedly untied it and unfolded it open. I recognized the handwriting right away, and my heart skipped a beat.

Amrita,

   *I received a note from your friend Varun. He
tells me (to my relief) that you are safe and on your
way to the Janaka Caves. For your sake, I hope
you trust him, because it is becoming increasingly
difficult to trust anyone here.*

   *I suppose by now, you've been to the temple and
learned of your true identity. I wish I could explain
to you why I never told you the things I knew. But
your father wanted you to find out on your own, when
you were ready.*

   *Looking back, I was delusional to think
that you and I might have had any kind of future
together. Sooner or later, you would have learned who
you are and found me unsuitable, unworthy of you.
Our little plot to run away together, it was a mistake,
all of it. I've forgotten it, and you should too.*

My surprise at Arjun's coldness must have registered on
my face.

"What is it?" Thala asked.

I simply shook my head and continued to read.

   *You should know that Shalingar is now a
colony of Macedon, and search parties have spread
out across the kingdom, looking for you. Army units
patrol Ananta, and people are being imprisoned
for reading books, speaking Shalingarsh in public.*

Women have been told to stay indoors at all times.
Shalingar will never be the same again.

"No, no, no!" I whispered.

"What is it?" Thala pressed, squatting next to me, reading over my shoulder.

> *You're temporarily safe with the Sybillines, but eventually Sikander's men will find the caves.*
>
> *My parents are safe too, but we haven't recovered from this series of tragedies that we never envisioned. I'm ashamed that I have no option but to do as Sikander instructs or he'll hurt my family.*
>
> *Please forget the past, Amrita. We have different roles now, we're different people. You are Maya. Perhaps someday, somehow, you can bring hope to your people, though I don't know what hope can do in the face of force.*
>
> *Please never come back to Ananta. If you do, I'll have no option except to turn you in to Sikander. I hope for this reason, and for both of our sakes, that we never see each other again.*
>
> *Arjun*

I felt anger, sadness, confusion, fear. I wanted to tear the letter up and scream. Forget what had happened? How could I? The letter made him sound like a completely different

Arjun, someone who had been brainwashed by Sikander and influenced by grief.

I realized then that I hadn't entirely given up hope in the desert. I had still believed Arjun and I would find our way back to one another, even if I never returned to Shalingar, even if I was no longer Princess Amrita.

But now I knew for certain that there was truly no way back.

I wiped tears from my eyes with the edge of my sleeve, no doubt smearing mud all over my face. I was self-conscious and didn't want to draw attention to myself, but the tears poured down my cheeks as though there was no stopping them.

"He's saying all that to protect you," Thala said.

But it didn't matter. Arjun's words devastated me. Shalingar was gone; it was no longer the place I had known. And Arjun was gone too, or may as well have been. It was over, whatever had existed for a moment between us, extinguished by the harsh gale of reality.

Kalyani sat down beside me. "I take it you've gotten some bad news. Come," she urged me, eyeing my filthy clothes. "You've had a long journey. Let's get you both a bath and some rest before we speak."

Instantly, I remembered why I was there.

"No," I said to her, squaring my shoulders. "We have to speak now. I'm here to tell you that you're in danger. Shalingar has been attacked, and I fear the Janaka Caves are next."

She nodded, unsurprised. "We've been preparing for this possibility for years," Kalyani reassured me. "We can never thank you enough for the sacrifices you've made to come here. You must rest. Even if these people you speak of are able to find the caves, it will take them some time. As you can see, they're very difficult to reach. Rest now, then we'll talk some more. You'll need all your strength for what's to come."

I looked at Thala, and she simply shrugged her shoulders at me.

I nodded, finally feeling my exhaustion, my muscles aching from our climb up the mountains.

"Are you the leader of the Sybillines?" I asked Kalyani.

She shook her head. "There are no leaders here, nor followers. But you could say that I am a kind of advisor to my people. If you wish, I can advise you as well. But that is your choice, and everything will be made clear to you in due time. Now Tamas will take you to the old guest quarters." She gestured to a young man who had been tending to the birds.

I nuzzled Saaras, grateful to be reunited with him, before I turned to Tamas.

Tamas smiled at us. "Welcome to the Janaka Caves," he said with an amused smile on his face. "What an exciting day it is for us. Visitors are an uncommon thing here."

"How uncommon?" Thala asked.

He frowned and took a minute to respond. "To be honest, I've never seen a visitor in my life," he said as he led us up a path that took us into the wall of caves. Hundreds of sets of eyes continued to watch us. "At least not of the human variety," he said, gesturing to the flock of birds by the lagoon. "And don't mind them," he whispered, jerking his chin toward the Sybillines poking their heads from their caves, watching us with curiosity. "They're all very friendly, just a bit surprised. Of course we all knew that eventually you'd come. It's part of the legend."

"The legend?" I asked.

"The legend about Maya's return. And also, we can sense these things. We have powers of sight." He turned to Thala. "You do too."

Thala nodded.

"You'll fit right in. But you must forgive our manners. We're not used to guests. It's difficult enough to find the caves, and then with Makara the Gatekeeper . . ." He shrugged his shoulders. "But it appears that you passed the test. You didn't try to kill him . . ."

"We considered it," Thala grumbled.

"Oh, Makara is indestructible. When the world ceases to exist, Makara will still be here. He'll outlive everything. But a good thing you didn't *try* to kill him. He wouldn't have taken to that well. And he needs occasional naps. His naps are when he's most productive."

"Does he really create, destroy, and sustain the world?"

"That's right. He's a very important axle of this world, the center of everything. And the saddhus tell us that the vast majority of people on the planet have never even heard of him. Strange," he said, smiling, "this world of yours. I'm told that there is so much progress, and yet, the roots of our existence on this planet have been forgotten, just as one forgets his or her birth."

We had come to a stop on the stone path that wound itself around the volcano.

Tamas gestured to an entrance in the rock leading to a grotto. "The old guest quarters. They've never been used. Well, only once. A long time ago. But . . . we've kept them ready for you."

"I have so many questions," I told him.

"And they will all be answered. But Kalyani is right. You should rest now. Everything will make more sense to you once you've had a chance to reset your mind." He grinned at us. "Just like Makara the Spider."

"I have a question," Thala asked. "If you never have any visitors, why would you have guest quarters?"

Tamas smiled. "The ancients built them. This is where Maya lived for a time, before she went to join—"

"Her lover?" Thala raised an eyebrow.

"The vetala," I corrected her, blushing.

"Not just any vetala. The Keeper of the Library of All Things," Tamas said to us.

We stepped into the cave, and under a curved ceiling of rock were two beds with white and blue striped linens. Next to one of the beds, a small heating stove. A mirror hung just above a basin. Perched on a wooden table, a wooden bowl overflowed with fruit. Two stone bathtubs had been filled with water. I dipped my hand in one. It was still warm.

I washed my face in the basin, taking in my visage.

I looked older, and my face looked gaunt even though I had been on this journey for only a few days. And yet, I could tell that I had aged, that I had changed so much already. Even though we had made it here, there was no end to my worries.

"They always knew something like this could happen . . . but where will they go, Thala?"

Thala closed her eyes. When she opened them, they were the color of sand. "Whether Sikander comes here or not, he won't be able to harm the Sybillines."

"There are at least a few hundred souls living here. Where are they supposed to hide? This is the last hidden place on the Earth."

"On the Earth, yes."

I shook my head at her cryptic response, and my mind returned to Arjun. My heart was filled with a desperate ache for him. "Do you know if I'll ever see Arjun again?"

Thala closed her eyes, then opened them. This time, they were the color of the lagoon at the base of the caves. "I think . . . you will." She looked confused for a moment before she turned to me. "It's harder and harder for me to see anything now. But he's right. It'll never be the same between you again."

Tears slipped from my eyes as I thought of him.

But there was something else on Thala's mind. "I don't feel safe here."

"But you said Sikander wouldn't—" The realization

struck me as I said the words. "Chamak," I remembered in frustration, burying my face in my hands.

"I don't think we should stay here very long."

I shook my head. "We won't." But I was overwhelmed with the thought of where exactly we would go next.

"Amrita?"

I turned to her.

"I know you feel like it's all lost right now . . ."

"It *is* all lost, Thala." I sighed. "Arjun is Sikander's satrap. My kingdom is a colony of Macedon. My father and Mala are dead. My people have been enslaved. And I've brought you into a place where you're surrounded by the very thing that could kill you. That almost *did* kill you, and I didn't even think of that till now. What's wrong with me?"

Thala shook her head. She was calm in the face of my panic, my outrage. "We won't stay here long" was all she said.

"And where will we go?"

"I don't know."

I felt helpless, lost.

"Listen to me, Amrita. Before a few days ago, you didn't even know of the Library, you didn't know about the Keeper. You didn't know you were Maya. You didn't know you could crawl through a tunnel or be lifted on a sandstorm or outsmart Sikander's men." She looked right at me with a conviction that surprised me. "But now you do. There are answers to all our questions," she said. "Just because you haven't found them and I can't see them doesn't mean they don't exist."

I didn't say anything more. Slowly, I removed my shoes before I undressed and stepped into the bathtub. I lingered there silently for at least an hour, still startled by all the revelations that had alighted upon me since our arrival here.

As the water cooled, my eyelids grew heavy. I reached for a linen towel on the side of the tub and stepped out, wiping myself dry.

Within minutes, I was in bed, wrapped in a warm blanket. My mind was blank. I didn't know where we would go next, how the Sybillines could help me, or even if they would. I was grasping for answers, for absolutes, trying to hold on to anything that made sense. But nothing did. *The Library, maybe it really* is *the only way*, I thought before I fell into the deepest slumber of my life.

Twenty-Eight

THE AFTERNOON SUN FELL into the cave in thick, honeyed sheets that warmed my arms and legs. I opened my eyes slowly, absorbing the light like a plant desperate for the sun's rays. I must have slept through the night and into the morning.

I sat up, noticing a stack of clothing at the foot of my bed. I reached for it. A white linen tunic and a pale blue salvar. Someone had lit the heating stove by my bed, and I watched the blue flames flicker and pop as I pulled the soft fabrics over my skin. Slowly, I ventured outside, my feet bare on the toasted rock.

From the ledge outside my cave, I scanned the bowl beneath me. Saaras was feeding with a flock of other birds. Thala was already up, dipping her feet in the blue lagoon by the falls, chatting with Tamas, who was sailing a miniature boat on the flat surface of the water. I noted the change in Thala's body language. She was relaxed, laughing. I felt a mixture of emotions: relief that she was with someone, and glad that she felt at ease, but I was also jealous of her in that moment, envious that she could feel light when I felt as though I carried the weight of the world on my shoulders.

I sat down, hanging my legs off the thick ledge. My eyes followed the whirl of the rock, and I wondered how far up it went.

Did it reach the heavens? Was there even a heaven? If there was, was that where my father and Mala were right now? Or were they at some way station? A place where they regrouped, waiting to be reborn?

What force in the world had made my father *my* father, and Mala mine too? What had brought them into my life instead of someone else's? What set of miracles, what magic delivered the people we loved to us? And what set of fates took them away?

Was it all connected to the Library of All Things?

I glanced at the mural of my own face. I felt as though it was mocking me. All I had in common with Maya was that we looked alike. She was magnificent, fearless, passionate. She inspired such hope in people, even hundreds of years after her existence.

But I was a girl on the run, terrified, guilty that I had managed to survive while almost everyone I knew had perished. And even those who did survive were suffering far worse than I was. Arjun's life was ruined. Shree and Bandaka were suffering too, along with all my father's subjects. And now I had brought Thala to a place that was dangerous for her.

"Peaceful, isn't it?" I heard a voice behind me.

I turned. It was Kalyani. I hesitated for a moment, trying to decide whether to tell her that I didn't know how to be at peace, that I didn't know how to be myself anymore. Still, I swallowed my words, grateful for the Sybillines' hospitality. "It's beautiful. Like nothing I've ever seen. I can't believe how secluded it is."

Kalyani sat down next to me. She moved like a young person, with grace and strength, fluidity in her limbs. "Secluded, yes. But we really have no need for interaction with the outside world. We're entirely self-sufficient. We build our own things, grow our own food."

"And you mine your own chamak too." I watched as a group of people collected the chamak from the walls and the floor of the caves, using comb-like tools to gather it, scrape it off the rock, and deposit it into bowls. "What is it, exactly? Chamak?"

"Some people here believe that it is what's left over from Makara's dreams. Perhaps the grit from his eyes? Me, personally, I don't know what it is," she said. "Anyway, after it goes through the ascetics, it eventually ends up in the hands of a few merchants who are taxed on it by the throne of the kingdom that we happen to be residing within."

"Shalingar," I said. "But how do you transport it out of here?"

Kalyani pointed to the flock of white birds nesting by

Saaras. The birds were of different sizes, some even larger than Saaras, but many smaller. There must have been hundreds of them. A man was carefully attaching and removing tiny sacks from their feet. Some of the birds sprang up into the air, flying out of the top of the volcano.

"Mostly bar-headed geese. They're small and sleek. They can fly at altitudes no other bird can. They've been trained to fly south, toward the forest where the monks take the chamak, feed them, and send them back to us with things we need."

"Things you need?" I asked.

Kalyani shrugged. "We have no need for money. Or material things. Although sometimes they send us seeds so we can grow fruits."

"In exchange for *chamak*?" I raised an eyebrow. It baffled me that the most valuable substance in the world—a material that Sikander had been willing to kill for—was being traded for seeds.

"Everyone has their own currency. Here, chamak is abundant. We harvest it during the day, and the next morning, the entire rockface is covered with it again."

"And outside these caves, it's liable to start wars," I said to her before I remembered what Arjun had said in his letter. "I . . . can't return home. My kingdom has been overthrown. I don't know where to go now."

"Let me show you something," Kalyani said, getting up.

I followed her up the swirl of the rocks, and we passed by people going about their own business in their cave homes. I don't know what I had expected of the Sybillines, exactly, but these people appeared to be no different from us.

A handful of them continued to harvest chamak, but most of the others were simply enjoying themselves, playing a game that resembled marbles but with pebbles made of volcanic lava, painting mandalas across the base of the volcano, or simply sitting by the lagoon near Thala, talking. Some fed birds while others hung wet fabric from clotheslines outside their caves or washed dishes in the waterfall.

"It's lovely here," I said. "I don't understand why anyone would want to leave."

"But people do leave. In fact, every moon, people leave. They wait for Makara to sleep, and off they go. Mostly the young. They want to be a part of the larger world. There's only one condition—they're free to leave, but they can never come back. My own children left. They must have children of their own now," she said wistfully.

"You've never left this place then?" I asked.

"No one you see here ever has. We're protectors of the Janaka Caves, of a way of life; it's one of our primary duties in this world."

We arrived at a cave that was so high up that looking down at the bowl made me dizzy. "I know you've been questioning who you are," Kalyani said as she guided me into the cave. "This might help you understand."

We emerged inside what appeared to be a shrine. A statue of Maya stood before me. I gasped, still struck by the resemblance. But what left me speechless were the murals around Maya. They moved and changed. There was Ananta, shrouded in mist, rain falling over Chanakya Lake. And the tall buildings and arenas of Macedon that appeared to reach the sky. There was the sun rising over the east and setting in the west.

"We're not just protectors of the caves," Kalyani said. "Makara might create and destroy the world. But who do you think sustains it?" she said.

My head whipped around to look at her. "So *you* . . . sustain it? Not Makara?"

"This is how the Earth speaks with us," she told me. She touched the mural of Ananta, and slowly, the rain stopped, and the sun peeked out from behind the clouds. "It's what we've been doing for years." She touched another wall where snow was falling over a landscape. All of a sudden, the snow halted.

"Come outside with me," she said.

We stepped outside the cave, and the sight before me left me speechless. Across the surface of the caves, the chamak moved and glistened into images of the outside world. There were projections of children being born, couples falling in love, elderly men and women on canes, crossing streets, children laughing, enemies fighting.

"This is where the whole world is recorded by the Earth. Every day is replayed here. Every birth, every death, every peal of laughter, every moment of despair," she said, and I watched as one of the murals morphed into an image of me sleeping in the caves.

"What if Sikander finds this?"

Kalyani laughed. "Sikander might find these caves, but he'll never learn of this operation. It'll continue long after we're gone, but it'll be hidden from him. He can't see it. Neither can your friend. But you can see it, can't you?

I nodded, unable to take my eyes off the rock face.

"You see, there's a reason you came here. A reason that was hidden from you. We were told that when Maya returns, we could leave."

"Leave the caves?"

"Leave the Earth."

I balked, remembering Thala's words the day before. "How will you do that?"

"Makara is the gateway to all places. He'll take us wherever we're supposed to go next."

I looked back at her, dumbfounded.

"You don't remember any of it, do you? The past, that other life? The Land of Trees, the Keeper of the Library?"

I shook my head. "It doesn't feel any more like my life than anyone else's."

Kalyani nodded. "We believe that there's a reason our minds forget the past. Do you know why we came here? Why we needed to be far from the rest of the world? Secluded, as you called it?"

I shook my head again.

"We came here to hone our abilities. We came because we knew how to speak to the Earth, to the sky, to the mountains, the desert, the rain. But our leader, Maya, was far more skilled at communicating with the Earth than anyone who has ever lived. We carried on practicing her gift, keeping it alive, like a language that could go extinct at any moment. It

took a village of people to do that. Do you know anyone outside of the Janaka Caves who knows how to do that—how
to speak with the Earth?" She looked at me pointedly.

All of a sudden, I was afraid of what Kalyani was saying.
I thought about our experience in the desert. Of the silver
tree in the forest that had somehow let down its shield when
I had asked for its help. She wanted me to admit that *I* had
such powers. That I had abilities.

But if I was so powerful, why hadn't I been able to save
my father? Why couldn't I have conjured up a storm that
destroyed all of Sikander's army? Why couldn't I have willed
the ocean to swallow up the men who had invaded the palace? If I had true powers, there was so much I *should* have
been able to do, I *should* have done already.

She must have read my mind, because she turned to me
then and said, "We forget our past in order to begin again. And
there are things we must lose in order for us to gain anything."

"So you're saying that I had to lose my father?"

She shook her head, compassion in her eyes. "All I'm
saying is that we had to give up certain earthly pleasures in
order to preserve what we thought was important. We lost
the forest of our beloved trees. We lost Maya because she
was mortal. We lost our connection to the rest of the world.
We had to forget our past in order to preserve the language
of speaking with the Earth. But now that you're here, we can
go. And you can teach others what you know."

But I couldn't shake my fear. "What if everyone is wrong
about me? If I'm so powerful, why am I so afraid?"

"Fear is actually the strongest evidence of our powers, the threshold we need to cross in order to reclaim them. All I know is that it's time for you to reclaim your powers, and it's time for us to begin a new adventure."

"I don't even understand where you'll go," I said to her.

Kalyani jerked her chin toward the wall before me. I followed her gaze. It was a mural of a starry sky. I could see purple galaxies, silver constellations twisting in whorls.

All around the cave, the Sybillines looked out into that magnificent vault of blue and cheered as though they had anticipated this moment their whole lives.

"Where is that?"

She shook her head and smiled. "I don't know."

"You're not afraid?"

Kalyani shook her head. "I've had a lot of time to untangle my own fears."

"I wish I were like you," I told her. "I'm afraid of everything."

"Kalyani?" a frantic voice called out for her as Tamas ran up the ledge. "We have a problem. I took my eyes off her for just a second and now she's —"

Before he even finished speaking, I felt a cold stab of panic in my lungs as I ran out of the cave and down the spiral path, looking for Thala, the conversation we had the night before replaying itself in my ears. She had expressed her fear to me, and I had done nothing about it.

She was lying next to the lagoon, her vacant eyes looking up at the sky.

"Thala?" I cried, shaking her.

"Step aside, please." Kalyani was already behind me, blending a mixture of herbs into a small mortar made of lava.

"Will she be all right?" I asked.

Kalyani's face didn't give anything away as she glanced down at the concoction in her hands.

Thala closed her eyes. She opened them, and they were a dark burgundy, so bright that I stumbled backward, startled at the sight of them.

"I wanted to know how to get to the Library," Thala said.

"She's hallucinating," Kalyani said, and placed a spoonful of herbs in Thala's mouth.

"The Keeper, Amrita—I know who it is," Thala whispered. "He's here. In this cave . . ."

Thala's eyes closed, and this time she didn't open them again.

Twenty-Nine

TAMAS WATCHED ME, concern on his face. "She'll be fine. She just needs to rest. Kalyani's seen situations like this before. The herbs should help. Once she's better —"

"Once she's better, we have to leave here," I said to him, and he nodded.

"Only, I don't think you can come with us to where we're going," he responded. "It's not a part of your journey."

"I know," I whispered. Leaving with the Sybillines, wherever they were going, would just be running away.

The evening was falling over us, a quilt of purple light illuminating the rose-colored mountains, the ancient honeycomb caves. The lagoon became a mirror for the sky, and around the edges of that mirror, the Sybillines sat on plush red cushions and golden carpets, lanterns lighting up their warm faces. Across the walls of the caves, images of the outside world flashed and disappeared like fireworks.

The Sybillines watched these images as they ate, laughing with those who laughed, crying when people in the images cried. But the caves buzzed with a kind of electric anticipation of the future. They were joyous, excited about the next leg of their journey. And yet none of them really knew where they were going. Neither did we.

I scanned the cave, wondering if Thala was right. *Was the Keeper of the Library really here?*

"You look as though you're unraveling a mystery," Tamas said to me.

I hesitated. "Thala took the chamak in order to help us, to help me," I said, feeling ashamed. "She wanted to find a way to get us to our next destination."

"Where did she want to go?" Tamas asked, taking a bite of his flatbread.

I watched him carefully. "To the Library of All Things." I took a deep breath, inspecting him for any signs that he was the Keeper.

But Tamas continued to eat his flatbread without a pause. "Why there?"

"She believes that we're meant to go there. I promised her that we would find it." I looked at Thala, sleeping on a cot beside a small fire, two Sybillines watching over her.

"You *promised* her?" I could hear the incredulity in his tone.

"She's desperate to change the past. And, in many ways, so am I."

"Is it because you have a . . . thing with the Keeper?" He grinned at me.

I rolled my eyes. *It's definitely not him. Someone who waits centuries for his beloved to return wouldn't make light of it.*

"But entering the Library," he added, "that's . . . impossible."

I turned to him sharply. "But Thala said she saw us, or me, in the Library."

Tamas looked confused. "The Library exists in another dimension from our world. There's no way for humans to access it."

"But vetalas can get in . . ."

Tamas nodded. "Because in order to go to the Library, you can't be living or dead. They leave behind their human bodies so they can get inside."

I thought for a moment. "But even if we can't get in, there's a way to convince the Keeper—"

Tamas shook his head forcefully. "To change the past? Change people's fates? He'd never do that."

After all the time I'd spent resisting the idea of the Library, I now found I couldn't accept what he was saying. "How do you know?"

"Because it's the Keeper's duty to guard the Library from humans. Humans are always tempted to break the rules. They do as they wish. Vetalas are different—they're . . . proper, fair. Even if he loves you, he's quite an ethical person. I doubt he'd be willing to—"

"Wait," I interrupted him. It was my turn to be incredulous. "You act like you know him."

Tamas sighed. "I know he's ethical because he could have

easily gone into the Library and changed *your* fate. That way, he wouldn't have had to wait hundreds of years for your return. Can you even imagine what it's like to wait for someone that long?"

I thought about how tortured I was over Arjun, and we had only been apart a few days.

And yet thinking of Arjun in that moment made me feel oddly disloyal toward this vetala who had been waiting centuries for Maya's return. I had to remind myself that in my own mind, I *wasn't* Maya. I was Amrita. I didn't know this vetala. I didn't owe him my loyalty and affection.

Tamas was still speaking. "Besides, whenever we've gotten a note from him in the past—"

"You've received *notes* from him?"

"Of course!" he exclaimed, gesturing to the birds. "My ancestors gave him the key to the caves. The key that you have in your possession," he said, gesturing to the dagger that was secured on my waist. "He has never used it, but he writes to us with details of his expeditions, his pilgrimages."

"So you've been communicating with him all this time?"

Tamas laughed as though I was playing some sort of trick on him. "It's *his* bird that delivered a dispatch for you."

I was silent as my eyes scanned the mountain for Saaras. "Saaras, you mean? The bird that Varun sent?"

"So you *have* met him," Tamas exclaimed.

Tiny electric spikes made their way up my spine. I could tell from Tamas's face that he understood I hadn't known.

And then he said the words that stunned me. "Devi,"

he said, taking my hand in his, "Varun is the Keeper of the Library of All Things."

My hands began to tremble, and my mind couldn't make sense of what Tamas was saying. All I could do was shake my head, tears spilling from my eyes.

"It's all right . . . ," Tamas said, touching my arm. "I thought you knew."

My head was spinning, and yet still, somehow, my eyes landed on him. He was standing on the far side of the lagoon in a dark corner, away from the cluster of Sybillines watching images flash and disappear across the walls of the cave. I got up as though in a trance, Tamas calling after me.

From across the bowl, Saaras flapped his wings.

And as he did, a familiar recognition crystallized within me.

With every step, I understood — I *knew* something in my bones that hadn't quite risen to the place of my consciousness.

He flapped his wings again, and I darted around the Sybillines, my bare feet on the cold rock in order to get to him.

Saaras was standing apart from the other birds, and I knew why.

He wasn't one of them.

As I approached him and stood before him, he flapped his wings one last time, and he was no longer Saaras. He was a person.

"Varun." I said his name, and he smiled back at me, his eyes fixed on mine.

I shivered in the breeze.

He reached for me tentatively, touching my arm, leaving

behind a shiver of goose bumps. He opened his mouth, but I could tell from his face that he was overwhelmed, as though he had been waiting for this moment a long time.

Forever.

Or what must have felt like forever: so many lifetimes. And now here we were, face to face in the white glow of the moonlight.

I felt shy and awestruck and moved, all at once.

There was only one thing I could think to ask him.

"Why didn't you tell me?"

Thirty

VARUN WATCHED ME with his blue eyes, his full lips pressed into a concerned line. "I wanted you to find everything out for yourself," he finally said. "I didn't want to . . . influence your choices. And I wanted you to learn about your abilities. You made it here all on your own . . ."

He waited me out before he reached for my hand, pulling me down beside him. We sat, facing each other, and I felt as though time had ceased to exist. All that remained were his fingers against my wrist, the sound of my heart beating in my ears. I took in his eyes, his familiar face. So familiar, and now I understood the reason.

"You still could have *told* me," I whispered.

"Would you have believed me?" he asked with urgency in his tone, as though he had longed to tell me everything on the trail to Mount Moutza. It must have been difficult for him, waiting, keeping it all to himself. And I understood then that there was so much he ached to share with me but couldn't.

I considered his words.

He was right.

I wouldn't have believed him. He had waited for the right moment to reveal himself to me, and it was now. I had needed to make the pilgrimage to the top of Mount Moutza, to see the statue of Maya. To observe the way Maya's devotees reacted in the temple. It was necessary for me to feel as though my old life was gone, to learn that I could speak to the sand and the wind. Finding the Sybillines, discovering the Janaka Caves for myself, was all a part of my journey.

Varun watched me carefully before he spoke again. "Vetalas are . . . no different than humans," he continued. "We *want* to influence those around us. We could change the fate of everyone on this planet. But we don't. We have great respect for human will. *I* have great respect for your will," he said, gently. I could tell that he was trying to gauge my feelings for him, that he was nervous and hopeful all at once.

I thought about the day that I had met him, the day he had told me the story of Maya the Diviner and her beloved. I never would have thought that he was sharing *our* story with me. Our story. It was strange to think we had a past that I couldn't remember.

For a long while, I couldn't speak. I turned to look at the Sybillines enjoying their dinner on earthenware plates, flatbread crisped and burnt at the edges after being cooked in a stone stove, juicy figs, and stewed pears. Tamas met my eyes from across the lagoon and put his hand up in the air, as though checking to make sure I was all right. I simply nodded at him, realizing that the Sybillines weren't thrown off by anything out of the ordinary. Perhaps this was because their entire existence was out of the ordinary; they believed in magic, and it was all around them.

Varun reached for my hands, and I felt an electric charge in his touch.

"You're cold as ice," he whispered, and I shyly took him in: his long, dark lashes, the cut of his jaw, his broad shoulders.

Out of the corner of my eye, I saw Thala stir awake on her cot. I realized that this was what she had been trying to tell me before she passed out.

"We don't have a lot of time," Varun whispered urgently.

I turned my gaze back to him, trying to refocus on all that I now knew, and all that lay ahead.

"The doorway will soon open, and the Sybillines will leave. You'll have to go as well—and it's up to you where that should be." His eyes bore into mine, his grip on my hands fierce. It was a challenge, and I would have to rise to it—only I had no idea how.

"Will you come with us?" I asked.

Varun shook his head. "Not this time. But I'll find you," he assured me, and I realized that I didn't want to leave him.

I could tell from the way he was watching me that he didn't want me to leave either. Even though we were together in this moment, it was temporary. The wait wasn't over for him.

"There's still more to your journey," he said wistfully. "And it's too important for me to get in your way. But you can ask me anything you want. I'll help in any way I can."

I remembered the last time someone had said this to me. *Ask me anything you want about your mother*, my father had told me, and I was dumbstruck, my mind a jumble of words.

This time, I knew what I wanted to ask.

"Why does Sikander hate my family so much?"

Varun stroked the back of my hand with his thumb, and I felt a wave of desire to be even closer to him. "Because hate and love are so tightly wound that they sometimes coalesce into one. He once loved your father, and your mother too, so fiercely that the cauldron of his poisonous mind turned that instinct to hate."

"Did you ever . . . hate me?" I asked. I wanted to understand how he felt all those years spent waiting for my return.

He hesitated, a small smile crossing his lips as he considered the past. "I was angry for a long time. Devastated. But now you're here. It was worth the wait. Just sitting here with you is worth the wait."

I smiled at him, and he went on.

"There's a reason we each have our own fate. Our own gifts, our own burdens. My fate was to wait for you. But sometimes fates can be altered."

I nodded slowly before I turned to look at Thala again. How would she fare in the long run? If she didn't change her fate, she would spend her whole life struggling, addicted to a substance that poisoned her body.

"I have another question," I said.

Varun's mouth quirked into a small smile. "Please."

"If I can't enter the Library, how can I change fate?"

"There's a way to change the past without entering the Library itself," Varun said.

I waited.

"You're not going to tell me?"

"All I can tell you is that there is another way. There are many ways, but you'll know in your heart which is right for you."

His fingers traced mine, and I could tell he felt what I did: an overwhelming need to be close. I shifted, moving beside him, his arm pressing against mine, my cheekbone against his shoulder.

"My heart wants to go back into the past and kill Sikander," I said.

Varun nodded, releasing a slow breath. "I understand the instinct, but I'd suggest that you try to understand him. Sikander is a part of the fabric of this world, just as you are. You think of yourself as separate from him, but whatever good or evil or cruelty or kindness he has within him, you do too."

"How can you say that?" I felt a wave of anger as I thought of what Sikander had done to my family. "There is *nothing* that Sikander and I have in common. And if I ever had the chance to destroy him, I would," I said fiercely.

Varun smiled, as though he admired something in me. He brought my hand up to his face. He held it there for a moment, and something in me softened.

"Follow your will, Amrita. Trust your instinct. It may not

turn out the way you wish, but your will has the power to lead you to new places."

I traced his face with my thumb, surprised at how at ease I felt with him. He leaned forward, and for a moment, I thought he was going to kiss me, but instead, he touched my mouth with his fingertips before his hand dropped into his lap and he slowly stood up.

I followed suit, uncertain of myself all of a sudden.

I remembered how annoyed I had been at him the first time we spoke. Now all I wanted was to be close to him.

His eyes continued to watch me. "I want to stay with you," he said, holding me in his gaze before he continued. "But if I do, I'll never be able to leave.

"If you ever need me, place the dagger in the moonlight and call for me. I'll come. I promise," he said, pulling my hands into his chest. "I think it's time for you to go now too," he said, nodding in the direction of the Sybillines.

I turned around to see that the images across the walls of the cave were beginning to fade.

"Now," Kalyani said to her people. She was looking up at the sky. "The moon . . . it's directly above us; now is the time to go," she said, getting up.

When I turned back around, Varun had already transformed back into Saaras. He nuzzled my hand before he flapped his wings and flew away.

My hands felt cold where he had touched them, and I felt a wave of disappointment. I didn't even say goodbye.

Thirty-One

"YOUR FRIEND IS ALL RIGHT. She's ready to go," Kalyani said, handing me two small satchels, each containing skins of water and some food. "I would invite you to come with us, but your story on this Earth is not yet complete."

I nodded, but I still felt a wave of uncertainty.

"Have you decided where you're going?" she asked me.

I shook my head.

"I should check on Thala," I told her and walked over to the cot. Thala was sitting up, stretching. She looked as though she was waking up from the most restful sleep of her life.

I hugged her. "I'm so glad you're okay."

But she had no interest in small talk. "Did you talk to him? Can he take us to the Library?" She pulled away, trying to read me.

I shook my head sadly.

"What do you mean?" She scrunched up her nose in frustration. "I *saw* you there, Amrita."

"He wouldn't," I said. "We have to find another way."

She appeared exasperated. "Did you even *ask*?"

"If it were an option, he would have offered."

"I hope you're both ready." I heard Kalyani's voice behind us. "We'll need to depart together. Makara is ready to transport you wherever you'd like to go," she said.

I nodded and thanked her, turning back to Thala.

"Well?" Thala glared at me.

"When he opens his mouth, don't be scared," Kalyani was calling out to the Sybillines who were lining up to exit the caves. They were talking among themselves, laughing, entirely unaware of where they were headed, and yet, they appeared blissfully happy.

Ignoring Thala for the moment, I got up and walked toward them.

"Kalyani, did you say we could go anywhere?" I asked.

Kalyani nodded. "Anywhere in the world. Makara is the gateway to all places."

"Can we travel to the past?"

Kalyani smiled. "I don't see why not."

I threw my arms around Kalyani, embracing her tightly.

"Thank you," I cried.

She laughed. "Thank *you*," she said to me, her eyes shining. She was carrying a small bag with a skin of water and a quilt.

"That's all you're taking?" I asked her.

"I think where we're going, we won't need very much."

"Do you think you're going where my father and Mala went?"

"No. Everybody who leaves this world doesn't die."

"But how can that be?" I asked her. "That's practically the only thing all human beings have in common. We're born. We die. If you're not dying, where are you going?"

"That's the mystery," she said. "We're going where only the Sybillines can go."

"Will I ever see you again?"

"That I can't tell you for certain, but I have a sense that you might." She smiled a mischievous smile, and I knew I would simply have to take her word for it.

Suddenly, Thala was beside me. "Are you going to tell me what your plan is?" she asked, but I said nothing. I knew my silence would annoy her, but I wasn't sure how she'd react if I told her the truth, and I couldn't think of any other option than to take this leap.

I watched as Kalyani threw open the door to the caves, exposing Makara, a smile on his blue face.

Kalyani turned to me one last time. "Wait for us all to leave. Then it will be your turn. Tell Makara where you'd like to go. Any place, any time. I wish you nothing but luck. And I'm honored to have met you," she said, bowing before me. "Choose wisely."

"Thank you," I told her, embracing her and Tamas one last time. "Good luck on your journey."

"And good luck on yours," she said before Tamas turned to Makara.

"Makara," he gently said, "show us the way."

Makara opened his mouth so wide that it was large enough to swallow any one of us. But when I looked into his jaws, I saw the same place that Kalyani had shown me earlier that day. A spiral of cosmos, the night sky, waiting for the Sybillines.

"Goodbye," Kalyani said, as she stepped into Makara's lips.

I gasped, and Thala gripped my palm tightly, but Kalyani was already gone. All that remained was a dark tunnel full of stars, a passageway into a place that was as mysterious as that sky.

I watched as Tamas followed Kalyani. One after another, all of the Sybillines walked through the portal until they had disappeared into that shroud of darkness and light, and the cave where they had lived for centuries was silent, deserted once again.

"It's just like how it was when they found it." I smiled, feeling an odd hint of recognition, a wave of déjà vu overcoming me. "Where do you think they're going, Thala?" I asked.

Thala softened for a moment. "To a place that I can't see. But it's magnificent, I know that. Maybe one day, we'll get the chance to go there too."

Slowly, Makara's mouth closed, and then we were looking into his face, playful and serene.

Thala turned to me. "But more important, where are *we* going?"

For a moment, I hesitated. I thought about all the places we *could* go. I could go back in time before Sikander came to Shalingar, but then Thala would still be a slave. I could return to my childhood, relive those blissful years, but what good was that bliss if I now knew what would come?

I turned to Makara. "Makara," I said to him, trying not to betray my fear of him, "I want to go back in time. I want to go to the place where my mother and father met. Where they first met Sikander," I said.

When Makara opened his mouth, the sight that I saw startled me. A pale blue sky. Buildings so tall that they grazed the clouds. Vast, bustling arenas, avenues so wide that they could contain a thousand chariots.

"Macedon," Thala cried, and I was stunned to hear a small sob escape her lips.

I hung back for a moment, taking it all in. I had never before left Shalingar. There was still a part of me that wanted to sidestep Makara, make my way through the tunnel to find a way back home. But my home no longer existed.

I remembered what Varun had said to me. *Follow your will.*

And in that moment, I felt a surge of that will, aching to make things right. I knew that if I could change the past, the future would follow.

"Why there?" Thala asked.

"We're going to find Sikander, the boy my parents knew. Before he invaded Persia and Bactria, before his armies and his slaves, before he destroyed all those lives. We're going to kill him," I said.

Thala's eyes were wide.

"Are you coming?" I asked.

Thala nodded and reached for my hand. I closed my eyes. Together, we stepped into the past. Behind us, Makara's mouth closed, taking us away from the Janaka Caves forever.

Thirty-Two

"WATCH IT." An elbow nudged me in the ribs, and I whirled around to see a girl my age with golden hair and determined eyes glide by me to join a long queue of young people. A row of tables flanked the top of the line, and behind the desks were adults in green uniforms, handing out leather satchels and books.

I looked around, taking in my surroundings. We were standing within a massive stone stadium with rows and rows of seats reaching the sky. Clusters of students my age stood in groups on immaculately trimmed grass. There was an electric crackle in the air, a heady excitement.

Beyond the crowds, beyond the stadium, I could see the tops of stone towers that reached the sky.

"I've never seen buildings that tall," I whispered.

My gaze traveled to a row of Macedonian flags flanking

one side of the stadium. Above them was a large banner that read:

MILITARY ACADEMY OF MACEDON

And then I put it all together: It was the first day of school.

"This is where my mother and father met . . ."

My father must be somewhere in this very stadium. I furiously scanned the crowds, my head turning this way and that. But it wasn't difficult to identify him. In a sea of blond heads and pale faces, there was a young boy with dark hair and dark skin like my own. He was standing alone, carefully regarding a map.

"That's him," I whispered to Thala, my voice breaking. I quickly wiped the tears that formed at the corners of my eyes. "How do I . . ."

But Thala didn't wait. She crossed the stadium, with me reluctantly trailing behind her.

Soon, we were standing before him. He looked up, taking us in. He was lanky, with the same dark wavy hair that I remembered, the same warm eyes.

"Hi," Thala said, holding out her hand. "I'm Thala. This is Amrita. Are you a first-year too?"

He smiled, and another overwhelming wave of emotion coursed through me. I never realized what a relief it would be to see my father smile again, to be near him again. I willed myself to stay composed.

"I *am* a first-year," he said to us. "Chandradev." He reached for my hand. "You look familiar," he said, furrowing his brow.

"She's from Shalingar." Thala raised her eyebrows, knowing that this would elicit a response from the sixteen-year-old version of my father.

"You are? Me too!" he said with such excitement in his voice that I had to grin. "I thought I was the only one. Is it . . . it must be your first time away from home too?" he asked.

"I've been away for a little bit," I told him. "We've been . . ." I looked at Thala, carefully considering my next words. "We've been traveling for some time. But I . . . I already miss it so much. People tell me it gets better, but it hasn't yet, at least not for me."

He nodded. "I'm so glad you're here." He smiled. "It's reassuring to know that there's someone else from home at the Academy. It's so different than anything I've ever seen," he said, glancing around. I noticed his gaze landing on a girl about my height. She smiled at us. Her eyes were green, just like mine.

"We don't know anyone here," Thala said, glancing from the girl to Chandradev. "Have you heard that . . ." Now it was Thala's turn to consider her words. "That the emperor's son is in our class?"

Chandradev nodded, holding out a piece of parchment and showing it to us. "It says here that he's supposed to be my roommate. Sikander is his name," he said. "I was going to try to find him before the induction assembly." He looked up. "I wonder which one he is."

"Let's go look for him," I suggested, instinctually grabbing for his arm and tugging at him to come along with us, as I remembered doing with my father when I was younger.

We made our way across the stadium, introducing ourselves to new students.

"Do you know Sikander?" I asked again and again.

Everyone we spoke to was acquainted with Sikander, or at least with stories about him.

"I heard he knows every famous person in Macedon," one girl quipped, while a boy turned to Chandradev and said, "You're his roommate? Lucky you, he can get you into any party in the city."

"He knows more people than Zeus himself," yet another boy told us.

But Sikander was nowhere to be found.

"Well, his reputation precedes him." Thala shrugged. She turned to me then, whispering under her breath. "Do you know that girl over there?"

I discreetly turned to look. It was the girl with the green eyes who had smiled at me.

"Why would I know her? Need I remind you of the circumstances that got us here?" I sarcastically quipped.

Thala shrugged. "Just . . . she looks familiar."

"Maybe she knows Sikander." I pulled Thala along with me until we were just behind the girl. I tapped her on her shoulder, and when she turned, I did a double take. Something about the shape of her jaw, the way she tilted her head and regarded me, was startlingly familiar.

She met my silence with a warm graciousness. "Hello,"

she said, gently extending her hand. "I'm Thea. What's your name?" Her wrists were small and bony, like mine. Her fingernails were the same shape as my own. Even her build, slight but strong, was so much like mine that I had to fight everything in me to stop looking at her. It was an instinctive knowledge, so clear that I couldn't shake it. I was holding my mother's hand.

"Amrita," I told her, even though it took a minute for me to get my name out of my mouth.

"Pretty name. It's a pleasure to meet you." She smiled, casually adjusted the bag on her shoulder, and tied her hair into a bun atop her head. I followed her gaze and realized that Chandradev had followed us too. He was standing behind me, watching Thea with curiosity in his eyes. I turned back to Thea. She was nervous, fidgeting—waiting to be introduced, I realized.

"This is Thala." I gestured to her, and Thea politely said hello. "And this is my . . . Chandradev." I caught myself.

"It's a pleasure to meet you," Chandradev said to her, reaching out his hand. They both stood for a moment, gazing into each other's eyes. Neither of them said anything. They just continued to grin at each other, their eyes locked.

I turned to Thala and shrugged, but she was determined to keep things moving. She raised an eyebrow at me before she lost her patience.

"Do you know a . . . Sikander?" she asked Thea, who quickly let go of Chandradev's hand and turned back to us, emerging from her trance.

"Of course I know Sik! We've been in school together since we were five years old. He should be here," she said, furrowing her brow. "Then again, Sik is always late. Maybe we'll see him at the dormitory. They put all the first-years in a residential hall together. So we'll be together quite a bit. But, yes, Sikander will show up when he wants. It's his way."

"He can just do that?" Chandradev asked.

"I guess you can do anything if you're the son of an emperor." She rolled her eyes.

"He's the son of an emperor too." Thala gestured to Chandradev.

My parents began to talk then and were so engrossed in each other that it was impossible to get a word in edgewise. I gestured to Thala and slowly walked away from them, looking around the stadium. It wasn't that I was losing my nerve, it was more that I hadn't actually considered how I was going to do this. Corner him and stab him? Find him in the dormitory and get him while he was sleeping?

Could I do this?

I turned back and saw my parents talking as though they had known each other their entire lives. Even Thala had the good sense to step away and find me.

"Look at them. They're completely enmeshed in each other," she said.

I nodded. "They seem so *happy*," I agreed, "and they've only just met. What happens to make it all fall apart, Thala?"

"Your mother has always had a soft spot for Sikander. The three of them will become inseparable. And Sikander will adore your father, because everyone does. They'll be roommates, best friends, till it's clear to Sikander that he's in love with a woman who doesn't love him back. A woman he's been in love with his whole life," Thala added, "who is in love with his best friend."

"*That's* how it all starts?" I could hardly believe that the source of the world's problems was a love triangle.

"That's how it all starts," Thala confirmed. "I suppose it's how all human drama starts. It's not overnight. It takes years and years. It takes . . . a recognition that you'll never be the hero of the story."

"So you choose to be the monster."

We were close to the edge of the stadium now, and I turned to look back at my father and Thea, animatedly gesticulating as they spoke to one another. Thea was laughing, and my father looked delighted at her laugh. I had to smile.

"Let's split up," Thala said. "We'll find him. He's close by. I can sense it," she said before she approached a tall boy who seemed pleased when she began speaking to him.

I sighed in frustration, sitting down on one of the benches at the edge of the stadium. Even though I knew what I had to do, my nerves were rattling me. A boy with shaggy hair and a rumpled tunic sat down beside me, lighting up a cillo.

"Want one?"

I turned and looked at him. "No thanks," I said, but I continued to stare at him.

He brushed his hair out of his eyes and grinned at me.

"Yeah, I don't much want to be here either," he said as though I had asked him a question. "I can't wait till I graduate from this holding pen," he said.

His voice was all I could think.

I turned to him, watching him carefully. I reached for the dagger in my satchel, wrapping my fingers around it.

"What did you say your name was?" I asked.

"I didn't." He grinned. "But *you* seem eager to find out."

My eyes narrowed. All I needed was confirmation. The moment he affirmed that he was, indeed, who I suspected he was, I would do what I came here to do.

My heart was racing, but I was resolute.

"What do you say we get out of here? I know a place by the water where we could get a glass of wine, maybe talk. Away from these . . . kids." He sneered at the crowd as though they all were beneath him.

"I asked you your name," I said, struggling to keep my voice steady.

He inched closer to me. "I'll tell it to you," he murmured, leaning in, "as soon as you tell me yours."

I was so deeply thrown off, I couldn't respond. All I could do was stare into the eyes of sixteen-year-old Sikander. It was him; there was no mistaking it. His teeth were intact, and his hair was long and dark, but I could tell from the way he moved, from his eyes, the entitled way that he spoke, that it was him.

I collected myself. "My name is Amrita," I said to him through gritted teeth. "Now tell me yours." The satchel was in my lap, my hand tucked into it, my palm sweaty from gripping the dagger so tightly.

He grinned, but before he could respond, I heard another voice.

"Sik! Stop antagonizing her. Ugh, he can be so annoying." Thea sat down beside me and put an arm around my shoulder. "I see you've met my new friend," she said to him. "And this is him, the man we've all been waiting for: Sikander."

Thirty-Three

"L ET'S GET OUT OF HERE." He directed this at Thea, but she answered as though he had addressed all of us.

Thea rolled her eyes. "The induction assembly is in an hour. We can't just skip it, Sikander!"

"What's going to happen? Are they going to kick us out?" He raised an eyebrow at Thea, who simply rolled her eyes again.

"It's the first day of school."

"Since when has that ever stopped you?"

As they went back and forth like that, I realized that Thea and Sikander had a familiar and intimate rapport. They were friends, and I could see from the look on my father's face that he felt excluded.

Thea must have noticed too, because she stepped back. "Sikander," she said, gesturing to my father. "Meet your roommate, Chandradev. Chandradev, Sikander."

"Good to meet you." Sikander turned to him. "I'll let you decide. Stay here for the induction assembly, or go explore the city. With me as your guide. What do you say?" He grinned and looked at my father expectantly.

I was startled by his friendliness, and his closeness with Thea made me question what I had to do. I had known that they had all once been friends, but seeing it before my eyes was startling. I had come here to kill Sikander, but when I saw the way he joked with Thea, his eagerness to befriend my father, I wondered for the first time whether I had it in me to kill another human being, much less someone my parents were once friends with. I wondered about how my actions—if I killed Sikander—would affect Thea and Chandradev.

But it was more than that. I reached to feel for my dagger in my satchel and imagined stabbing Sikander with it, as I had once considered stabbing Nico that day on the hilltop. Except that was survival—a moment of desperation—and besides, I hadn't actually gone through with it. For some reason, in this environment, with a friendly Sikander joking with my parents, I couldn't find in myself the urgency to kill another human being, even if it *was* him.

Chandradev shrugged nervously. "Yeah, let's get away from here," he said, and Sikander got up, slapping him on the back.

Thala pulled me aside. "He was right next to you, and you did . . . nothing?"

"I . . . wanted to make sure it was him."

"Look at him!" she exclaimed. "How could you *not* know?"

"I can't just go around stabbing people," I hissed.

Thala grew serious. "You have to act fast," she said, her voice low.

"How can I . . . I can't kill him in front of his friends," I whispered to her.

She looked me in the eye, her voice almost a growl. "Remember what he did."

Her words stunned me. As though I could ever forget. But before I could respond, the others turned to look at us.

"So . . ." Sikander glanced from me to Thala. "Are you two coming?"

It wasn't that difficult to sneak past the campus guards, because Sikander appeared to actually know all of them. He joked around with them before handing them some coins, and when he asked if they could get us a taxi chariot, one of them ran out into the street to hail us one.

"Where to?" the driver asked.

"The Shipmakers District," Sikander told him as we all stood behind him on the street.

I looked around at the massive thoroughfare before us, so opulent and awe-inspiring that it took my breath away.

"The Avenue of the Gods," Chandradev said as he glanced up and down the street. "It's amazing, isn't it?"

It was a grand boulevard with elaborate marble statues of Macedonian gods every fifty paces or so. Golden chariots pulled by magnificent stallions carried the country's elite to and fro, while the less privileged begged for change by the side of the road.

On either side of the avenue, vertical structures made of stone and glass shot into the sky. I was awestruck, till I was hit by a handful of coins flying out the window of a chariot passing us by.

Thala averted her eyes as people emerged from squalid tents and huts in rags to palm the coins, but I couldn't help but look.

"I've never seen a place like this before," I said to her. "So much wealth, and yet, these people are starving. It makes no sense."

"Welcome to Macedon," Thala said to me. "The entire world wants to remake itself in this kingdom's image."

"It's actually more like *Macedon* wants the world to remake itself in its own image," I said.

Sikander was still speaking with the driver of the chariot. The driver hesitated. "You're sure that's where you want to go?" He turned to us, a worried expression on his face. "You won't get there till dusk."

Sikander reached into his pocket and pulled out a small golden coin, pressing it into the driver's hand. "Just drop us off on Santori Street. We'll take it from there."

The driver looked at the coin, biting it between his teeth before he nodded and we all hopped inside, Thala and Chandradev on either side of me, Thea and Sikander facing us.

We made our way down the Avenue of the Gods and

then farther, past the stately marble government buildings, past the Grand Palace made of stone, the armory and the capitol, to the Royal Temple, a round structure surrounded by stone pillars with an open roof that drew in the light. We drove past the botanical gardens and the financial district, filled with men running up and down the streets. Markets stretched so long down the street that I realized that Macedon lacked for nothing.

But it was those tall buildings that I couldn't take my eyes off. My father was taken in by the sights too, his eyes fixed on the window of the chariot anytime he wasn't looking at Thea.

"It's nothing like home, is it?" he asked me.

I shook my head. "But there are wonderful things about Shalingar too." As I said it, I realized how strange it was, to be talking to my father about our home.

"I don't know. Home is . . . humble compared to this. Macedon is so grand, so impressive," he said. "I've never seen such wealth, such opulence."

"Don't be so fooled by it," Thea said, pointing out a group of squatters under a bridge. There must have been hundreds of them, a village of people living in desperation, hunting for food in the streets. "Macedon is a place for the wealthy. If you're wealthy, life is good, but if you're poor, or disabled, if you're a foreigner, or even a woman, Macedon isn't so kind. This country is built on the backs of the disenfranchised."

"But you're a woman, and you managed to get into the Macedonian Military Academy," I pointed out.

"I come from wealth." Thea shrugged. "My family is well-connected, and we've been attending the academy for ten generations. They couldn't turn me down. But I plan on using my training here to do something different. To institute change." She turned to Thala. "You're from here. You understand."

Thala nodded. "I do." She hesitated before she said, "I come from a family of seers. They live in poverty too. I'd like to do something for my people."

I was sitting next to Thala, and I had to turn to look at her face. She had never expressed anything of the sort to me, but I realized that just being here, not perceived as a slave for the first time, had empowered her. And she was right. She *could* change Macedon from within.

"Seers, eh?" Sikander grinned. "So you can see the future?"

"And the past."

He watched her for a moment before his face broke into a smile. "Can you see my future?" he asked.

Thala held his gaze for a long time before she closed her eyes. When she opened them, they were yellow.

Thea and Sikander appeared taken aback for a moment.

"There are many futures," Thala thoughtfully replied, sitting up taller. It was as though she was no longer Thala, a slave who had been taken from her family. She was powerful—she always had been—only now she knew it. "Your future is changing," she said. "I can see . . . a few possible outcomes."

"Let me guess: I become emperor of Macedon, and my father's words come true, that I'm a profligate and useless ruler and ultimately drive my empire into decline."

"Or you might be dead by tomorrow morning," Thala casually said.

We were all silent for a moment before Sikander burst out laughing. The rest of us followed suit, but I could feel beads of sweat forming on my upper lip.

Sikander grinned. "Looks like we're going to have to get a few glasses of wine in you before you make any more predictions."

We were on the road for a couple of hours, and I wondered the entire time whether I could kill Sikander. With every minute that went by, I was losing my resolve to carry out my plan, but not my determination to right a horrific wrong. I just didn't know how to reconcile the two impulses warring within me.

By now, we had left the lofty avenues and lush gardens of the capital. The sun was setting over the seedy part of town we had ventured into. In the distance, I could see the clear blue of the ocean, and docks with wooden ships bobbing on the surface of the water, like toys left behind by a careless child.

Before us were crumbling buildings made of stone and streets that looked as though they had been deserted for centuries. The buildings here were low and squat, made of stone that had been overtaken by moss. They looked dark and imposing.

We followed Sikander through a maze of cobblestone streets that smelled like salt and fish. It occurred to me during this walk that I was trusting *Sikander*, of all people, as he navigated us through the empty lanes. Broken bottles and bits of scrap metal and wood littered the cobblestone, and the town was so quiet, our footsteps echoed in the alleys.

Finally, the empty streets gave way to a line of shops selling metal scraps and parts for boats.

"*This* is where you've taken us?" Thea asked.

"Patience is a virtue," Sikander called back at us, and I hoped he was right.

We turned down a dark alleyway and then another, arriving at a building with a conspicuously red door. The door was flanked by two windows that were muzzled by metal grills. Sikander knocked on the door three times.

Finally a gruff voice. "Who is it?"

"Emperor Amyntas is a fool," Sikander said loudly, and the door was opened by a short, balding man who smiled at us with broken teeth.

"Right this way, sir," he said to Sikander.

Sikander tipped the man a coin, and we walked through the drawing room of someone's home, the walls a pale pink, a settee in one corner and a forlorn-looking table with no chairs in another. Dusty, stained lace curtains hung from the windows.

"Come this way." Sikander gestured to us to keep moving, and we walked through the small house. At the back, behind a filthy kitchen, was another door.

Sikander opened it, leading us to a courtyard enclosed by four stone walls.

Across from us was the stone exterior of another building. The entrance to it was a yellow door. Sikander opened it, and we emerged in some sort of abandoned factory. The bones of a large ship sat squarely in the middle of a high-ceilinged room, and we walked past it as though this was an everyday occurrence.

"What is this place anyway?" Thala asked.

"It's the old ship factory. Or at least it used to be. Now they make few ships. But it's the center of Macedon's nightlife."

"That's so obvious," Thea quipped, and we all laughed nervously. "Sikander, my parents had better be able to find me tomorrow if they need to," she called out.

"Is it true your parents are revolutionaries?" I blurted out, and Thea smiled.

"I wish they were. They're part of the country's aristocracy. They have a . . . complicated relationship with Sikander's father . . . a friendly rivalry." She smiled at him.

"So they tell us . . . as they bicker with one another at state dinners. But my family has been entangled with Thea's for generations." Sikander shrugged. "Just one big, warring, feuding, loving family." He smiled.

Thea nodded her head and turned back to me. "My parents . . . they've spent years questioning the leadership of our country. They believe in equality and justice for all. They don't like the rigid hierarchy of Sikander's father's government, and after all, a governing body can't be run by a single man . . . or at least, that's what they tell him. They want a more democratic Macedon."

"But unfortunately, my father is a megalomaniac." Sikander shrugged. "Still, he can't get rid of them, because they're old aristocracy, and they're the only thing between him and a revolution."

"A revolution would be good for this country," Thea went on. "I fear my family is all talk, all concessions. They haven't really made a dent in the way things are run here. Maybe it's on me to carry on their legacy, to actually *do* something for Macedon's people."

"Now, *she* should be the leader of Macedon," Sikander said, pointing to Thea, a smile on his face so wide that I was embarrassed by how obviously he loved her.

I tried, in my mind, to make sense of what exactly went wrong, when or how things went awry for Chandradev, Thea, and Sikander. They all appeared to get along so well—could it really have been Chandradev and Thea's relationship that broke them apart?

By now, we had approached another large metal door with a massive handle. This time, I could hear loud drum-beats coming from behind it.

Chandradev stepped forward, pulling at the large handle with both hands. The door finally opened, and we were standing in the middle of a raucous party. Purple, green, and blue lanterns were suspended from string that hung far above us, and beyond those, just the sky. Women spun around wildly, wearing brightly colored bandeaux and skirts. Bodies writhed on the dance floor as music echoed off the walls, making my heart race faster.

Sikander led us through the mass of bodies to the other side of the packed courtyard to yet another door guarded by a large man. He whispered something to the man, who nodded at us. Sikander gestured for us to follow him.

We followed the large man up a circular flight of stairs for at least five stories. I was practically out of breath when we arrived at a place where I could see the sky again.

Thala reached for my hand in fear, but the others simply laughed in delight.

I looked around. We were standing on an empty, flat rooftop. A string of white lights hung just above us. On the edge of the roof was a modest wood table.

"I'll be right back, master," said the guard to Sikander before he ran back down the stairs. By the time we were seated around the table, an entire staff of men had appeared, bottles of wine in their hands, plates of cheeses and breads and olives and sweets.

I looked out into the distance at a view of the ocean. In fact, there was nothing but ocean with a few dots of light scattered across it.

"Ships sailing away from Macedon. Sailors leaving behind their lovers and all that," Sikander said.

"It's . . . beautiful," Chandradev said.

"*I* think so. I think you ought to trust me more often," he said, grinning, placing his hand on Thea's shoulder. Once again, she pulled away and turned to Chandradev.

"You know . . . I've always wanted to travel to Shalingar," she said.

"Perhaps I'll take you there one day," Sikander said to her. "Maybe for our honeymoon," he added causally as he poured each of us a glass of wine.

I began to laugh. "Your honeymoon?"

I looked around the table, waiting for the others to join me in laughter, but no one did.

"Yes, of course," Sikander said with a hint of annoyance in his voice. This time, he placed a possessive hand on Thea's elbow. "She hates talking about it. And half the time she hates me," he snickered, but there was a hint of nervousness in his laugh. "But one day"—he turned to Thea—"you're just going to have to accept it."

"Accept what?" I asked, my heart racing.

"That we've been betrothed to be married since we were children," he said. "I told you . . . just one large, bickering, warring, loving family."

I looked from Thea to Chandradev. They both reached for their glasses of wine, avoiding each other's eyes.

Thea downed her entire glass, and Sikander refilled it, spilling wine all over the table.

"Sorry," he said without looking at her. "My mistake."

Thirty-Four

I WAS STILL IN SHOCK by the time we arrived back at the dormitory, Thala and I sneaking into the stately stone building in the dark with the others. We silently followed Sikander and Chandradev to their room, exhausted from the night. Only I was more than exhausted. I was confused and unnerved by what I had learned.

So Thea had followed her heart, and in the process, Sikander had gone mad. My parents had separated, I had been left motherless my whole life, and my father had been assassinated. But that wasn't even all of it. Sikander's rage had caused him to destroy so many lives — Thala's, the soldiers we had encountered in the desert, the citizens of all the empires he had overthrown, even his own subjects.

Here and now, he was simply an entitled party boy: well-connected, wealthy, and profligate, but ultimately harmless.

But I understood that losing Thea must have turned him into a crazed despot.

In the chariot on the way back, I had been quiet, pondering what I was here for, and yet, every time I turned and caught my father's profile or my mother animatedly told me something about herself, I felt overwhelmed with a kind of gratitude I never expected to feel. I was content, happy. Sitting between my mother and my father, I felt at home, loved, almost moved to tears. I had found it—the simplicity of being with my parents and enjoying their company, the feeling of family. The strange thing was that when I saw the way that Sikander interacted with them, I realized that he had once been a part of their family too, that he considered them his own.

I knew that I couldn't kill him.

But I didn't know what else *to* do.

"We'll see you in the morning." Sikander yawned as he and Chandradev headed into their room. Thea hugged us before she took off.

"I'm so glad you're both here." She smiled. I watched her walk away, realizing that it was just Thala and me again.

We walked to the end of the hallway together and turned a corner, finding an empty spare room with two beds, two desks, and two chairs. A bare window overlooked the campus.

Thala collapsed on the bed. "At least we have a place to stay the night."

But I was furious at her. "When were you going to tell me?"

"I didn't know."

"You know everything, Thala. How did you not know that Thea and Sikander were betrothed?"

"Does it make a difference?" She sat up to face me. "You still have to kill him, Amrita."

"You told me he *loved* Thea! Not that they were betrothed!"

"He does love her." I continued to glare at her, and finally she sighed. "Amrita, I can't see the future anymore. Or I should say, I can't see it from here. I didn't know about their betrothal. I can't see what happens to Sikander. That's why I said what I did when he asked me about the future. Coming back here . . . it's done something strange to my abilities."

"What do you mean?"

"We're actively rewriting the future now because we're rewriting the past. I don't know what the consequences might be. I can see hundreds of different possibilities."

"Does that mean you're having second thoughts? About killing Sikander?" There was a hint of hopefulness in my voice.

"I don't know what it means. All I know for certain is that if Thea and Chandradev marry, Sikander goes mad. He kills his father, overtakes the throne, starts invading every territory from the north to the south."

I sat down on the window ledge. "And what if they don't marry?"

"What do you mean?"

"What if she ends up marrying Sikander, just as she's supposed to do?"

Thala fidgeted in her chair. "I don't know." She shook her head. "Maybe I just need to sleep. But I don't have any answers for you anymore. I can't help you with this, Amrita. I'm sorry."

I couldn't sleep, and after tossing and turning for a couple of hours, I got up, grabbing the dagger in my hand and sneaking off campus. I found a small park in the center of the city, placed my dagger in the grass, and looked up into the moon.

Varun, I need your help.

But there was only the night sky staring back at me. I closed my eyes, praying he'd answer, and soon heard the sweeping of wings. My heart swelled with anticipation.

I opened my eyes to see that Saaras had landed before me. He flapped his wings until he transformed into Varun. My heart raced at the sight of him, and for a moment, I wasn't sure what to say, my thoughts clouded by the thrill of seeing him again.

"You've been watching me," I finally said. I wasn't sure how I knew this, but I did.

He nodded his head, his mouth curling into that welcome smile that had by now become so familiar. "I sensed I'd find you here, in the past. I told you there was another way." He sat down before me in the grass, and once again, we were face to face.

This time, the desire within me spoke even louder than

before. I wanted to touch his face again. I wanted his mouth against my own, his body against mine.

And yet, I didn't want to forget why I had called for him.

"I can't kill him," I said. "I just can't find it in myself."

Varun nodded his head, his warm eyes assessing me. "You should consider that a blessing."

"What do I do?" I looked back into those eyes, trying to find my center.

"That I can't tell you."

"I had a feeling you'd say that."

"And yet you still called for me . . . ," he teased, reaching for my hand. "Sorry. It's instinct," he said. But I shook my head, squeezing his hand before he could retract it. "It's been hundreds of years, and yet it's still there. Some part of me can't forget."

"I don't remember the past, but right now, this thing between us . . ." It was impossible not to acknowledge, but difficult to articulate.

He fought back a smile. "I know" was all he had to say.

We both felt it—as though there were a magnet pulling my body to his, and the only thing resisting this pull was our own will in the face of a task at hand that was far too important.

Varun continued to watch me, and I saw the way his eyes took me in. With a desire so strong that it took everything for him not to act on it.

And yet, when he spoke, his tone was pensive. "Something has to be sacrificed in order for something to be gained."

For a moment, I thought he was talking about us, but I recovered quickly. "I'll sacrifice whatever I need to . . . but *what*?"

He didn't have to answer. As soon as the words came out of my mouth, I understood what Varun was saying. I thought back to the revelation I had before I tried to sleep.

What would trigger the horrific events we had experienced in our lives, what would start a chain reaction that would lead to the suffering of so many people, the tiny flame that would eventually turn into the conflagration, was Chandradev's growing love for Thea and Thea's growing love for Chandradev. It was their relationship that needed to be stopped. And if they were never together, never a pair, if they never got married, then I would cease to exist.

I inhaled quickly. "It's me," I realized. "I'm what must be sacrificed."

Varun nodded.

"Thea is a . . . leader. She could be good for Macedon. Good for the world. And if she simply goes ahead and marries Sikander as she's expected to . . ."

"She becomes the queen of Macedon," Varun confirmed, "And Chandradev returns to Shalingar at the end of school. Just as he's supposed to."

"I can't stop them from falling in love," I said, thinking aloud.

"It's already beginning to happen."

"But I can stop them from being together."

"You have the power to."

"So . . . it'll be like—"

"Like you never existed."

I imagined myself nowhere, floating in a sea of black. I shuddered. "But where will *I* go? Will it be like dying?"

Varun shook his head.

"Will I go where the Sybillines went?"

He shifted, lying down in the grass and gently pulling me down with him. We lay there for a moment in silence, looking up at the stars. I leaned into his arm, and he wrapped it around me.

"No," he finally said. "You're not going where the Sybillines went."

When it was clear that he wouldn't explain, I said quietly, "It's the only way, isn't it?"

"There are many ways, but you have to ask yourself if this is the one that feels right."

I hesitated for a moment, taking it all in.

"I want you to enjoy it," he said. "Your time here on this Earth. You don't want to end it by taking someone's life."

"I don't want that either. So my life really is about to end." I let the thought sink in.

"You don't really know how it ends yet," he said before he slowly disentangled his body from mine, propping himself up to look into my eyes.

As he did, I sensed the end of our meeting, and once again I felt bereft, alone.

"Find me again once you've carried out your task," he said. His hand cupped my cheek, and I nodded, watching him transform back to Saaras before he took off.

I sat in the grass for a long time by myself, realizing that there wasn't just one death. There were hundreds, if not millions of deaths in a person's life. They varied in degree; they took on different forms. But they were ultimately all variations of the same few things: saying goodbye, change, sacrifice.

I realized something else as I sat there: There was a part of me that wanted to stay forever with Chandradev and Thea. I wanted to watch their affection and love for each other grow. I wanted to know my parents, every part of them. I wanted to feel like a normal person, but I knew I never would again.

Maybe nobody ever really gets that chance.

When I returned to our room, Thala was up, reading a book, waiting for me.

"I have to prevent my parents from ever being together," I announced.

She put her book down and took a deep breath. I braced myself for an argument. "I know what I came here to do, but I'm sorry, I can't," I told her. "It's not who I am."

"I know," she said.

I was taken aback. "What do you mean?" I asked. "Can you see anything?"

Thala closed her eyes, and I realized how much I'd come to rely on her extraordinary gift.

When she opened them, they were gray. "All I can see is that it won't last between Thea and Sikander. That they don't have to be together forever in order to change Sikander's fate. Just long enough that Chandradev can return to Shalingar."

I walked to the window, and Thala followed me.

In less than an hour, a new day would break over Macedon.

But right now, the moon was still full, and the campus was drenched in a radiant silver light.

"Where will I go, Thala? If I'm never born in this new version of time, where do *I* go?"

"I don't know," she said, and we were both silent for a moment. We hadn't slept in ages, and we were weary and still looking for answers to questions that baffled us.

And then, I heard a voice.

"Who are you?" it said.

We both turned at once. Thea was standing by the door, her hand against the doorframe, fear and confusion in her eyes.

Thirty-Five

"I . . . DON'T KNOW if you'd believe me," I told her.

"Try me," Thea said, sitting down on the bed across from us.

Thala glanced at me before she got up. "I'll leave you two for now," she said before she walked out of the room.

"I don't know how to put this," I said to Thea, "but I come from the future." I looked at her to see if she would simply laugh at me, but she didn't.

"I never knew my mother," I started.

She was watching me carefully, waiting for me to go on, and so I continued. I told her about my childhood, about my father, about Shalingar. I told her about the betrothal to Sikander, about Arjun, about the attack on Shalingar Palace. I told her about meeting Thala and going on a journey. I told her about the temple at Mount Moutza and the desert and the Janaka Caves and Varun.

As I did, and as she listened, it was the strangest thing: I could feel myself disappearing. Maybe it was that I already sensed things wouldn't be the same after I told her everything, but it was more real than that. I was asking her to do something that would erase me from the universe, negate me from the record of time, and I was hoping with everything inside of me that she would concede.

Finally, I finished my story.

"I'm the child that you and Chandradev will—would have had one day. Except, in that version of the story, Chandradev leaves Macedon . . . without you. And he raises me alone before he's killed by Sikander's men. I never get to be with or even meet my mother. We were separated amid this . . . tragic turn of events."

I looked up at her, still trying to make sense of it: the fact that we were sitting face to face in a dormitory, me from the future, her from this present. A mother and a daughter meeting across time.

"You're saying I have to marry Sikander? Otherwise, he turns into some . . . despotic ruler?" she quietly asked. At first I thought she was mocking me, but when I saw the look on Thea's face, I could tell that she believed me.

"You don't have to do anything. But I had to tell you what happens if you don't marry him."

"And if I do stop speaking to Chandradev? Cut him out of my life?"

I couldn't predict the future like Thala, but I knew what would happen, how things would unfold.

Thea would stop spending time with Chandradev. It

would be a decision she made with her will, rather than with her heart, and she would pay a price for it. She would distance herself from him, even as it pained her. She would spend weeks and months and years wondering what that other life—the one she desired—might have looked like.

She would watch Chandradev return to Shalingar at the end of his four years at the Academy, and she would spend weeks lamenting his absence. She would marry a man she didn't love, and she would harbor an intense pain and longing for the one she did.

"I suppose, no matter what, I'll be fine," she said to me after a long silence.

"You will?" I asked, surprised.

She smiled. "I don't know." There were tears in her eyes. "The thing is . . . I know we've only just met . . . but somehow, the idea of being with Chandradev is already rooted in me."

I nodded, trying not to cry. "I know he feels the same way."

In preventing one particular form of disaster, the absence of that other reality, the one we knew and expected, the one that we felt was our own, was slowly becoming a gaping hole in each of our lives, searing us with its edges.

"Will he be all right?" Thea asked. She was asking about my father.

In some part of me, I knew the answer to this too: Chandradev would suffer, wondering what he had done wrong. He would hold tightly to a secret, buried in the deepest recesses of his heart: That he loved Thea. That he couldn't have her.

But perhaps that was always the case.

"In the version of time that I came from, that I experienced, he spends years away from you, missing you anyway. It seems that loss, or at least the experience of being torn from each other, is a part of your lives no matter what you choose."

I remembered Thala's words: *Some things are fixed, some things are changeable.* Maybe it was never Thea and Chandradev's fate to spend a lifetime together, to raise a family together. Maybe fate is a puzzle that nobody truly understands, not even the vetalas.

She nodded. "I know what you're asking me to do. But it's still difficult to swallow. That I have a choice, but I really don't. That my actions have unintended consequences."

"I'm sorry that I'm the one to deliver the news to you. We're altering the course of nature," I explained to her. "And I don't know all the consequences. I don't think anyone ever does. And I know that in your heart, it doesn't feel right. It probably won't for a long time."

"What about you?" she asked. "What happens to you?"

"I'm not sure."

"Do you just . . . disappear?" she asked carefully.

"I don't know. But most likely, it all just . . . ends."

As I said this, I realized that I felt broken too. I was close to exiting this world that I had been a part of, and it was difficult to let go. It was as though the pain that Sikander must have felt in that other version of this story had somehow been divided among us.

That was the moment that Thea began to cry, her shoulders trembling. It was actually hitting her now — she wasn't just letting go of a moment or a person or an outcome that she wanted. She was closing the door on an entirely other life, and I could tell that she felt the loss of that future as though she had actually lived it.

And she had, in some other version of time. I understood this now.

"Thea?" I quietly asked, getting up and sitting down next to her. "Are you . . . all right?"

She turned to me, and her skin was blotched red, her eyes crimson. She was crying the kind of tears where the sadness threatens to choke and engulf you. I knew this kind of sadness well.

"One day, I'll make peace with it, I suppose. But it's a lie. And the saddest thing is . . . he doesn't know."

"Who, Sikander?" I asked.

She shook her head. "Chandradev. He'll never know how I feel about him. It's as though there's a hollow in my life now that can never be filled. And I just know I'll spend my years searching the world, looking for pieces of him in everyone I meet. Does that make sense to you?"

I realized then that she was looking to me for strength. My mother wanted *me* to comfort her. I swallowed hard as I thought about Arjun. I sat down beside her. "I loved someone like that once."

"Arjun?"

I nodded. "There's another version of this story where he and I run away together," I said. "Where we actually succeed at running away."

"And probably another where you marry."

"And another where he loves someone else, and so do I."

"How do you make peace with that?" she asked. "With all the possibilities? With everything that could have been?"

But for once, I couldn't will myself to consider all the fates that were out of my control, all the lives I had lost or couldn't have. I simply wanted to spend the last precious moments of my existence with my mother.

She was right: Sooner, rather than later, it *would* all end. It would end for all of us. I just didn't know what that would look like for me. But perhaps that's always the case anyway.

"Amrita?" she asked before she left my room that night. I turned to her, and she pulled me into her arms, holding me tightly.

"I love you," she said. "And I'm sorry. I'm sorry I couldn't be there for you the way I should have," she said.

I couldn't fight back the tears that flowed easily from my eyes. We both cried, together, for all that had been lost, in this life and in that other life. And we cried because I think we both understood that there was no life without loss.

But mostly, we cried because through some great mystery of the universe, through forces beyond our understanding, we had been returned to each other, and for that, I was grateful.

The sun was rising over campus now, and it was a new day: an opportunity for another future.

But I was thankful just for this moment.

"I love you too, Mama," I said before I reluctantly let her go.

Thirty-Six

I MUST HAVE SLEPT the entire day, because it was dark by the time Thala woke me up. I had no energy; I felt as though I was made of air, like my bones were glass.

"How did it go?" she asked, slowly sitting down beside me.

"We spoke for a long time," I said, "About . . . everything I could think of." I turned on my side to look at Thala.

She closed her eyes before she opened them again. They were gray, and I watched her as she spoke.

"I can see again. It's like the future is forming, becoming more solid. Thea and Sikander won't have children of their own," she said, as though this was some sort of consolation. "They'll be together for some time . . . many years. Sikander will inherit the throne organically, after his father dies a natural death. He'll have been so influenced by Thea that he'll be a benevolent, kind ruler, beloved by his people. Thea knows what she wants for this nation. She and Sikander will build schools and hospitals. They'll tax the rich, make sure the poor are taken care of. She'll start a movement to empower women. This is her chance to make Macedon the kind of place it should be. And Sikander will carry out her will. This is all wonderful for the people of Macedon. And the people of the world."

I nodded, but I didn't feel happy. I came here to do what I needed to, but it had left an indelible scar on me. Perhaps there wasn't a version of life that one could sail through unscarred, but I felt as though I knew too much, understood too much, had seen too much of the complexities of the world.

"And my father?"

"He'll marry eventually. But many, many years from now. He'll go back to Shalingar and rule the way he was always meant to. When he dies, he'll leave the throne to Arjun, whom he'll treat like his own son."

"Arjun." I smiled. Arjun felt so far away now, as though I had known him a lifetime ago. I didn't even feel as though he was mine anymore. And he wasn't. We had forged entirely separate paths. The probability that he would eventually meet someone else, love someone else, smarted only slightly. I knew he was the very last thing I had to let go of, and once I did, perhaps another world waited for me beyond my own attachments.

"It's all because of you, Amrita," Thala went on. "You've saved your kingdom. You've saved so many people. You've . . . undone years of war, of slavery, of injustice."

Still, I felt unconvinced and depleted. "Imagine if I had actually killed Sikander . . . none of this would have been possible." The nearness of that version of events was chilling.

Thala shrugged. "But you didn't. You did the right thing."

I thought about the last couple of days. I had traveled to the place of my birth. I had gotten to know my mother. I had spent time with my father again. I had done more than just the right thing. My heart was full, even though I was a different person now.

"Now there's the matter of my own fate," Thala added.

"What do you mean?" I asked. "Sikander won't come find you in the woods now, he won't kidnap you or break apart your family—"

"We're not . . . real, Amrita."

I looked at her quizzically.

"We came here to do what we have to do, but if we keep hanging around here, then we become vetalas ourselves."

"I don't understand."

"When my mother has a child, a few years from now, it won't be *me*. It'll be another child. Because I'm here, in this odd, in-between space. And so are you. We don't . . . belong here."

The reality of her words hit me hard. *Varun*, I realized, sitting up. That was why he had followed us into the past. Perhaps he had even led us here. Either way, we still weren't done, not quite yet, but only Varun could show us our fates now.

◻

The moon was low in the sky when we arrived at the base of Mount Spinakis, and we hiked all the way to the top in the silver light, taking in the blanket of stars above us. The bright lights of Macedon sparkled beneath us, and chariots whizzed this way and that on the Avenue of the Gods. I looked at the river that we had raced across, the campus where I had met Thea and Chandradev and Sikander. I took in the sight one last time, and smiled.

I didn't know where I was going, but just being up here was somehow freeing. I realized that I didn't really *belong* anywhere or to anyone anymore. Not Sikander or my father or my mother. Not Arjun either. I had somehow become my own person.

"Ready?" Thala asked.

"Ready," I told her, and I fished the dagger out of my satchel and placed it under the moonlight.

"Varun," I asked. "Please come help us."

We waited.

I watched the moon, until I saw a small speck growing and growing against the light.

It was flying toward us. A bird. Not just any bird. Saaras.

He landed before us, flapped his wings, and transformed into Varun.

This time I ran to him, embracing him, a mixture of relief and desire coursing through me as I felt the warmth of his body against mine. But there was something else: I ached to be comforted. Only Varun could understand how world-weary this journey had made me. He wrapped his arms around me and held me closely for several minutes.

Finally, I looked up at him. "We've done it—what we came here to do," I told him.

He smiled, tracing my jaw with his thumb. "So you're ready?" There was excitement in his voice. But something more, a release, as though it was finally here—the moment he had waited for over the span of so many lifetimes.

I looked from Varun to Thala, and a small laugh escaped my lips. "I'm not entirely sure what I'm ready for. I don't know where I belong. All I know is that I don't belong here anymore."

Varun nodded, still holding me, so close that I could feel his breath on my hair. Goose bumps prickled my neck. "I can take you to the Library. There, you'll collect your book. You've finished one leg of your journey, but there are many places we can go to next."

"But I thought that humans can't enter the Library," I said.

"Humans can't. Only the vetalas. And those who are no longer of the Earth."

My heart felt as though it stopped as he said that. "What do you mean, I'm no longer of this Earth?"

"You're no longer Amrita. No longer human. You've sacrificed your life for the greater good. How do you think gods and goddesses are created?" he asked. "They're anomalies. People who have sacrificed themselves for something bigger than themselves. And that's what you did. It's time that you become Maya. But you can't do that without going to the Library and taking back your book — if you're ready," he said, pulling away from me for a moment. He watched me carefully, taking in my reaction.

I still wasn't entirely sure what he meant, but something was propelling me forward into the very Unknown that had once frightened me. Now it had somehow become my friend.

"What about Thala?"

He turned to her, his eyes full of apology. He fished in his pockets and drew out a piece of silver bark, handing it to her.

"If you take this, you'll fall asleep. You won't wake up till you're born again."

Thala accepted the bark in her hand, hesitating for a moment. I felt a swell of affection for her when I saw the uncertainty in her eyes, but Varun caught her apprehension too.

"Don't be afraid. It's the only way you can depart this plane and end up where you belong once again. A life awaits you, a body waiting for you to slip into it. But you can't be in two places at once. It's what you must do."

But something within me ached at the idea of saying goodbye to Thala. She had helped me escape the palace. She had come with me through the desert and to the caves and all the way to Macedon.

But I also knew in my bones that I had to take the last leg of the journey on my own, that Thala and I had different destinies now.

I wanted to comfort her, but instead, it was she who comforted me.

"Don't be scared, Amrita." Thala squeezed my shoulder. There was tenderness in her eyes. "You brought me to Macedon. You changed my fate. I owe you everything."

"I couldn't have done any of it without you," I said, reaching for her hand.

She choked back her tears before she looked at me and said, "You're the only friend I ever had. This isn't how I expected it to turn out, but—" She shook her head as though she had already said too much. "Just know that I'll miss you. I don't know if I'll see you again, but I'm glad our paths crossed."

It wasn't till that moment that I realized how much Thala had needed me too. We had both needed each other through this time, and now I wouldn't join her for the last leg of her journey either. She would have to go it alone.

I threw my arms around her and held her tight as she wiped away her tears. I thought for a moment. "You'll come visit me one day," I said.

"How do you know?"

"Because I'll make sure of it," I told her.

Thala stepped back and smiled. She was still holding my hand. She looked to Varun.

He nodded, and we watched Thala as she placed the bark under her tongue and lay down in the grass. I placed my scarf over her. She fell asleep quickly, and soon, I could see that she wasn't breathing anymore.

I wiped tears from my eyes. "I'm going to miss her," I told Varun.

"I know," he said to me, pulling me close to him. "But I promise you: Nothing is ever lost."

My eyes were still on Thala. "What do I do now?"

"Simply ask. Ask the Library to reveal itself to you."

"That's it?"

Varun nodded his head, a small smile crossing his lips.

I closed my eyes and asked, and when I opened them, we were there.

The shelves reached all the way to the sky, and they were filled with more books than I had ever seen in my life. The books appeared to be speaking, whispering, no different than the sound of birds chirping in the morning at Shalingar Palace.

"Where do we go?" I asked him before he took my hand and led me to a shelf that held a series of leatherbound books. My father's. My mother's. Sikander's. Arjun's. Thala's. Bandaka's. Shree's. Tippu the gardener's. Mala's. Everyone I had ever known. I found my own book, bound in green.

When I opened it to the first page, there was a stamp across it.

OUT OF CIRCULATION, it said. I smiled and tucked it into my satchel before I reached for my father's book.

I spent that day reading their stories, one after another. Maybe it was a day. Maybe it was days. I couldn't say. All I knew was that time didn't exist here. I was never tired or hungry or wanting. There was no day or night.

I read and read and marveled at all the lives of everyone

I had ever loved: the richness of their experiences, the tastes they relished and remembered, the smells that were imprinted on their senses, the pleasures and pains of their bodies, the wisdom they acquired, the people they loved and lost, the fears that they hid, the identities they carried like masks.

Varun watched me read those words. He looked content just to be sitting beside me for all those hours or days, or whatever it was. Some space that existed between day and night, between dream and waking.

At the end of it, I took out a pen and added only one line in Thala's book.

"That's it?" Varun asked.

I shook my head. "I don't need to change anything else," I said. "This world"—I gestured to the books—"it's as perfect as anything can be. I was lucky just to be a part of it."

Varun smiled before he took my hand. Now it was his turn to share his story.

He told me about all those years without me. He told me about the world and how it had changed, what he had seen and heard on all those pilgrimages to Mount Moutza. He told me the entire universe as he knew it.

And when he kissed me, it was with longing and desire, the kind that can only come of hundreds of years of waiting.

I understood then why he had seemed so familiar that day on the road to Mount Moutza. There had always been a deep and magnetic power between us. Only, I didn't know it.

The world was full of mysteries, abundant with magic. Now I knew.

Epilogue

I COME HERE TWICE A YEAR, when the veil between the living and the dead, the gods and the mortals, is lifted. I sit, with Varun by my side, offering up my blessings. People say that I am an irreverent goddess. I don't necessarily believe in the power of my own blessings, but others sometimes do. I don't fault them.

I don't believe that anyone is more powerful than anyone else. I believe that anyone can change. I believe there are mysteries built over even more powerful mysteries, and it takes lifetimes to unearth them.

When I am not here, I travel to other places, other worlds that I never imagined existed.

But this is still one of my favorite places. It's my old home, the kingdom that I once lived in.

Chandradev is older now, in his forty-fifth year. He comes twice a year to greet me, but this year, he brings along a woman whose face I instantly recognize. She is older too, but she still has those green eyes, that gait that is so familiar. When I reach for her hand, I feel as though I am holding my own hand.

Chandradev introduces her as Thea. He tells me that his old friend Sikander the Great has died. His throne was handed to a distant relative, a nephew. "Thea and I knew one another a long time ago, in Macedon," he tells me, and I listen to their story, even though I already know it.

I know that Chandradev will marry her. That they'll live many more years together. That they've earned their love for each other after all these years apart.

Perhaps I look familiar to them, but they don't recognize me. That's the thing I've learned about humans: Their minds are too fixed. They see me only as Maya, or as the Goddess. They have no idea that in another life, I was their child. That in another life still, in this life, a long time ago, I was their friend, their classmate.

I bless them and ask about their plans for the next season, for the year. It's one of the things I miss most about being human. There were always plans.

"I'm handing the throne down too. My successor is like a son to me."

"Arjun?" I ask, and Chandradev nods.

Arjun visits the temple sometimes too. He still brings small gifts for me. Sometimes a scarf, or a bracelet made out of jasmine buds. Another time, a seashell.

"He'll make an excellent maharaja," I tell Chandradev.

And I know that he will, that he gives every part of himself to the things and people he loves. And he loves this kingdom.

After the pujas, I watch people tuck parchment into the crevices of the temple. They bring gifts: garlands of marigold, boxfuls of juicy golden jalebi. Mangoes and pomegranates, guavas and figs. I distribute the food to anyone who comes to me, asking for my blessings, asking for advice.

I've learned that it's best not to interfere too much. The best I can do is be there and listen to anyone who needs to be heard.

By dusk, Varun and I watch the last caravans leave the temple, making their way down the Silk Road. The sky is almost crimson, so beautiful that it's impossible not to look at.

And then, right as we're about to depart, a chariot arrives. It stops just outside the temple, and Varun goes out to meet it.

A woman hops out. "I know the temple is closing," I hear her say, "but I'd just like to see her once. You see, I've traveled all the way from Macedon to see her, and I know it's her last day for another six months."

I recognize her voice and come out to greet her.

"My name is Thala," she tells me. "I don't know why, but for some time now, I've had this feeling . . . as though I need to come see you," she says, and I smile at her, nod my head.

"It is written," I say to her, and she smiles as though we understand each other.

"Would you like to join us for a cup of chai?" Varun asks

her. "You've come all the way from Macedon—that's quite a journey."

She nods, looking relieved. "I'd love to," she says, as Varun ushers her into the temple.

"I went to Macedon once," I tell her as she begins to sit down by my feet. "No, no, not there," I say, taking her hand and pulling her into the chair beside me. "You're like an old friend."

"It certainly feels that way, doesn't it?" she says. "I grew up hearing stories about you from my mother and my aunts. Perhaps that's why. I love a good story," she tells me, and I have to smile.

"Would you like to hear my story?" I ask.

And she nods her head, her eyes wide.

"It begins right here, in Shalingar," I start. "Another time, another place. Have you ever heard the Parable of the Land of Trees?" I ask her.

"I think I have," she says as she leans in, and I begin to tell her the tale.

ACKNOWLEDGMENTS

WHEN I WAS A JUNIOR IN COLLEGE, I had the opportunity to meet my favorite author, Arundhati Roy, and somewhere in between my fangirling over her, she said something to the effect of, "Don't bother trying to learn how to write. Learn to see the world. That's your only job as a writer." I'm tremendously grateful for a vibrant community of friends and family who play an enormous role in how I see the world every day.

Enormous thanks to my editor at Razorbill, Jessica Almon, for her brilliant and insightful feedback, for her tireless support, and for her friendship. I wish every author had an editor as thoughtful and caring as Jessica. Razorbill has been a wonderful publishing home for my books, and I'm thankful to Ben Schrank for welcoming me into the Razorbill family and to Lauren Donovan and Jennifer Dee for all their support and hard work bringing this book to the world.

I've been lucky enough to have Theresa Evangelista design two gorgeous covers for my books, and every time I receive a compliment about either of them, I think of her.

Thanks to the wonderful Jenny Bent who has always

been an enormous champion of my work, whose feedback I have come to rely upon. She's also super fun to talk to on the phone about feminism, politics, and books.

While I was writing this novel, Jolene Pinder and Clint Bowie visited from New Orleans on a handful of occasions and made my home the scene of numerous slumber parties. I am ever so grateful for their friendship and love and for their fantastic hospitality and the drive-thru slushies and movie nights when I visit them in NOLA.

Payal Aggarwal-Scott and Andrew Scott came out to book events and went taco tasting with me in Tijuana while I was working on this manuscript. Their encouragement and kindness (and love for food-related adventures, big and small) have truly enriched my life.

Jeff Perry saw me through the process of publishing my debut novel as well as writing my second one. I am ever indebted to him for his love and kindness and for his lovely notes, emails, and letters.

I'm thankful for friends like Jen and Sam Sparks for their general wonderfulness, because they are always suggesting cool places like the Roger Room for drinks and for making me laugh when I most need it.

Thanks to Dan Lopez for his support, amazing eye for detail and beauty, aesthetic advice, and the great articles he sends my way. Thanks also to Edgar the rescue dog, who basically makes everyone's day better.

I will never be able to thank Bridget Jurgens enough for

all she has done for me, but I'm forever indebted to her and grateful for her friendship and love.

In no particular order, these fantastic human beings have always been there with the perfect words, book recommendations, or tasty meals right when I most needed them: Dee Montealvo, Nathalie Huot, Linda Sivertsen, and Tabby Nanyonga. If past lives really do exist, I have a long history with these folks. On a regular basis, they nurture my soul with their spirit of generosity.

Thanks also to Kate McClelland, or Mrs. Mac as we all knew her, who ran the Young Critics Club at Perrot Library and nurtured my love of books. Even though she's not with us anymore, I think about her regularly and hope that I've made her proud.

For their friendship, support, and love, thanks also to Stephanie Watanabe, Veronica Ho, Akriti Macker, Jenny Rosenbluth, Julie Fulton, Meredith Hight, Kirsten Markson, Jaime Reichner, Julia Ruchman, Susanna Fogel, Taryn Aronson, Dahvi Waller, Shelley Marks, Smitha Khorana, Lizzie Prestel, Kristie and Brian Kim, Krupa Desai, Priya and Sanjay Nambiar, Lizzy Klein, Alessandro Terenzoni, Melissa Brough and Chris Marshall, Adam Chanzit, Katie Robbins, Daniel Berson, Jessica Poter, Romina Garber, Tansy Meyer and Brian Lauzon, and Nell-Rutledge Leverenz.

Thanks also to Percy for making my life run smoothly and for her warmth and kindness, and to Ginny Fleming for keeping me level and sane through the difficult times.

Thank you to Amanda Petrocelly, Zoe Owens, Nick Paliokas, and Miriam Brummel and everyone at Cafecito Organico for daily news/laughs/TV recommendations/ astrological forecasts. Seeing them is often my favorite part of the day.

Thanks also to Heidi Heilig for her support and encouragement and for all she does to promote diverse books and #ownvoices authors.

My first book was dedicated to my grandparents, and even if it's a cliché, I've always believed that even though they're no longer *here*, they know what I'm up to. I hope I've made them proud.

Last, but certainly not least, *Library of Fates* is my second novel, but one of the best things about publishing my first novel was seeing my parents' reaction to this enormous career transition I decided to make in 2012 and everything that's come with it. As with most creative ventures, it was looking a little touch and go for a while, but they offered so much support and wisdom and love during the hard part and so it's been fun sharing the good stuff with them too. Seeing their faces in the crowd at my first book launch was one of my proudest moments. Having them come out to book events, getting texts from them with pictures of my books in bookstores, and learning that my mother is the best publicist I could ever have asked for has been an enormous delight. I hope they know how grateful I am to them for creating so many amazing and enriching possibilities for our family.